CANDLELIGHT
Supreme

**"I WOULD KILL ANY MAN WHO TRIED TO
TAKE YOU AWAY FROM ME, CHARITY."**

She stared at him, hearing the silky menace in his
voice. "Tell Layton, you're . . . crazy."

"About you? Perhaps I am."

"What's gotten into you? I've hardly seen you these
past few years, and all of a sudden, you're talking like
this. It's unreal."

"I want to marry you."

Charity's eyes widened. "You're taking a lot for
granted."

"You can turn me down or accept me. That's your
prerogative. But you better know now that I'm going to
do everything in my power to convince you to be my
wife."

CANDLELIGHT SUPREMES

QUANTITY SALES

Most Dell Books are available at special quantity discounts when purchased in bulk by corporations, organizations, and special-interest groups. Custom imprinting or excerpting can also be done to fit special needs. For details write: Dell Publishing Co., Inc., 1 Dag Hammarskjold Plaza, New York, NY 10017, Attn.: Special Sales Dept., or phone: (212) 605-3319.

INDIVIDUAL SALES

Are there any Dell Books you want but cannot find in your local stores? If so, you can order them directly from us. You can get any Dell book in print. Simply include the book's title, author, and ISBN number, if you have it, along with a check or money order (no cash can be accepted) for the full retail price plus 75¢ per copy to cover shipping and handling. Mail to: Dell Readers Service, Dept. FM, 6 Regent Street, Livingston, N.J. 07039.

SAPPHIRE HEART

Hayton Monteith

A CANDLELIGHT SUPREME

Published by
Dell Publishing Co., Inc.
1 Dag Hammarskjold Plaza
New York, New York 10017

ISBN: 0-440-17652-2

Printed in the United States of America

July 1987

10 9 8 7 6 5 4 3 2 1

WFH

To Our Readers:

We are pleased and excited by your overwhelmingly positive response to our Candlelight Supremes. Unlike all the other series, the Supremes are filled with more passion, adventure, and intrigue, and are obviously the stories you like best.

In months to come we will continue to publish books by many of your favorite authors as well as the very finest work from new authors of romantic fiction. As always, we are striving to present unique, absorbing love stories —the very best love has to offer.

Breathtaking and unforgettable, Supremes follow in the great romantic tradition you've come to expect *only* from Candlelight Romances.

Your suggestions and comments are always welcome. Please let us hear from you.

Sincerely,

The Editors
Candlelight Romances
1 Dag Hammarskjold Plaza
New York, New York 10017

SAPPHIRE HEART

CHAPTER ONE

Meow! Meow!

The intrusive yowls broke the somber, almost inaudible murmurings of the minister conducting the funeral service for Cyrus Publius Bigham, the sounds ripping through the air like a cacophonous underworld choir. They were coming from the car of Charity Bigham, Cyrus's granddaughter.

Tell Layton felt a barbarous humor rise up in him as Charity, who was late, hurried across the lawn toward the knoll where the service was being held. She was even more lovely than she'd been four weeks ago, when he'd seen her last. He had managed to see Charity at least once a month in the years she'd been away from Bigham House, but never in all that time had he contacted her face to face or let her see him. But that was ended. Now he was going to take her. He'd waited too long as it was . . . and she could fight him all the way. It wouldn't make any difference. She was his.

Charity Bigham felt all thumbs, arms and legs moving disjointedly. It was as though her footfalls across the well-trimmed green lawn in the Upstate New York cemetery resounded like a herd of elephants. She kept moving forward, her eyes straight ahead. One, two, three.

Keep counting the steps and don't look at anyone. Four, five, six. Almost there!

Grief had her in its grip because she would miss her beloved grandfather, though she hadn't been able to see him as often as she would have liked in the last months of his life. Along with the sadness there was a nervousness that all her self-scolding could not dissipate. Charity didn't relish confronting most of the people who would be gathered at the mausoleum. Curling her hands into fists, she raised her chin. She was the only grandchild, the only blood relative, and she had every right to be there! And she would pull herself together and face them all.

The day had been a surrealistic nightmare anyway. She had driven up from Manhattan in her rusting Mazda with the two kittens she'd adopted a few weeks ago in the car and they had loudly complained most of the way, just as they had done as she'd approached Bigham Park Cemetery where her grandfather would be interred.

Of course, she didn't usually drive between the high wrought-iron gates of Bigham Cemetery, the words scrolled in metal on the tall barriers that were now thrown open. She and her grandfather had often walked through the well-kept burial place when she'd been a child, studying the dates and names on the gravestones.

"Gravestones are one of the earth's most valuable history books, child. Nothing scary here, just good learning," he would say to her.

She was late! And for her grandfather's funeral. She must stop this silly ruminating and hurry now that she'd finally arrived. Though she had started early enough she had run into a snag on the thruway leading north from New York City toward the small town of Bigham some fifty miles from the outer perimeter of the metropolis. She'd forgotten that when the weather was warm the

10

repair crews would be out on the highway as they tarred and resurfaced the much-used road.

Finally, twenty minutes later than she should be, she had arrived in Bigham Park. As her car had crept through the tortuous narrow lanes of the hilltop burial ground, she had taken no notice of the stands of pine and fir that delineated the passageways. Charity had been too intent on the cluster of cars on the grassy knoll on the far side of the area.

Bigham Cemetery was large considering the size of the town of Bigham Park. There were Bighams buried there from the Revolutionary War, and today, the last of the male Bighams was being laid to rest. Though there were other family names listed in the large park-like area, most of them were related to the Bighams in one way or another.

Charity had jumped when the two kittens had yowled again in protest from the backseat of her car. "For heaven's sake, behave. You're in a cemetery." Charity had hoped the kittens would pick up the message to be quiet from her urgent tone of voice. "Would you like to have been left home in that stuffy apartment on this hot August day?"

Another yowl had answered her and Charity had groaned. "Just be good a little longer, then I'll take you to the motel and you can play there."

As surreptitiously as was possible with a broken tailpipe and a rattling muffler, Charity had wound her way along the tree-lined lanes toward the family stone and cement structure where her grandfather would be buried.

Charity had done all her crying when she'd heard the news of his death, but as she had drawn closer to the place where they had often walked when she was a child, her eyes had grown misty all over again. If only she had been able to say a final farewell to the only

11

mentor and father she'd ever known. She had felt less welcome at Bigham House in the last year than she'd ever had and if what her stepgrandmother had told her was true, her grandfather had not been anxious to see her even when he'd known the end was near. That had been a raw pain. It was true that things had subtly changed for Charity after her grandfather's marriage to Kathleen Beech, and after she had left the house to go to college she hadn't seen much of him outside of short visits at Christmas and his birthdays. But they had talked at least once a week on the phone until his illness had worsened . . . then more and more Kathleen relayed the messages.

"I want to speak to Grandfather, and perhaps come up and see him this weekend, Kathleen."

"Ah, I don't think that would be advisable, Charity."

Each time she'd called, Kathleen had put her off with some excuse.

Charity had known he was dying but when she'd been informed of the death it had been a tearing, wrenching blow. Grief had hit her like a tidal wave. All of what she was and had been was gone! She, Charity Bigham, was the last Bigham. Grandfather Cyrus had been her only relative. Her mother, Cyrus's only child, had died when Charity had been twelve years old. Charity had been born out of wedlock and she and her mother had lived on a good-sized house on the grounds of Bigham House. Her mother had been perfectly satisfied with the arrangement, content to paint the landscapes she loved and look after her daughter. On many evenings the two of them would go up to the big house and dine with Cyrus and he would often walk down through the pine trees to visit them.

After her mother's death Charity had gone to live with her grandfather in the main house and she had been happy. She'd had a fine tutor in the basic subjects and foreign languages even though she attended the local school. With a dog of her own and a horse to ride she was a contented person . . . until Cyrus married again.

Charity had stopped living at Bigham House when she'd been seventeen and ready to enter college. As the illegitimate granddaughter in a subtly hostile atmosphere created by her stepgrandmother and her relatives, she had found her position untenable. As soon as possible after graduation from high school she had sought her fortune in New York City with her grandfather's blessing and a good-sized stipend.

Columbia University had been an exciting place for an eager teenager but she had been inexpressibly lonely many times. She'd had to steel herself not to return to Bigham House . . . or to reach out to Tell Layton.

Though her grandfather had shown her care and as much attention as a busy industrialist could, it had not been a happy five years for Charity when she'd lived at Bigham House with the Beeches in residence. Charity had learned to be very wary of Kathleen and her three children and brother who had moved into Bigham House when she was thirteen.

Charity had parked behind the long line of cars, her rusty, faded-blue Mazda standing out like an onion in a petunia patch among the glistening stretch limousines. She walked toward the cluster of people dressed in gray and black, aware that her coral-colored voile dress that lifted in the breeze was like a waving flag in that sea of drab. How her grandfather would have hated all that gray and black that contrasted so sharply with the flowers and the green trees and grass!

Charity was almost to the group when she heard the yowl behind her. The kittens, Oregano and Sweet Basil, the Herbal Twins, were protesting their confinement. She stopped in her tracks, willing the kittens not to

13

make any further announcements of their displeasure. Awareness of the sounds rippled through the onlookers.

Meow! Meow!

Startled faces swung Charity's way for a moment, then turned back to the droning minister. The one visage that didn't turn back to the reading of the funeral service drew Charity's eyes.

Tell Layton! Why should she be surprised that he was at the gravesite? He was watching her, not Reverend Pike. He stared at Charity, holding her in place with that look that had stymied her as a child when she'd had a fierce crush on him.

What was Tell Layton doing these days? Buying Pittsburgh? Investing in Africa . . . like putting a down payment on Kenya, for example? Charity smothered her tangential thoughts and kept moving toward the group, the minister's voice becoming audible.

". . . and so we consign the soul of Cyrus Publius Bigham to the rewards of a better life . . ."

Would her grandfather think that the afterlife was better than this one? Only if he could subscribe to the *Wall Street Journal*, Charity thought. A giggle escaped her, but most of the people didn't hear it because at the same moment the Herbal Twins yowled again in strident protest. The sound seemed to ring up into the trees, loud and long, an intrusion on the solemn event.

Again all heads turned but Tell's, who hadn't looked away from her since she'd stepped from the wreck she was driving. He had watched her approach, his eyes screened by dark glasses. Her walk had the graceful hips-forward, shoulders-back easy gait of a model. With her it was so natural; he knew because she'd walked that way since childhood.

Charity heard the murmur of questioning irritation that went through the watchers as the kittens sounded their clarion call once more just as she took her place

14

next to a person she didn't know. She smiled at that frowning person, then her glance slid to Tell Layton, who cocked his head in recognition.

Why should she feel so defensive all at once? After all it was her grandfather, and Cyrus would have understood why she couldn't have left the kittens in Manhattan. Tell Layton was no relation to any of the Bighams, after all, though Cyrus Bigham had treated him like the beloved son he'd never had.

Of course he'd be at the graveside. Though he was rich in his own right and a busy executive of his own holdings, including a bank and a string of marinas up and down the East Coast, he had been her grandfather's closest fiscal confidant.

In the five years she had lived at Bigham House she had seen Tell often, but rarely since she'd lived on her own. Tell Layton had been her ideal even though he had never given her much more than a half smile and a few tennis lessons all the time she'd lived at Bigham House —except for that one time that not all Charity's diligence to do so had quite banished from her memory, graduation night from high school.

The crowd moved and shifted and Charity was jolted from her daydreams. It was over! And she had barely heard one word of the service.

Meow! Meow!

"What on earth is that screeching?" Kathleen Beech Bigham demanded.

"Nothing to worry you," Tell Layton told her quietly. "Ambrose, take your mother to the car and then the others will leave and gather at the house. It's useless to mill about here."

Ambrose Beech, called Amby by his mother, glared at Layton, whom he didn't like, but he took his mother's arm and led her to the front limousine.

The people filtered away, moving around Charity,

15

some speaking to her, others just leaving. She stared at the darkened opening of the mausoleum where the coffin rested on a pedestal just inside the door.

"You could go in if you like, Charity."

Without looking at Tell, she nodded and stepped into the stone room. She didn't notice the dankness as she placed her hand on the coffin, whispering her good-byes, the sounds strangling in her throat.

She hurried from the stone room when she heard the kittens making louder noises.

Tell faced her, his familiar twisted smile touching her from head to toe. "I assume the wildlife is yours."

"Yes." Charity coughed to clear the huskiness from her throat. "I found them on the sidewalk outside of Promise House and—"

"Since no one took them in, you had to, of course."

"It wasn't like that . . . it's just that . . . well, they were so tiny and that neighborhood—"

"Is one of the worst in the country," Tell finished for her, his face grim. "Why don't you find a job on Fifth Avenue?" Tell held up his hand, palm outward. "Never mind answering that. I don't want to get into a philosophical brouhaha with you . . . not here at any rate."

Charity fumed silently, feeling herself outdone as always by his quick mind.

"You look ready to dismember me."

"I just think you should know that there was no one to take them in and that this weekend they would have been alone while I came up here. And since I have very faulty air conditioning it could have been torture for them. I hadn't planned to stay in the area but when Jacob Henry said that the reading of the will would be directly after the ceremony, and there would be papers to sign that would involve some time I thought I should get a motel room for the night and—"

16

"Dammit, you know you can stay at Bigham House." Tell glared at her.

"No, thank you. I wouldn't relish the remarks made."

"It's your grandfather's home."

"I know that." Charity gulped a sob, then felt herself hauled against his Savile Row suit. She closed her eyes as she inhaled the elusive lemony scent of his after-shave; hot tears stung behind closed lids. "The kittens are almost twice the size they were when I took them in but they're still babies and I was afraid to leave them alone in my apartment since I would be staying away overnight. The motel allows pets, you see . . ."

"You're babbling, Charity." Tell kissed the top of her hair.

"I know," she muttered into his shirt front.

"We should go. They'll be waiting at the house."

Charity nodded her head, her face still pressed to the fine fabric. With a sigh she pushed back from him and looked up. "I've dampened your shirt front."

"So you have."

All at once, Charity fell silent, hearing the buzz of bees busily taking nectar from the wildflowers that grew at the side of the mausoleum. The whirr of a female cardinal as she swooped by in a graceful ballet was accompanied by her scarlet-mantled mate singing sweetly in the top of a pine tree.

Memories of the man in front of her crowded her mind, pushing her back, stonewalling her against her bittersweet past so that her emotions clotted and logjammed there, immobilizing her. Charity was a person of action but now she felt paralyzed in mind, body, and spirit. Go away Griffith Tell Layton, go to Asia, to Africa, but don't stay here.

Tell touched her face. "Your face is like a movie screen of emotions, lady. That much hasn't changed."

"Has the rest of me?"

"Oh yes, very much on the outside, and your spirit is that of a woman's, though the little girl is still there." Tell leaned down and kissed the corner of her mouth. "I've missed you."

Charity didn't move. "I was only a phone call away."

"And several light-years." He moved back from her, but his eyes didn't leave her. "There were always too many complications between us, Charity, but that's going to change too. Shall we go? The others will be waiting."

Charity wished she could read his expressions as easily as he seemed to read hers. Damn him, he was a sphinx! "What do you mean when you say the complications are going to change?"

"I don't think I put it quite that way. Let's just say I don't want any more barriers between us. Do you?"

"Maybe. I'm not sure I understand you."

"You will."

She made one small effort to free her elbow from his hold, then decided it was fruitless to rebel against him. More than once she had tried it in the five years she lived at Bigham House and she had always been thwarted. "I don't know why I'm going there or even why I'm staying overnight."

"It's ridiculous to have gotten the motel room . . ."

"It was necessary."

". . . but it was best that you stay overnight because the will reading will be rather involved."

Charity tried to stop walking so that she could ask him more about the will but Tell wouldn't let her. "There's no need for me to be there for that."

"Don't be naïve, Charity. You were Cyrus's granddaughter and only blood relation."

"And he also has a family by Kathleen who have been closer to him than I these past ten years."

18

Tell shrugged. "Is this your car?"

Charity looked around, surprised at where they were standing. She was about to answer in the affirmative when the loud, protesting concert of the twin cats resumed. "Stop that. Soon you'll be out of there." She leaned her head in the open window and looked at the two of them sitting in the airy carrier. "See, you're nice and cool under the pine trees," she told them in crooning tones. She looked up at Tell. "Thank you for walking me back to my car. I'll see you at the house."

"I'm riding with you." Tell opened the driver's door and ushered her into the seat. Then he went around to the passenger side and bent his length into the front seat. Muttering to himself, he worked at the lever under the seat.

"It doesn't work. Everyone has to sit with their knees on their chest. And you're taller than most, so you'll be uncomfortable for a while. It's a good thing we only have a short drive. Of course, I didn't expect to chauffeur you either."

With a creak and bang, Tell's seat shot backward. "There. Now your passengers will have room."

"How did you do that? The cats will have less room now." Charity looked over her shoulder at the tiny harlequin cat and her brother, a marmalade tabby. They stared back unblinkingly, seemed contented now that she was back with them. *Now* they had to behave perfectly, just when she wanted them to yowl. Charity looked back at her dashboard and prayed the motor would turn over on the first try. Sometimes it was temperamental. With a roar and bang of muffler and tailpipe she started the car, wincing at the ear-bending noise the engine made. "Have to get that fixed."

"Why don't you junk this?"

"Because it's a perfectly good car." Charity flinched

when the kittens protested again. "I don't think they're too fond of traveling."

"Not in this bucket of bolts anyway," Tell asserted.

Charity lifted her chin, not deigning to answer, steering her car along the narrow lanes leading to the front gate. "Where is your Ferrari?"

"Do I hear sarcasm? Actually I drive a Lamborghini now."

"Pitiful."

"Are you being patronizing? Should I get into my coveralls and paint old buildings to house the homeless?"

Charity's head shot his way, resentment building at his steely tones. "Don't you denigrate helping the poor. How did you know that we do that at Promise House anyway? It's only one of the projects that we've tackled, by the way."

Tell shrugged. "Good guess."

Tell Layton propped his long legs against the dash and slouched in his seat, cocking his head her way so he could study her.

Charity had always been beautiful, but now her spectacular coloring and her natural womanliness made her breathtaking. Her red-gold hair shone with health, swinging around her face like a curling silken swath. Her skin was the whitest he'd ever seen but he knew that it could turn a pinky bronze from the sun. "Tell me about Promise House and what you do there." He knew what her answers would be, just as he had always known what she had been doing from the time he'd first seen her when she'd been a small child. She'd fascinated him from the start.

"You're so pompous I should tell you to stuff it, but I'm too anxious to get a donation out of you to keep quiet." Her huffy tone elicited a chuckle from him. "You are a very irritating man, Tell Layton."

20

"So I've been told."

"Promise me a donation and I'll tell all."

"Mercenary, aren't you? All right, you've got a donation."

"You won't regret it. Our work is very worthwhile." She paused and shot him a glance. "Not that I don't know that you give to other good causes."

"Ah, thank you for pulling me back into the human race."

"Stop being so caustic or I won't talk to you at all."

"Think of the generous check."

Charity laughed. "I don't know why I'm laughing, because you really annoy me."

"Stop running on and tell me about your work."

"It's wonderful. And I love what I do. Actually, I've done about every job there is at Promise House but now, mainly, I counsel unwed teenaged mothers. Sometimes I see more down curves than up in my job, but I won't give up because the ones that we're able to help make it all worthwhile." Charity frowned.

Tell chuckled. "That sounds familiar. You were always a persistent brat, not to mention a world-class softy. I can't even begin to count the number of creatures that landed in Cyrus's kitchen after you took residence there."

Charity glared at him for a second. "And you are a cynic."

"Not really, pet." One strong finger stroked down her soft cheek. Tell felt a tightness in his middle at the touch of her. "Tell me about Promise House and I won't interrupt again."

"Do you know since I started there our fiscal picture has brightened? We have twice the donations we once had and many more offers of jobs and private homes for our kids."

"Is it still mostly twelve to sixteen as far as ages?"

21

"How did you remember that? I don't think we've talked for ages about this."

"It's been a while."

"Our kids are getting younger, sad to say. Many are throwaways plus the usual runaways. Throwaways are the ones whose families have kicked them out of the house. Usually when they arrive in New York City they're pretty battered, both physically and emotionally. The rule of thumb is that if we don't get them off the street in the first weeks, we've lost them."

"I've heard that."

"You seem to be well informed."

"There's the turnoff."

Charity jammed on the brakes and swung into a turn, bringing a muttered curse from Tell. As she drove through the large gates leading to Bigham House she thought how similar the landscape was to the cemetery they'd just left, the same well-kept lawns and flowers surrounded by wrought-iron fencing. And now there was a similar flash of pain that she'd experienced in the cemetery as the upward curving drive brought them into full view of Bigham House. The beautiful mansion clung to the knoll like a huge gray stone monster, the windows winking gemlike in the fading sunlight like a collection of bizarre eyes.

Charity let the car idle for a moment, staring. "It's still very beautiful, isn't it?"

"Cyrus and I always thought so, but I think Kathleen and her family consider it an extravagant white elephant."

Charity remembered how often her stepgrandmother tried to persuade Cyrus to sell. "She always preferred the house in Saratoga Springs and the other in Palm Beach."

"Not to mention the townhouse in New York," Tell said smoothly, then opened his door before the car had

22

fully stopped, going around to her side before the tall white-haired man in the black suit could come down the steps to the car.

"Macon, how are you?" Tears welled in her eyes when she saw how the elderly retainer's hand shook as he approached her. "Oh. Macon, you'll miss him so much too." Charity hugged the elderly man.

"Miss Charity, how much you look like Miss Julia, your mother, more each time you come, I think."

"Thank you, Macon." Charity thought of her dainty blond-haired mother and couldn't see the resemblance, but she would never tell the butler that.

"But you must come inside. Mrs. Bigham is getting anxious," Macon fretted, looking over his shoulder as though someone would be coming out to censure him.

"Not to worry, Macon. We'll go right inside. Are they all in the sitting room?"

Charity saw the palpable relief cross the older man's face at Tell's words. Macon nodded in answer to his question.

Tell took Charity's arm, feeling it stiffen as they entered the air-conditioned home, the coolness refreshing after the sticky air outside.

"Oh wait, I must bring the kittens in. It's too hot for them in the car." Charity stopped and tried to retrace her steps.

"You wait here. I'll have Macon take them to the kitchen. They should be fine there." Tell gestured to the butler.

Charity nodded, smiling at the puzzled butler as he passed her a few moments later with the cat carrier.

"I shall have to find a litter box for them, miss, then everything will be fine."

"He didn't sound too sure," Tell told her dryly, coming up behind her. "Shall we?" He ushered her to the double doors that led to the sitting room and opened

23

them to the sound of querulous voices. "Let the games begin," Tell murmured.

"Thank you, Caesar." Charity could feel a beading of moisture on her upper lip as those assembled turned as one to watch her enter the room. Tell's hand at her waist gave her a measure of reassurance. "Hello."

Kathleen Beech Bigham dabbed at her eyes and took her daughter Jennifer's hand. "You were late today, Charity." The mild censure, though breathed softly, carried to everyone there.

Murmured assent rippled through the room.

"Shall we get on with this, Jacob?" Tell queried brusquely, bringing all eyes to him as he stood behind Charity's chair.

"Ah, of course. The will is rather lengthy and some of it is recorded electronically. I will read this short statement first as dictated by my late client, Cyrus Publius Bigham . . . ahem."

The faintest sigh of impatience escaped Kathleen Bigham's lips, though she kept her eyes on the lawyer.

"If anyone attempts to contest this will, which Jacob and his entire firm assure me is airtight, then that person will be automatically disinherited, and every penny accorded him or her will be absorbed back into the estate."

Irritated mutterings waved over the room until Jacob Henry pushed a compact disc into the player and Cyrus's voice came from the speaker directing the remembrances to his staff both in Bigham Industries and his home.

At the end Jacob picked up a sheaf of papers and cleared his throat. "This segment is also on discs, one for each member of the family, but Cyrus wished me to read this to all of you when you were gathered together after his funeral."

A light sob was heard, then silence.

24

Monies were designated to Ambrose Beech, his sister Jennifer, and younger brother Gareth Beech. A small money bequest was made to Lyle Clausen, Kathleen's brother who had come to live in Bigham House some years after his sister had married his long time acquaintance.

". . . and to my wife Kathleen I leave the house in Palm Beach, the one in Saratoga and the sum of . . ."

Tell let his mind drift away from Jacob as he watched Charity to see how she would take the estate of her grandfather being sliced up among Kathleen's relatives. She looked serene. His eyes drifted over the purity of her profile, the straight, short nose that emphasized the small-boned structure of her face. If she were looking at him, instead of just being a little in front of him and to one side, he would be able to look into the most remarkable green eyes he'd ever seen, the outer edges just lifting at the corners, giving her a sultry, gamine look that she'd always had. Now that she was a woman, her sensuousness had increased a hundredfold. Yes, now she was a woman and he was damned glad of it.

A gasp of surprise brought his head up, his eyes pinioning the others in the room who were now staring at him. He felt his mouth twist upward. So! They had come to the bequest Cyrus had made him. Tell knew all about that, but he was damned if he would explain anything to them. Not that he understood everything. None there would believe that he had tried to talk the old man out of the bequest to him. Tell's mind flashed back to that day, his conversation with Cyrus still a puzzle to him.

"No! Tell, you are getting the money and the business. It's the only way I can protect Charity. She must be safe."

"What do you mean, Cyrus?"

"Nothing. Believe that I know how to take care of my granddaughter."

"For God's sake explain yourself, man."

"Perhaps I'll tell you of my fears one day, Tell."

But the day had never come. Cyrus had died and his secrets with him.

Tell shook his head feeling the frustration he always did when he thought back to that conversation. He ignored the still hot glances cast his way by the Beech family, wishing Cyrus hadn't been so secretive about some elements of his life.

"No, that can't be. This house is mine." Kathleen's voice rose shrilly. "You're wrong, Jacob Henry."

Tell stared at her, then his glance moved to Charity, who was staring at Jacob Henry, mouth agape.

"I assure you, Mrs. Bigham, I'm reading the will properly just as it was dictated to me and to my associates who witnessed the writing and signing of this will. Cyrus Bigham was so careful, madam, that he also invited an outside firm to witness this."

"I shouldn't think you would quibble about your share, Kathleen. It's considerable." Tell stared at the woman whose eyes flashed animosity.

"None of this is any of your concern—and you should not have been mentioned in the will at all," Kathleen blurted, then she reddened and sat back in her chair, her daughter Jennifer patting her hands.

Charity shot to her feet her mouth opened to retort. Tell's voice cut across her like a whip, keeping her mute.

"Kathleen, you're overwrought or I'm sure you wouldn't have made such a tactless statement. Cyrus wouldn't have liked it." Tell looked at each person seated near Kathleen, his glance lingering on Cyrus's widow.

The room fell silent. Myriad scowls and frowns were

fixed on Tell before the glances fell away. Mouths opened and closed but there was no retort.

Kathleen's nostril's flared as though she had inhaled brimstone, and her cheeks reddened.

"I think you can get on with it, Jacob," Tell drawled, his hand on Charity's shoulder gently pressing her back into her chair.

"And to my granddaughter I bequeath the rest of my estate . . ."

"What the hell . . ." Amby Beech was barely restrained by his uncle who clung to his arm, whispering urgently to the angry young man.

". . . which includes Bigham House, the apartment in New York and all monies with which to support both places and the staff they require . . ."

Tell felt Charity go slack under his hands. So she really didn't know what Cyrus had planned. Tell frowned. Damn the man for being hell-bent to hide everything. If he had confided in Charity or himself, some of the things he was trying to protect his granddaughter from might have surfaced and Tell would be on his guard and not feel so helpless as he did at the moment. Why had the man always been so cryptic when speaking on the subject of Charity? What were the secrets he took to the grave with him? Tell doubted anyone would ever know.

Charity blinked as though she had just wakened, the rustling of papers as Mr. Henry sorted them and began returning them to his briefcase sounding loud in the quiet room. Her hands felt flaccid and useless as they lay in her lap. She felt as though she'd lost the power to move. Owner of Bigham House! Incredible!

Her grandfather had left her his beloved Bigham House and the apartment overlooking Central Park. How she had loved both places and yet never thought to even visit them again. Many times her mother had

27

brought her into New York and they had stayed at the apartment, raiding the well-stocked refrigerator, sitting cross-legged on the floor in front of the fireplace and rehashing the play or show they'd just seen. Often grandfather had accompanied them . . . at first. Then later it had been just she and her mother who had stayed there even though her grandfather would meet them for dinner and a show. Sometimes she would ask her mother why Cyrus did this. Even as young as she was Charity could see that it had puzzled and bothered her mother somewhat, though her mother had never alluded to that.

"Businessmen have funny habits, child. Don't worry, we'll be seeing him this evening at the play."

And that would be that. Charity had felt her mother was not telling her everything, but she'd accepted what she was told because she was with the person she loved most in the world, her mother, and after her came Cyrus whom she would see that evening. Her world was beautiful with the two of them beside her.

Jacob Henry approached Charity Bigham. It was hard to believe that the child whom he'd bounced on his knee was now a woman. Where had the years gone? What a beautiful young lady she'd turned out to be. No wonder his old friend, Cyrus, had loved her so much. How like Julia, her mother, she was. He didn't like to think of her. It started him thinking of his own son, Jake, who had been one of Julia's closest friends and who had died several months before Charity had been born. He missed his son still. Jake and Julia had had so much fun together, moving in the same circles and always laughing and enjoying themselves, whether on the tennis court or the dance floor.

The older man sighed. Life could be so complex, taking so many unexpected twists and turns. Look at what had happened to Cyrus and Charity. Whatever it was that had estranged them shouldn't have occurred. How sad Cyrus had been at the end when Charity had not visited and yet his dying friend hadn't let Jacob call and insist that she come. In fact, Cyrus had forbidden his lawyer and good friend to call her. It had all been so fruitless and beyond Jacob's comprehension.

Jacob leaned down in front of her and took her hand in his. "My dear child, you have my sincere condolences. Please believe that your grandfather loved you."

Charity fought tears as she nodded. "And I loved him —so much."

It crossed Jacob's mind to say that she should have been with him when he'd been so ill, but he couldn't censure her when she was obviously deeply distressed. He had always had a soft spot for Charity. How sad it was to see the grief of one who had been alienated from a loved one. Nothing was worse than that uncrossable void. "It was your grandfather's wish that I remain as your lawyer—unless of course you would prefer—"

Charity squeezed the surprisingly strong hand that held hers and shook her head. "I don't want anyone else, Mr. Henry. I would like you to remain my lawyer."

"Remember that you should be very sure whom you want to represent you, Charity," Jacob Henry told her.

"I think Jacob is just reminding you of how important your decision is," Tell leaned over her and said.

Jacob Henry smiled. "Tell is right, Charity."

She shook her head. "No, you've been Grandfather's lawyer for years." She looked up at the older man. "And wasn't your father his father's lawyer also?"

Jacob Henry nodded in assent. "Yes, indeed. Our families have been closely connected for many years, child." He leaned over and kissed her hand in his slow, dignified way. "Good day, my dear. Please remember

29

that I'm only a phone call away if you need me. My office in New York is . . ."

"I know. You can see the Statue of Liberty from the window."

Jacob Henry looked taken aback for a moment. "What a good memory you have, Charity. You can't have been there in years."

"Mother and I stopped to see you one day shortly before she had her accident."

Jacob nodded. "I remember. Dear Julia. How beautiful she was." Jacob shook his head and moved slowly away toward the widow who had her family clustered about her. Jacob had never felt close to Kathleen Beech Bigham, even though he'd known her for years, just as Cyrus had. Her younger brother, Lyle Clausen, had been an acquaintance of his son Jake and of Julia Bigham, Charity's mother, so he actually knew him better than the widow. Lyle had often been in the same groups as Julia and Jake. He had been a polite young man but a little wild, Jacob had always thought. He shook himself from his musings and bent over Kathleen's hand. "I assure you that I will be glad to assist you in any way that I can."

"And how can you do that if you're Charity's lawyer? No, never mind answering, Jacob. I have already contacted March and Day. They will be representing me—in any further legal business I may choose to contract."

Jacob straightened, looking down at her tight-lipped face. "Of course you must do as you see fit, but I feel I must remind you of the provisions of the will . . ."

"I remember. Thank you for coming." Kathleen turned her head away to say something to one of her children.

Jacob wasn't sorry to be leaving the house. It hadn't been a happy place the last year or so. Ah well, it was best to let the Bighams handle their own problems.

30

They would anyway. He left the house, pausing on the fan-shaped steps, waiting while his car was brought around to him. It was a hot day, but already there was a smell of autumn from the mountains. Perhaps he would go fishing up at Old Forge on Saturday.

Charity looked up at Tell when he moved around to take Jacob's place in front of her. "What will I say to them, Tell?" She tipped her head in the direction of Kathleen and her family.

Tell shrugged. "You needn't say anything if you don't choose. I can handle it, if you like." He frowned. "Kathleen could have been nicer to you."

Charity's head shot up and she wondered at the grim look on Tell's face. He had never before made any comment on her grandfather's wife to her, or any of the family for that matter. "Tell, is this house really all mine?"

Tell stared down at her, seeing the disbelief on her face even as he nodded. "He loved you so much, Charity."

"Then why did he keep me away from him when he was so ill?" she blurted, not able to mask the hurt in her voice.

Tell frowned down at her. "I thought you would know the answer to that better than anyone."

"Well, I don't, and you can stop looking so incredulous, because it's true."

Tell didn't answer her because he saw the movement in his peripheral vision that signaled someone else had approached them. "Ambrose. What do you want?"

"Cordial as always aren't you, Tell?" The younger man barely masked his dislike, the sneer on his face marring his even features. "You act so superior, don't you. Well, you can forget it as far as I'm concerned. I'm not taking it anymore."

"You either keep those thoughts to yourself or I'll toss you through that window," Tell said evenly.

Ambrose's ruddy complexion darkened and mottled but he didn't respond to Tell. "My mother would like to speak with you, Charity."

Charity rose to her feet at once, her eyes sliding toward Tell as Ambrose turned on his heel and retraced his steps to his mother's side.

Tell took her hand, accompanying her across the spacious room to the place in front of the Adam fireplace.

Kathleen looked up coolly. "I am sorry to inform you, Charity, that it will be impossible for any of us to leave Bigham House at this time." She made a sweeping movement with her hand to include her family. "My home in Saratoga is undergoing extensive renovation and it won't be livable for some time."

"Oh."

"How about the place in Palm Beach?"

"That, Tell, is a foolish question. I never go to Palm Beach until October," Kathleen told him frostily.

"I'm sure you could find lodging somewhere, Kathleen . . . you and your brood."

Charity saw how her stepgrandmother stiffened. "Ah, that's no problem. You can stay here until your house is ready."

"Thank you. We'll do that," Kathleen said abruptly.

"And how long will that be?" Tell put his arm around Charity's waist when her head swiveled his way. He ignored Jennifer's gasp.

Kathleen rose to her feet. "I couldn't say."

"In the meantime, Charity might feel that she would like to take over her grandfather's suite of rooms." Tell's hand dug into Charity's waist when she would have spoken, silencing her. "Since there is ample room on the third floor where the other guests will be residing, it shouldn't be too much trouble for the staff to help you move."

Kathleen seemed to stiffen. "I did not think that I would have to move from my own wing."

"Oh, but . . ." Charity began.

"Since this house became solely and completely Charity's less than an hour ago, I think it would be appropriate that she occupy the owner's rooms." Tell released Charity, who was staring at him in fulminating silence, and pressed a button on the desk console. No one spoke until the butler entered the room. "Macon, will you and some of the staff please assist Mrs. Bigham to move her things to one of the best guest rooms. That should be done at once, with your supervision of course. Thank you."

"At once, Mr. Layton."

Seemingly as one, Kathleen and her family moved to the door.

Ambrose, who was at the end of the procession, whirled to face Tell. "You have no right to tell people what to do in this house." Then he left the room in a rush, reaching back to pull both the double doors shut behind him.

"Ambrose is right." Charity glared at Tell. "Why are you being so . . . so bossy, outspoken? And what right do you have assigning rooms in this house?"

"Sorry, I didn't mean to ride roughshod, but I could see you were going to let Kathleen maneuver you into letting her remain in the master suite."

"I don't see the need to get in a snit about who sleeps where. All you've done is alienate Kathleen and her family from me even more than they were."

"What you might not have known is that your grandfather had Kathleen moved to one of the other bedrooms in the master suite and did not allow her into his room that often when he was ill."

"Oh."

"Does it bother you to be at cross purposes with them?"

"No, but—"

"There you are then. It will work much better this way. The master suite is very large and comfortable. You'll hardly have to see any of the Beech family." Tell watched the thoughtful look return to her face. He had seen a similar expression more than once since the will had been read. "You look as though you already had plans now that you're quite rich. Taking a trip around the world?"

"Don't rule it out, but not for a while. I was just thinking that my girls, who are packed together like sardines at Promise House, would love a stay in the country. Why they could even deliver their babies here, in a pinch. There's a good teaching hospital not far from here."

"Olivet Memorial," Tell said faintly. "You're thinking of turning Bigham House into a haven for unwed mothers?"

"It would be ideal. We could open the old Green and Pink wings that are unused now. I have the money to refurbish." Charity faced Tell, her hands clasped in front of her. "It would be perfect." She frowned when Tell burst out laughing, his face turning red. "What's so funny?"

"You have found the perfect shoehorn to lever the Beeches out of here, my sweet."

"I'm not your sweet." Charity noticed how the dimples appeared at the corners of his mouth when he laughed. "You are disgustingly good-looking, do you know that?" Charity squeezed her eyes shut, then opened them. How could she have said that!

Tell stopped laughing and moved closer to her in one stride, so that he was staring down into her eyes. "I

34

never want to disgust you, pet—or frighten you." His one finger stroked the camellia texture of her skin.

At his touch, memory flooded back to that other warm summer day when she had gone down to the small lake on the property and found Tell swimming there in the nude. Charity knew that he was reading her mind and remembering that day as clearly as she did. She had been fourteen. He'd been twenty-four. Not even thinking twice about it she had stripped off her clothes and flung herself out toward him in a splashy surface dive that had turned his head her way. He had treaded water, watching her, neither moving in her direction nor away from her.

"Dammit, Charity, you had better be wearing your underwear."

"Why? You're not." She blew water from her mouth and grinned at him, treading water not fifty feet from him. "What difference does it make? I'll just get out of the water around the bend and you—"

"What the hell do you think you're doing? Get out of here now."

"Nope."

It was then that Tell seemed to explode with rage. He had swum to her side, hooked an arm around her, almost drowning her when she struggled, and dragged her to shore.

On land she had pushed back from him, uncaring of her nakedness as she vented her fury. "Damn you to hell, you bastard!" Charity had shouted when she had been able to get a breath. "You're a rat, Tell Layton."

He had stared down at her as though he hated her, his eyes running over her from head to toe and back again. "Don't ever swim naked here again or you'll regret it, I promise you that." His words lanced through her, drawing blood from her spirit.

"What are you going to do? Kill me?" Charity's laugh

35

had faded at the murderous look he'd given her. "Stop that. Your eyes look like the holes the woodpecker makes in the dead oak tree."

"Damn you, Charity, if I ever catch you like this again, it will be the end of you." Tell had shoved his towel at her with enough force to push her backward. Then he'd stalked past her without another word, his hands clenched.

Tears had rolled down her cheeks as anger and bafflement had rocked her. She had loved Tell and been sure that he had loved her. Now she knew that he hated her. He was the bastard, not her!

After that Charity had avoided Tell as much as possible, but sometimes that was hard since he seemed to be at Bigham House all the time, day, night, weekends. It was as though he lived there, had a right to come and go as he pleased on the large estate. Even when he spoke to her pleasantly during the following years, she would snub him or glare at him. It was vinegary satisfaction but the only one she'd had with Tell.

"Don't you have a store to mind?" Her fifteen-year-old tongue had been deliberately insolent with him one afternoon in autumn.

His eyes had gone over her like razors, slicing where they touched. "It's too bad your mind isn't developing as fast as your body, pet."

"In your ear." Charity had sprinted for the door when she saw the golden fire in his eyes. Tell would have thought nothing of turning her over his knee right in the foyer, not caring if her grandfather or Macon, or anyone saw.

Being scathing with Tell was her only armor. She felt poisoned around him, as though her system were reacting in order to throw off a toxin. Her blood thumped painfully through her, her limbs felt heavy and feverish as though all movement had atrophied, that she was paralyzed by him. She wanted to kill him. Anyone else in the world she was able to forgive slings and arrows, but not Tell. He wounded mortally. It would have been wonderful to see him dragged down the street by a team of horses, tied to a railroad track. Visions of his grisly death were comforting in her teenage years.

Boyfriends began appearing in Charity's line of vision about the time of her fifteenth birthday. They stopped being nuisances and began to become intriguing all in one moment, it seemed. Relishing the attention, she threw herself into the new life with verve and gusto.

Sports, especially tennis and swimming, began to play a big part in her life in high school and this carried over into college. All along the way were the intense relationships with boys and young men, deathless passions that fizzled in weeks.

It wasn't until she met Buzz Lasker when whe was a senior at Columbia that she ever had sex with anyone. She loved Buzz and had wanted him to make love to her. Charity had found it disappointing, but since some of her friends confessed that they had found it a big nothing after the buildups given by others, she had not worried about her feelings. Still, after that, she had avoided physical relationships with men, figuring that one day she might marry and have a family and by then she might look on sex differently. Maybe what the Victorian ladies said was true, that if you closed your eyes and thought of duty—Good Lord, what a future. Charity consoled herself with the fact that when she chose her husband she would care for him enough to make their sex life good for him. After that assessment, she put the whole subject into the back of her mind.

When she'd returned home after her college graduation she'd found a gift wrapped in silver paper on her bed, the silver card slashed with only a signature. Tell. The fine gold chain with the small sapphire heart had her gasping. She had put it on and had never taken it off except for the annual jeweler's check on the clasp and the gem prongs. Whenever she was agitated or upset she would put her hand to the heart and feel strong. Tell had left power in the sapphire.

"Come back to me, Charity, and tell me about your daydream."

Tell's voice jarred her into the present. "It's nothing. I was just remembering—Bigham House."

"I'm sure you have many memories, my sweet." He laughed when her mouth dropped. "Why do you look so surprised? Is it the endearment?"

"Well, you have to admit that you have been less than cordial to me a few times since I arrived at Bigham House as a child. I can still recall my seventeenth birthday." The arrested look on his face telegraphed to her that he recalled the incident as clearly as she did.

Tell had given her a wrought gold watch and she had thrown her arms around him in gratitude. When he had smiled down at her, she had taken hold of his face and pulled it down to her and kissed him. He had thrust her back from him, red-faced and furious, flailing her with words. Charity had turned and run from him upstairs to her room, crying and cursing him.

"Times change, people grow."

"Don't they." Charity was about to turn away from him when Macon returned to the room.

"Miss Charity, I thought you would like to know that the maids have moved Mrs. Bigham to the guest wing with the other members of her family." Macon cleared his throat quietly. "I put Mr. Layton's things into his regular room. If that's all right, miss?"

That would put Tell in her wing. She was tempted to tell Macon to put Tell in any of the other wings, but she could tell by his twisted smile that he expected such a response from her. Damn him for the know-it-all he

38

was! "Ah, that would be fine, Macon. Thank you for your trouble."

Macon looked startled. "Trouble, miss? I am always glad to serve you. After all, you are the only Bigham left."

"Not quite, Macon. My mother is one." Ambrose Beech stepped into the room, pausing to stare very hard at the old retainer who had turned to face him when he spoke.

Charity opened her mouth to retort even as Lyle Clausen entered the room behind his nephew.

"Calm yourself, Amby. Macon meant only that Charity is a Bigham by blood. Didn't you, old fellow?" Lyle gave Macon a friendly smile as the butler inclined his head woodenly at Charity and left the room, his slow dignified stride unchanged.

Charity took a deep breath, then spoke in measured tones. "In the future, Ambrose, I would rather you didn't use that tone of voice to Macon. He has been a member of this family since my mother was a girl and he merits respect."

Ambrose Beech's color fluctuated between pasty and mottled red. "Quick to take over, aren't you?"

"Yes, I suppose I am, but if you don't like the way I'm doing things, you have the freedom to pick up your option." Anger at the way Beech had talked to Macon rippled through her. Charity recalled how many times those same sarcastic tones had been directed at her. No more!

Ambrose took a step forward, his hands curling into fists.

"Don't be a fool, Beech," Tell drawled, not straightening from his lounging stance next to Charity.

Ambrose stared into Tell's face, his own features working in frustrated ire.

"Tell's right, Amby," Lyle told his nephew lightly, his

39

eyes flicking over Tell and back to his nephew. "Why don't we get a drink and relax? Could I fix you one, Charity?" Lyle jerked on his nephew's sleeve, urging him toward the corner of the sitting room near the scrolled oak bar.

"Ah, no, I'm going to my room to freshen up."

"I'll have an Irish whiskey with ice," Tell told Lyle, his head to one side. Then his glance slid to Charity. "What time are we having dinner, Charity?"

Charity stopped in mid-stride, swinging around to face the three pairs of eyes.

"My mother has ordered the dinner for seven as always," Amby told Charity abruptly, lifting the drink that Lyle had set on the shiny surface of the bar and taking a hefty swallow.

"Fine. We'll eat at seven." Charity didn't trust her temper if she remained in the room any longer. Ambrose Beech was trying to bait her, much as he had done when she was a young girl and he had come to live at Bigham House with his mother and his siblings.

She stood in the huge foyer with its Italian marble floor and looked up the wide fan-shaped staircase that led to the second floor where the master suite was situated. As though pulled on a string, she moved upward, looking at the pictures of Bighams that lined the staircase, all the stern visages comforting her as they had always done. She belonged here, just as the pictures of her ancestors did. Charity put her foot on the first stair, looking upward at the French plastering that was in itself a work of art.

Halfway up the staircase she could see the outer edge of the scrolled oak door that led into the master suite. Nothing was above that wing as it was a two-story suite, but there was another stairway across the spacious second floor hall that led up from that level to the third floor.

The second floor had two smaller sections separate from the master suite. They were roomy apartments consisting of sitting room, bedroom, and bath. One was once used in conjunction with the master suite by her grandmother, Cyrus had told her. The apartment had then been used by Kathleen. By the time Kathleen was in Cyrus's life, Tell was using the other suite exclusively for his own since he had become Cyrus's closest business confidant and friend.

On the third floor, in another wing, there was ample room for guests and it was here that Kathleen and her family would reside until they moved to her house in Saratoga.

Charity sighed. It would go against the grain of all Bigham tradition to make her guests uncomfortable. She would never do that, but she knew it would be a relief to have Kathleen and her family out of the house, especially since she fully intended to bring some of her girls from Promise House out to Bigham House for their pregnancy stay.

Charity felt the thrust of anger that was always there when she thought of the girls at Promise House who were pregnant. Most of them were babies themselves. Teenagers weren't meant to be mothers! The work at Promise House with the disadvantaged teenagers was just the tip of the iceberg. There were so many they couldn't reach, who wouldn't, for a host of reasons, get help, who would fall through the cracks. Blinking against the hopeless feeling that such thinking brought, Charity concentrated on when she would bring some of the girls to live in such wonderful surroundings and when the Beeches would be gone.

Charity had never felt at ease with the Beeches and especially not with her stepgrandmother in the later years of her grandfather's life. Kathleen was the one who'd kept her from her grandfather, Charity was sure of it, otherwise Cyrus would have called her to his side when he was dying. She could never doubt the love her grandfather had for her and he would have wanted her with him.

Charity paused on the landing, facing her grandfather's room, then crossed to the oak scrolled door, her shoes sinking into the luxury of the cream, green, and coral Aubusson carpet. The door handle turned with ease and she pushed it open and stepped inside to stare about the cavernous octagonal room with the mammoth four-poster bed. "Grandfather. Grandfather," Charity called as she often had as a child.

Then the tears came, the sobs tearing from her throat as she stood in the center of the room, both hands pressed to her mouth, the void in her life looming black and cavernous.

Dinner was as Charity remembered it, with everyone dressing up. Since she had brought little with her, her one suitable outfit was a pleated silk skirt with cream and blue horizontal stripes and a double breasted blouse in cream silk.

Since she'd fallen asleep on the king-sized bed and had been late showering and dressing, Charity was the last person to enter the sitting room.

"We do dine at seven, Charity. It is now six minutes after the hour." Kathleen's soft reprimand had the effect of lifting Charity's chin and steadying her nerves.

"Then perhaps we can adjourn to the dining room. If anyone wishes another drink I'm sure Macon will bring it to the table." She spun on her heel and left the room.

When she felt a hand at her elbow, she looked up, startled.

"To the manner born, my pet. Let me escort you to the table." Tell didn't allow her to protest when he led her to the head of the table, pulled out her chair and all

42

but thrust her into it, then he seated himself at her right.

"Shouldn't we have waited until the others were at their places before we sat?" She wanted to throw her crystal water goblet at him.

Tell smiled blandly. "Another time." He turned and gazed at the others who all seemed to be bunched in the doorway. "Come in, Kathleen. I'm sure you're as hungry as I am and when you're all seated, Charity will ring for Macon to begin serving."

Kathleen strode to her chair at the foot of the table, removing her napkin from the wrought pewter ring and shaking it over and over again before placing it on her lap. "I do hope the menu meets with your approbation, Charity."

"I'm sure it will," Tell interjected. "She's always had an appetite like a horse and a stomach for anything." Tell grinned at her when the rest of the Beeches craned their necks to look at Charity.

"You—are—a—swine," Charity whispered between locked teeth, not gazing at him, but trying to maintain a serene smile. She jammed her finger on the button on the table and almost immediately the heavy doors leading to the kitchen corridor were pushed open and the heavy carts were wheeled into the dining room, the soup quickly and quietly served by the understaff and supervised by the sharp-eyed Macon.

"Black bean soup? I ordered French onion." Kathleen shot a hard look at Macon.

"So you did, Madam." Macon inclined his head and gestured for the staff to continue serving.

"It's my very favorite, especially with a dollop of sour cream on top." Charity breathed in the aroma of the hearty soup before spooning a small portion into her mouth. "It's delicious, Macon. Tell Rumrill it's perfect."

43

"She knew you would say that, miss." Macon looked smug as he gestured at his underlings to clear away the soup tureens and ready the next course.

Tell chuckled, pulling Charity's gaze his way. She saw that he was looking at the Beeches and she followed his gaze her stomach flip flopping when she saw the antipathy aimed her way. "Ah, Kathleen, perhaps in future you will let me order the meals for the day. My mother taught me about that when I was quite young and I should get used to the duties of Bigham House."

"Of course," Charity's stepgrandmother answered frostily.

CHAPTER TWO

Somehow Tell hadn't really believed that Charity would turn Bigham House into a haven for homeless girls until the Monday that Gareth Beech phoned him in New York.

"I suppose you'll be going out to the house on Thursday, Tell."

Tell heard the thread of laughter in the other's voice. He and Gareth had gotten along the best among the Beech clan, but Tell felt that caution was in order. "Why do you ask?"

"Because if you are I'm going to ride to the country with you." Gareth laughed out loud, the sound bursting from him as though he couldn't hold it back any longer.

"Sounds like you're going to a hanging. Mine, maybe?"

"That would be diverting, but unfortunately this entertainment is of a different nature. It involves my mother and the rest of the family. I think Cyrus is the only person in the clan who would have enjoyed this."

"Out with it, Gareth." Tell figured it had something to do with the bequests, since Gareth worked for Jacob Henry in his law firm. "But be sure you're not crossing the line on client-lawyer confidentiality."

"I assure you, old boy, I'm not, since the announcement will be made in the papers this afternoon."

"Go on." Tell bit back his impatience with his caller because he recognized that Gareth was enjoying himself and would be downright gleeful if he detected even the slightest irritation in his voice.

"It seems the new owner of Bigham House will be installing five—teen-age—pregnant girls in the home as of next Monday." Gareth sounded out each word. "I assume that Charity will utilize the weekend to inform my family, and the staff—and you, since it would seem you are ignorant of her plans." Laughter burst from him again.

Humor and anger warred in Tell. Nothing would have given him more pleasure at that moment than to wring Gareth's neck. Why the hell hadn't Charity warned him it would be so soon? "So, she's going through with it," he mused.

"You knew about this?" Annoyance laced Gareth's voice.

"She mentioned that she was thinking of doing it." But not so damned fast. Damn her, the way she charged into things, she should be wearing brass knuckles from head to toe.

"My dear mother will have a calf over this, maybe twin calves. Umm, maybe it won't be such a good idea to go up there this weekend."

"Suit yourself. I'm going to call Charity and see if she wants a ride."

"Wouldn't miss it. Pick me up."

Tell stared into the phone long after the connection was broken. On impulse he dialed Charity's office number.

"Promise House. Charity Bigham speaking. How may I help you?"

"Have dinner with me tonight?" The sound of her voice had sent a sensual sensation running over his skin. He had to see her.

46

"Tell? Is that you?"

"Yes. How about dinner?"

"You sound a bit irked. Should I have known your voice at once?"

"Stop laughing, pet. I might decide to come over there and paddle your backside."

"Ooh. Tough man. Did you forget that I'm no longer a twelve-year-old that you can lecture?"

"I've forgotten nothing about you, Charity."

"I think you do want to harangue me about something. Your voice sounds as if you're biting through steel."

"Does it? I assure you I just want to dine with you and listen to some soft music. All right with you?"

"Sounds good, but I can't. I'm getting some of the girls ready for the trip to Bigham House . . ."

"But that isn't until for a week."

"Oh? You know? Did you read the article about us? Wasn't it a good one? Only one thing was in error. It said I was taking them down on Monday. We're going this Thursday."

"Does Kathleen know?"

"I told her that I'm bringing some people to the house . . . and she was bound to see Macon and his staff cleaning the Green Wing, so I don't think it will be a surprise."

"But you haven't come right out and told her that you're bringing five teenage, pregnant girls to Bigham House?"

"Not in so many words, no."

"It will be interesting. Did you say the Green Wing? That hasn't been opened for years. You can't even be sure you don't have termites in that area." Tell knew damned well that Cyrus took very good care of his property.

Charity laughed. "You're joking."

47

"Of course." Her voice had an amused remoteness he didn't like. He wanted to reach through the wire and pull her through it into his arms. He sensed Charity's hesitancy before she spoke again as though she felt his temper.

"Thanks for the invitation, Tell, but I do have to coordinate a few things if we're to leave on Thursday morning. Maybe another time. I'll be back in the city next week for a day, I think."

"You'll see me this weekend," Tell said abruptly. "I'm driving up with Gareth." All at once the vision of five young girls and Charity driving to Bigham Park in her heap jumped in front of his eyes. "Ah, I know where I can get a passenger van so that you can travel in comfort. I'll have it dropped off on Thursday morning early." He could get someone on his staff to round up a safe vehicle for her.

"Thanks for the offer. I've already hired a trailer and one of the volunteers on staff is driving a pickup truck behind me. He'll be taking two of the girls, the other three and the cats will be going with me."

"I see." Damn her, she would go off the road in that rattletrap of hers. "Since I will be leaving early that day, I'll come over and follow you in my car."

"Oh, but that won't be . . ."

"Good-bye, Charity."

Charity fumed for the next two days at Tell's high-handed manner with her. Not even all the preparations she had to make to transport the girls, patch their records into Olivet Memorial Hospital, arrange tutoring for high school equivalency for four of them and college entrance for one, plus planning their counseling sessions could take her mind off the most irritating man in the world. Tell Layton had been her bête noire since adolescence and he still was!

48

Thursday morning she was up at six, checking the last-minute items on her list that she would need for her stay at Bigham House, then packing everything in two cases. The kittens were at Promise House; the rest of her belongings would be moved to the apartment that had been left to her by her grandfather some time in the near future. She looked forward to the safe neighborhood and having a lot of closet space.

Charity locked her place behind her, hefting her purse and two pieces of luggage and pressing the button for the elevator with her elbow.

One of the few good things about the apartment house she lived in at present was that it had an underground parking facility with a security person patrolling the area. It was scarcely maximum protection but still safer than trying to park her car on the street.

When she stepped from the elevator into the underground facility, she wrinkled her nose as she always did. Dampness, the odor of engine fuel plus the yellowish gloom of the safety lights gave the garage a noxious, nether-world aura that repelled her. Charity moved as rapidly as possible to her car to get out of the area as soon as she could.

She wouldn't be sorry to leave the rather ramshackle apartment building. The thought of the apartment her grandfather had left her in the area of Manhattan overlooking Central Park buoyed her spirits. It would be almost as wonderful as returning to Bigham House. Both places held happy memories for her.

Out of the blue the thought came to her that Tell had a place in the same general area of Manhattan as her new place. She would be close to him. Her heart thumped in her chest. That was silly. People came and went in Manhattan who lived in the same building and never saw one another. Chances are she would never see Tell.

It didn't enter Charity's consciousness when she heard the sound of a revving motor, the protesting squeal of brakes suddenly released as an engine exploded into forward motion.

"Hey—look out!"

The security guard's surprised shout alerted Charity who turned openmouthed to see the car with the black windshield bearing down on her. Throwing herself sideways, her luggage and purse flying from her hands, she landed on the hood of the nearest auto, the reflex action pulling her out of the path of the roaring vehicle. The speeding car just grazed the tip of her shoe, catching it for a millisecond, but it was enough to yank her leg back painfully. Then the black auto disappeared up the exit ramp and was gone.

Charity lay where she was on the hood of the blue Chevrolet, her head almost touching the windshield, her body shaking so much that she barely noticed the throbbing in her left leg. She tried to lift herself but her quivering muscles wouldn't support movement.

"Take it easy, lady. You'd better not move. I'll call an ambulance."

"No, no wait. Aren't you Cassidy?"

"Yep." The man came around and leaned down so that his head was even with Charity's. "It's too early in the morning to be blitzed, but I'll bet that guy had a snootful. He must have had cause he never even slowed down even when you were right in front of him. Jee-zus, he's dented and scratched Mr. Lathmore's Chevy. Damn, I bet I'll catch it for this. Lady, ah, Miss Bigham, you'll have to be my witness."

"I will, if you'll just give me a hand getting off this car."

"Oh sure, but I don't think you should move if you've been hit."

"I wasn't struck. I think, maybe, his side mirror

caught my shoe, but I don't think I've got anything more than a bruise. Could you help me down, please? I'm getting numb."

Cassidy leaned up and took hold of her waist, edging her to the side of the hood, so that she could swing her legs around, then he lifted her to the ground.

"Ow, damn, I think I did pull something. It hurts like hell. I'd like to give that tenant a piece of my mind. Whose car was it, anyway?"

"Gosh, I don't know, Miss Bigham. I've never seen that Caddy before. We don't have much call for them here—well, except for the pimp's car in stall eleven, but that's a Continental with a pink lady hood ornament. Nope, I never did see that black Eldorado before today. Might be a new tenant."

"A pimp? In our building?" Momentarily diverted, Charity stared at Cassidy.

"Been here a year," he announced importantly as he helped her toward her car. "Gee, you're limping a lot Miss Bigham. Maybe you'd better see a doctor."

"I can't, not today, but it would be a help if you could retrieve my purse and two pieces of luggage over there." Charity answered grimly, her teeth gritted against the pain in her lower leg. "I have to drive to the country in half an hour."

"Jeez, I don't think you can drive when your leg hurts." Cassidy hustled after her things then put them in the trunk of her car when she handed him the key.

"I think it's my ankle and since it's my left and I have automatic, I should be fine. My right foot will do all the work."

"If you say so." Cassidy helped her into the car and closed her door, leaning in her window when she rolled it down to get some air. Even the heavy atmosphere of the garage was preferable to the stifling car. "Don't forget to tell the super it wasn't my fault about Mr. Lathmore's car or it could be my job."

"Sure, I'll tell him. And you do me a favor, will you? If the guy in the Caddy comes back, tell him I want to talk to him."

"I'll do that and I'll remember the car, too. I always wanted a black Cadillac."

"Good-bye, Cassidy." Charity shifted the car into drive, trying to place her left foot in as comfortable position as possible. It had started to throb.

By the time she'd reached Promise House, she was biting her lip at the discomfort. She would have to get an ice pack from the kitchen at Promise House and strap it to her ankle.

Charity made good time in the early-morning Manhattan traffic and reached Promise House ten minutes before she was due.

"Hi. We're all ready." Priscilla Bailey, who was fourteen years old and the most outspoken of the group, came up to Charity's parked car. "Hey, you look funny. Been car sick? I used to get that way when—oh well, it was a long time ago."

"No, Pris, I wasn't car sick. I've pulled a muscle in my ankle, I think. Get everybody together and in the car and truck and we can get going. Is Lionel here?"

"Yeah. Inside. Everything is set. Wait a minute, let me help you, Charity. Gosh, your pants are all dirty."

Charity grimaced and nodded, trying not to lean on the pregnant girl. "Don't say anything to Lionel, will you. If he thinks I have something wrong, we won't get going for hours. All I want is an ice bag and a bandage."

"I can get that for you if you want to get back in the car, then if Lionel comes out he won't notice anything."

"Thanks, Pris. Call the girls together while you're in there then we can be ready to roll as soon as Lionel comes out of the house." Charity settled back into the vehicle with a pained sigh, biting down on her lip when she saw how anxious Pris became. She and the other girls had enough on their minds without worrying about her ankle. "Hurry up. I'll be fine."

Pris ran up the steps and into the brownstone that had a tattered, bruised look to it, as did many of the fine old buildings on West Forty-first Street in New York.

In short order the girl was back with Charity, helping her with the ice pack and bandage.

"Gosh, it's swollen." Pris pointed to Charity's ankle when the pant leg was raised.

"Never mind that. Let's get the bandage on before Lionel gets wind of what we're doing."

It was makeshift at best because Charity was sitting behind the steering wheel, but finally the leg was wrapped and the wrinkled cotton pant leg pulled down to cover it.

"Hey, you two, what's up?" Lionel stuck his head in the passenger window of the car, the other four girls standing around him.

"Waiting for you. Let's go." Charity gave her puzzled-looking friend a wide smile then noticed that his attention was on something behind her.

"Wow. Look at that. A Lamborghini. What a great machine. I'd like to save my pennies and get one some day," Lionel breathed.

"Dammit, no, not today." No one heard Charity's disgusted comment. There were too many remarks on the dashing Italian vehicle.

Charity didn't have to turn around to know that Tell was coming her way. A burning, electric sensation on the back of her neck telegraphed his nearness. Taking a deep breath she looked up and out her open side window. Though it was early in the day the August heat was already coming off the pavement. "Hi."

"Hello." Tell frowned. "Is something wrong? You

53

have an odd expression on your face and you're pale. What's bothering you?"

Nothing except her leg that was thumping like a drum. "Just anxious to get going. Nice of you to see us off. Good-bye. C'mon girls, get in the car."

"We'll only be taking two in this car," Tell told her, going around to the passenger side of the car and pulling the front seat forward so that two of the girls could get in the back. "Gareth will be driving my car and taking one of the girls and the other two can ride in the truck."

"Manipulator. I didn't plan a safari." Charity glared at him, reaching forward to switch on her engine. It roared and rattled to life. "My appointment to get a new muffler is on next Wednesday." It irked her that she'd explained that to him.

"Why don't you have this thing shot, give it a funeral and get a new one?" Tell glanced at her. Instead of a tirade she was biting her lip as though concentrating on something. "What's wrong, Charity?" Wariness chilled him.

"Ah, nothing."

"Yes, there is. Charity—" Pris interjected.

"Never mind that, Pris."

Charity's quick interruption brought Tell around in the seat so that he was facing her, his one arm along the back of her seat. "Charity. Tell me what's going on. Now."

"When we get to Bigham Park. Right now I have to keep my mind on the traffic." Charity pulled out, checking that the other cars were behind her. Conversation died as she maneuvered her way to the bridge that would take them to the thruway and north to Bigham Park.

For the first time in her life Charity was grateful for the press of cars going in and out of Manhattan. It

54

allowed her to keep her mind totally on her driving, ignoring Tell, who hadn't taken his eyes from her, and the pain in her left leg that seemed to be thumping more each mile despite the ice pack.

Never had the trip in a car seemed so arduous to her. The journey loomed endlessly.

"Charity, you're perspiring and it's not that hot in this damned car."

"It's cooler in the truck. That's why Lionel is driving the kittens in his space behind the seat."

"Find a place to pull over and I mean now."

"Now listen, Tell—"

"I mean it, Charity."

Perhaps she would have given him an argument if it wasn't killing her arms to steady the car while pulling a trailer that was jammed to the rafters with the girls' personal things. Her leg throbbed more and more and even though she didn't need to use her left one for driving, the pain had increased, clouding her thoughts. She was not in the best shape for driving or having an all-out verbal battle with Tell, especially with Pris as an avid witness. It would be heavenly to elevate her leg, then soak in the hot tub, something she was going to do as soon as she reached Bigham House.

Signaling and cursing under her breath at the same time because of the sway of the car, Charity sighted a hole in the press of cars. Edging over to the side of the highway, the car and trailer rocked when she hit the cindered shoulder. She saw in her mirror that the truck and the Lamborghini had followed suit. With an angry sigh she turned to face Tell. "Now will you tell me what's itching at you so much that I had to pull over and stop. We have a distance to go—"

"Get out of the driver's seat. I'm taking the wheel."

Charity was still sputtering her outrage when Tell

came around to her side of the car, opened the door and lifted her from the seat. "Now, listen—"

"Stop arguing or we're liable to have an accident. Those cars whizzing by are damn close." Tell looked down at her when he shepherded her around the car. "You're limping. Why? Is that an ice bag in your hand?"

"You said we shouldn't dawdle out here on the highway, so let's not."

"Damn you, Charity. I'll find out what the hell is going on, and you can bet your next check on it." Lifting her in his arms, he strode to the passenger door that he'd left open, smiling his thanks at Pris when she leaned forward and closed the glove compartment door that popped open all the time in the old car, then he placed her in the seat and shut the door with a decided bang.

"Did you tell him what happened, Charity?"

"No, Pris." Charity looked out of the windshield, aware that Tell had leaned in the car and had heard what Pris had said. "Shouldn't we be going?"

"This isn't the end of it, pet." Tell wrenched her chin around and planted a hard kiss on her mouth.

"Wow," Pris breathed. "Where did you find him, Charity?" Pris watched as the grim-faced man went around the car again to get in the driver's side.

"Under a rock," Charity muttered as Tell opened the car door.

Tell had signaled the vehicles behind them that he was ready to go, then maneuvered back into traffic. "What's so amusing, Pris?"

"Charity said she found you under a rock."

"Did you say that, my sweet?" Tell put his hand on her knee and squeezed gently.

Charity nodded. "You're a toad, Tell Layton, a bossy toad."

56

"Why, darling, how you talk."

Charity could hear the gravel in his voice, telegraphing his irritation. She decided it wasn't the time to trade words with him. Turning around, she caught the bright-eyed looks that Pris was shooting from Tell to her and back again. It was definitely not the time for a contretemps. Biting back a wince she edged her left leg into a less cramping position and leaned back, closing her eyes. She definitely needed an aspirin and a long soak in the hot tub in the master suite at Bigham House.

The noise of the passing traffic was deafening. Charity rolled up her window and bent forward to turn on the air conditioning, praying it would work for a change. It rattled into life. Charity sighed her relief, slamming shut the glove compartment door again.

Already she regretted letting Tell into her car—into her mind—into her life. Many of the barriers she'd buttressed her life with crumbled in his presence. It was as though she stood naked in the Gobi Desert, racked with chills and fever whenever he was with her.

"What happened to your leg, Charity?"

"Ah, nothing, really."

"I can tell you. She hurt her ankle, maybe pulled a muscle." Pris leaned forward from the backseat, smiled at the two adults then settled back in her seat next to Rita, who had fallen asleep the moment the car had begun to move.

"Details," Tell said grimly.

Charity was about to tell him to stuff it but she knew he was quite capable of pulling over the car again and staying put until she told him. Glancing over her shoulder at Pris who was leaning back watching the traffic, her eyelids fluttering, and the soundly sleeping Rita, Charity took a deep breath and sketched the morning's incident in the garage of her apartment.

57

"Christ," Tell muttered. "You should have called the police at once."

"It was just a stupid accident." Charity looked sideways at him as he began berating her actions, watching that strong mouth move. Though she didn't listen to the words, his hard face telegraphed his anger. He was a damned beautiful man.

"And don't think I don't know you've skated over what happened, because I do."

"Don't be a bear, Tell." Charity bit back a flinch, grateful he was driving. Just recounting to him what had happened made her body quiver in reaction. Added to his presence that was always disastrous to her nervous system, she felt as weak as one of the kittens Lionel was carting in the truck. Not since the early days when she'd arrived in New York by herself had she felt so helpless, so at sea. She hated the feelings that Tell created in her because she felt she had no defenses against them. He had instilled a self-confidence in her which was good, but there was also that reckless, sexual sensation of wanting to chuck everything and run away with him on a journey—say, to Mars or Pluto—that was always just under the surface. It was so stupid! So many times when she had first started Columbia University she'd had the urge to call Tell to help her, to take her away, but she'd fought it. Not that she'd had a bad experience at college, she hadn't. Her luck in many ways had been phenomenally good. Jacob Henry had gotten in touch with her when she was apartment hunting and had given her the name of a friend who owned a building near Columbia. She had stayed there for the four years she was at school. It was only after she'd begun working at Promise House that she sought and found another location, on her own this time. That had satisfied her even if the apartment had not.

The check her grandfather sent her each month easily helped defray the cost of her rent. Though she had been adamant at the amount of money she would take from Cyrus, she had been most grateful to Jacob Henry when he had come forward with the added bonus of the monthly stipend that she assumed had come to her from her mother's estate. At least she was pretty sure that was the source because when she'd mentioned that fact to Jacob he hadn't denied it. Charity remembered how embarrassed he'd been, mumbling something about lawyer-client confidentiality.

How far away those college days seemed even though she was just twenty-four years old now. It was eons ago, not just a few years. Charity had learned a lot about herself and the world around her in those times, how to guard herself, protect her emotions, be wary of relationships. Those early years of being the illegitimate daughter of Julia Bigham had been hard lessons too, but valuable just the same. Trust was not something that Charity gave easily.

Now, in just a few seconds, all the bolstering she'd done on her mind and emotions had been eroded just because one gorgeous man had touched her again, and, much as he'd been like an aura in her early life, he seemed to be becoming a cloud about her again. Since the funeral she'd hardly been able to banish him from her mind. Like the ticking of a clock he would enter her brain at least once an hour and not all her struggling against it had mitigated the damned power of Griffith Tell Layton.

Charity opened her eyes, then closed them again. God! Her schoolgirl crush hadn't resurrected itself, had it? No! It was far more involved than that. She wanted him, woman to man, one on one. There were no childish sentiments included. Damn! It wasn't love, it couldn't be! True love took time, involved deep friendship, com-

59

mitment. This was just a case of adult lust, not lasting, and dangerous if not handled with care.

"Why are you glaring at me, pet?"

"Stop calling me pet."

"I think it's cute." Pris leaned forward from the back, her forearms resting on the back of the front seat. "Is Tell your el primo man, Charity?"

"No!"

"Yes, we're getting married," Tell answered blandly, overriding Charity's explosive negative.

"Gosh, that's great. Why didn't you tell us, Charity? I love weddings. So do the other girls. Don't you want us to come?"

"Of course you want the girls to come, don't you, darling?"

"And he calls you darling, too," Pris sighed, her glance sliding away from Tell to settle on Charity. "Gosh, Charity, your face is so red. Did you get a sunburn or something?"

"No."

"And you sound like you're choking. Maybe we should stop again, Tell." Pris leaned forward and smacked Charity on the back. "There. Is that better?"

"Much," Charity responded hoarsely.

"Of course she's all right, aren't you, love?" Tell put his hand on Charity's knee, feeling the anger quiver through her flesh to his fingers. "She's always been a bit high-strung." Tell took perverse satisfaction in angering Charity. She damned well was always setting his teeth on edge. It still infuriated him that she had refused his dinner invitation. Thinking she might be involved with another man was anathema to him.

"In your ear," Charity breathed as Pris settled back on the seat.

"Darling, I recall you said that to me one other time . . . and I chased you." He could tell by the way her

60

breath caught that she remembered the time just as clearly as he did.

"You didn't catch me."

"This time I will . . . and keep you. I meant what I said about getting married."

"Why would you want to marry me?"

"For all the usual reasons," Tell drawled.

"It can't be money. You're dripping with the stuff."

"True."

Charity's head shot his way. "Or have you made some bad investments and you want to recoup?"

"That must be it." Tell kept his voice even with an effort. He could have strangled her at the moment. "I won't even bother to mention that I am now chief stockholder and managing director of Bigham Holdings."

"That was a stupid remark. Sorry." Charity slumped down in her seat and looked out her side window.

Tell glanced her way, barely able to see her profile. "Things will work out for us, Charity. I'll see to it. Now tell me more about this morning and the car that struck you."

"I told you it was a near miss."

"So you did, but I'd like to know more."

Charity turned to look at him, jolted anew by him, the crisp, clean black hair, the taut hard line of him from eyebrow to ankle. "There really isn't that much to it, Tell. I was in the underground garage of my apartment and a car came out of nowhere and almost struck me. A warning by the security guard alerted me and I threw myself on the hood of a car, one of my neighbor's actually. I suppose it was the side mirror, I don't know really, that hooked my shoe and yanked it hard enough to almost topple me off the car and . . ." Charity's voice trailed as she realized that she'd told him that she turned her ankle when jumping on the car the first time.

"What?" Tell's anger exploded around the car, his foot trodding hard on the accelerator, jerking Charity against her seat belt and waking the snoozing Pris from her nap.

"Why are you so hyper?" Charity glared at him. "You startled me and probably scared Pris and Rita out of their wits."

"He didn't really." Pris covered her mouth with her hand to stifle a yawn. "I always fall asleep in cars and Rita is still zonked."

"Go back to sleep, Pris. I'm sorry I woke you." Tell's measured tone masked the anger inside. Charity could have been badly injured or even killed! The thought was like a blow to his solar plexus. He could have lost her. "You're not staying there another day. You're moving to the apartment." He coughed to clear the hoarseness from his voice. "And don't argue with me."

Charity opened her mouth to speak, then closed it. "Tell, are you all right? You . . . you're gray-looking."

"I'm fine. Give me your word you'll move into the apartment as soon as possible."

"Well, I would, but you see I'll be running back and forth from Bigham House to the city and it would be too much work to move my things at this time."

"Not to worry. I'll have my staff do it. Better yet, move in with me. It will be safer."

"No." Charity lowered her voice. "No, that won't be necessary. I'm perfectly safe. It was an accident."

"So you said."

Charity found him such an enigma. Half the time she couldn't fathom his attitude toward her, but when he'd mentioned that she move in with him, her heart had ricocheted painfully. Move in with him? Was he out of his mind? She'd have to be out of hers to contemplate such a thing. Seeing him every morning over her coffee cup, staring at his tough-planed face as they ate dinner. The ambivalence of hurt and joy such a vision conjured had her catching her breath.

"Does the leg pain you? I heard you gasp."

"A little." Keeping her guard up seemed to be second nature with her when talking to Tell.

"We'll go right to Olivet and have it examined as soon as we unload the girls and their belongings."

"I can't leave them alone to face the family."

"From the look of him, your friend Lionel looks as if he could handle himself pretty well." Tell frowned. "He looks familiar to me."

"He should. Lionel Bevins was a linebacker with the Miami Dolphins before injuries sidelined him and then he came back to New York to run the restaurant business that he'd started. He came to Promise House because he'd studied sociology at college and he wanted to give a helping hand."

"He's Beast Bevins? I've seen him play. He was the best." Tell's voice was harsh. "You seem to be fond of him."

"I am. He's one of my dearest friends."

"Oh?"

"Stop looking as though you swallowed worms. Shouldn't I have good friends? I'm sure you do."

"Everyone should have friends. Is he more than a friend to you?"

"You don't have the right to ask that."

"We disagree on that, my darling. I assure you I would kill any man who tried to take you away from me."

Charity stared at him, hearing the silky menace in his voice. "Tell Layton, you're crazy."

"About you? Perhaps I am."

"What's gotten into you?" Charity shot a quick glance over her shoulder but both girls were sleeping soundly. "I've hardly seen you these last few years, and all of a sudden, you're talking like this. It's unreal."

"I want to marry you. Think about that. When we have more privacy we'll talk again."

Charity's eyes widened. "You're taking a lot for granted."

"You can turn me down or accept me. That's your prerogative. But you better know now that I'm going to do everything in my power to convince you to be my wife."

"Oh."

"Charity, we know each other well and have no illusions about each other and that's a great deal more than many people have when they marry."

"Really? No one knows you, Tell. There's an invisible shield around you that lets no one in, so there's probably a hundred versions of what kind of man you are."

"Whatever I am I want you in my life, Charity. You'll soon know all of me."

"What will you do with that string of ponies you've been keeping for years? Let's face it, Tell, I couldn't pick up a paper and not see you with a gorgeous creature draped over you. Blond, brunette, redhead, you had them all."

"True."

"So there you are. I don't want to be married to a man with a host of beauties that he can run to whenever the little woman becomes boring."

"You'll never bore me, Charity."

"Thank you."

"You're welcome. Oh damn, this conversation belongs in Bellevue." Tell chuckled.

"That still doesn't mean that I go along with this. I'm serious, Tell. I wouldn't want a man who needed other ladies in the wings." Why was she even conversing with him like this? It was asinine. She didn't want to dwell

64

on being Tell's wife. It would make her break out in hives. The man had been her life long menace!

"There won't be anyone but you, pet."

Panic sent a fission up her spine at the sensuous peril she saw in his face, the sexy magnet of his voice drawing her. She had the childish desire to run like hell, climb a mountain, take a plane to Katmandu.

Tell saw the disbelief in her eyes when they locked glances just for a second as he was about to turn in the wide drive that led through the open gates up the gently curving slope to Bigham House. Charity didn't trust him. That put him into a towering rage. He wanted to shake her, kick the daylights out of her wreck of a car, read her the riot act. "We made it, without this heap collapsing. Another modern-day miracle."

"Stop being so pompous about my transportation just because you're angry. This car gives me very little trouble."

"What have you had to compare it with, lady?" Tell stopped the car under the portico at the foot of the steps leading to the main entrance. He pulled far forward to give the vehicles behind him the room they needed, then he turned off the ignition and faced her. "Let me get you a car."

"You made that offer before and again I'm going to tell you I don't need it." Charity felt bound by just a look from him, she didn't need a gift to tie her to him even more. He would act as though he owned her body and soul if he as much as gave her a lollipop. No way! He'd had her strung up emotionally as long as she could remember. At this time in her life she was free of encumbrance and staying that way.

"Never mind." Tell felt that unaccustomed thrust of frustration and anger that only Charity could create in him. He didn't want to hear her rebuff him another time.

"Sometime you might get me a truck though," Charity murmured as Tell was opening his door.

"What?" He looked over his shoulder at her, noting the run of color up her face.

"Nothing."

Tell touched her chin. "You're lovely when you blush, pet, and I have very good hearing."

"Oh my God. It's a freaking palace," Pris whispered from the backseat, breaking the spell between Tell and Charity. "Why didn't you wake me when we were coming up the driveway so I could have seen all of it?"

"You'll have plenty of time to explore the whole place, since you'll be living here for a while."

Tell went around the car and helped Charity and the two girls alight, then he went to the rear of the trailer and opened the small door, almost getting buried in the mini-avalanche of things that fell toward him. "Christ! Who the hell packed this?"

"The girls and I did and it was perfectly all right until you opened the door." Charity covered her mouth with her one hand when she saw how tight-lipped he was. "You look very silly with that scarf draped over you."

"I'm going to paddle you, darling. Count on it," Tell told her silkily. It pleased him when her jaw dropped and she took one step backward.

The door opened and a wide-eyed, though otherwise expressionless Macon moved in measured dignity down the steps toward them. "Let me help you, Mr. Layton. I'll send for some of the stable personnel to give a hand as well, sir."

"Fine, Macon. Ring for them. I'll just get started unloading."

Charity watched the girls get out of the truck and Tell's car, their wide-eyed stares almost the exact replica of Pris's. "Heidi, Marybeth, Liz, over here girls, with Pris and Rita. We'll go up and check your rooms. Only carry your lighter bags. Nothing heavy."

The girls turned as one and started toward her, all of them seeming enthralled with Bigham House.

"Gosh, Charity, I never thought it would look like this," Heidi muttered. "All we need now are some Dobermans to race around the house and eat us and I'd know we were in the Sherlock Holmes story on the English moors."

"The Hound of the Baskervilles was a bull mastiff, Heidi. You should stop watching those old movies on cable, you nut." Liz nudged her friend and laughed.

"Yeah? Well, I just hope you don't get killed in your bed, Liz."

"I wish you wouldn't talk that way, Heidi. It gives me goose bumps."

"Girls, we have no ghosts and no murderers," Charity told them, smothering a yawn. She had been up since six that morning. "Let's look at the rooms."

Hauling two suitcases, Tell approached Charity again. "I think they like their new place. What could be better than to have a good old-fashioned crime to make them squeal and dive under the bedcovers?" His heart thumped hard against his chest wall when Charity laughed and nodded.

"But don't encourage them. I don't want them in my bed every night while I try and convince them that Bigham House doesn't have ghosts."

"I'll get into bed with you instead." Tell chuckled when Charity glared at him and blushed.

"Stop talking that way." Turning away from him, she smiled at her group. "C'mon, girls, I'll lead the way and remember, don't carry anything heavy."

"Oh, we're all right, Charity." Pris grinned, her eyes shining, the smile fading when Macon stepped out of the door again, his black-suited, stern person stopping conversation. "Jeez, if it ain't Jeeves. I saw him on cable."

"That's not the real Jeeves. Is it?" Marybeth breathed.

"Almost." Tell smiled at each of them, noting that Gareth was taking the things he'd toted in the Lamborghini and hoisting the back packs on his shoulders.

Tell didn't wait to be introduced to Lionel Bevins, figuring that he and the ex–football player would meet shortly anyway.

Following behind Charity as they climbed the stairs to the third floor, he couldn't help but notice the graceful sway of her body, the long legs that moved so cautiously, the richness of her hair that swung on her shoulders. Charity had been a lovely but lost child. Now she was a self-assured woman with a deep commitment. The love in her had given her great beauty and he wanted it all. She was his and he was going to keep her. Nothing was going to interfere with that.

As Charity had her hand on the doorknob that led into the Green Wing, Kathleen came out of her suite.

"I want to speak to you, Charity. Now. In here."

"I'll be glad to talk to you after I settle the girls Kathleen, but I'm too busy at the moment."

"I said now." Kathleen's face was mottled an unbecoming red. "It's about bringing ragamuffins into my house. My lawyer has informed me that—"

"You are speaking out of turn, Kathleen." Tell stepped around Charity and spoke before Charity could force out a word. He turned, keeping his body between the two women. "Go into the Green Wing, Charity. We don't want the girls to hear any of this. You can tackle her later."

Charity turned on her heels and walked down the

gallery, now freshly painted, that was a bridge from the Green Wing to the main body of the house.

"I'll—I'll—I'll toss her out on her ear, even if she is grandfather's widow. What's the matter with her? This is my home and there are a battery of lawyers who will swear to it." Charity exhaled all the words in one angry breath. "How dare she talk about the girls in that fashion? Aren't they facing enough in their young lives without her scathing denunciation? Besides, this is my home and she's a guest here at my sufferance. And I can have anyone here that I choose."

"Atta girl. Now move out of the way so I can get through. Whose suitcases are these and where do they belong?"

"Oh. Sorry. The name's on the handle tag." Charity looked around her all at once as they stood on the wide octagonal-shaped landing with the many rooms leading from it. "It looks wonderful, so clean and fresh." She threw open some of the suite doors and laughed out loud. "My goodness, Grandfather would be so pleased at what they've done. He had always said that one day he would renovate the Pink and Green wings." Charity stared at the many paintings on the walls that were framed in the fancy golden scroll as were the many in the gallery. "You know, Tell, I'm going to have the paintings cleaned and refurbished too. So many of these meant a great deal to Grandfather."

"Good idea. I think I might know someone at the Metropolitan Museum who could point you in the right direction." Tell flexed his shoulders and stared at Charity. "But for now could you just direct me so that I can unload some of these things."

"Whoops." She turned to Pris. "This is the Chartreuse suite. You can share it with Marybeth and Rita. Heidi and Liz will take the one next door to you." Charity led the way through the spacious rooms that made

69

up the wing, describing the portraits and pointing out the many lovely porcelain pieces. "The Pink Wing has a large collection of jade pieces that are quite wonderful," she told her entourage. "I hope that the workers were careful with them."

"They were. I had my staff oversee the renovations." Tell saw the dimple quiver at the corner of her mouth. "What's so funny?"

"I'm sure if your people saw to everything, all is in excellent order."

"Bet on it." Tell grinned at her. "I'm going downstairs to supervise the rest of the unloading of that trailer. We'll bring most of it up in the elevator, I think."

Charity watched him retrace his steps down the corridor that would take him to the lift, swallowing a sigh at his lithe movements, the easy swing of his tough, lean body.

"You have an elevator in this place, Charity?"

Charity looked at wide-eyed Liz who wasn't much shorter than she. "We do, but, though it's always kept in good repair, we never used it much."

"Gosh, a house with an elevator in it. What do you think of that, Rita?"

Charity watched the more slender, blond girl who was the great enigma of the five. Charity knew that she had been well grounded in literature and history and was quite sure that she had gone to a fine school. Rita was a little older, seventeen, than the other girls and far more reserved, yet the desperate, panic-filled characteristics shown by most of the other girls were no less in her by being more carefully masked. If anything, Rita seemed the most vulnerable and surprisingly more fearful. Charity had spent a great deal of time with the girl but she had not achieved as good a level of trust that she'd been able to build with the others. Instead, Charity had the feeling that the least push to unravel Rita's personal mystery would send the girl into headlong flight.

Rita shot a glance at Charity, then smiled at the younger girl. "Yeah, it's great to have an elevator in the house, but it would be better for us if we used the stairs. Exercise. Remember?"

"Ugh."

Everyone laughed and the awkward moment passed, but Charity was left with the feeling that Rita was not impressed.

"Ah, excuse me, Miss Bigham. I'm Nadine. Macon said that I was to be in charge of the young misses' rooms and to help them when I could."

Charity spun around and stared at a rather buxom young woman. "You're from Bigham Park, aren't you? I seem to remember you," Charity questioned.

Nadine reddened. "My father is Macon's brother, miss. I'm Nadine Macon."

"Of course. You used to come and take lessons in riding with me."

"That's right, miss, though I still don't like most of the filthy beasts." Nadine wrinkled her nose making the other girls laugh.

"I should like to ride, I think."

"And so you shall Marybeth, if the doctor says that you can, but you will also help in cleaning up your rooms, making your beds just as you did at Promise House. We have the same rules here."

"Oh jeez." Pris grimaced, then smiled. "But I bet the food will be better."

"It couldn't be worse." Heidi joked.

"All right, group. I'm going to leave you to settle yourselves with Nadine to help you. Whenever you're through up here, feel free to wander the house or come down to the first floor, or even go outside. Your chore list will be in the kitchen and, as in Promise House, it won't be heavy work but it will have to be done according to schedule. See you." Charity walked along the wide corridor leading to the stairs, the girls remarks singing around her. They did sound carefree . . . Rita would take a little work, maybe, but the others seemed fine.

Charity let her glance touch the beautiful sculptures in the wall niches in the corridor. Bigham House was like a museum with its fine collection of objets d'art and now it belonged to her and she would keep it as her grandfather would have wanted.

As she approached the staircase, she pulled up short when Kathleen and Lyle came out of her step-grandmother's suite of rooms. Clenching her hands at her sides, she tried to summon up a smile though she wasn't feeling too friendly toward Kathleen at the moment.

"We've been waiting for you, Charity," Kathleen said accusingly.

"It would seem so." Charity lifted her chin, staring straight at her stepgrandmother, aware that Lyle was smiling. "Well I'm here." She glanced at her watch. "I can give you a few minutes but I want to shower and change for dinner."

"Watch your mouth, young lady. Whether you know it or not, I do have the legal power to have you removed from this house, you and your gaggle of street urchins."

CHAPTER THREE

Charity reeled with the information that Jacob Henry gave her when she called him immediately afterward. Kathleen was not bluffing!

"Yes, my child, I'm afraid, in spite of the safeguard your grandfather insisted on to protect your estate, Kathleen and her family actually have a few cannons they can use against us. It's much more complicated than we had thought. If she and her lawyers try to make a case for incompetency, there are questions she could raise before a magistrate that might cause some problems, anything she could dredge up that might question your ability to handle your estate could bring about a legal confrontation." Jacob had coughed lightly. "Of course, if she decides she wants to do battle in court I'm sure she couldn't win, but the case could be in litigation for years. It could tie your hands as far as taking care of the girls you now have and the use you wanted to make of Bigham House in the future. All the work you wanted to do with the Promise House girls . . ."

". . . could go down the drain," Charity finished the sentence for the lawyer, her voice taut and charged with fatigue.

"Yes."

To Charity, Jacob's affirmative was like a death knell over the phone. For a moment her mind went blank, then her mounting fury burst forth in grating commitment. "Jacob, I'm not sending those girls back to Promise House. They love it here. The small jobs they do make them feel that they are contributing, that they belong. They need that. Enough has been taken from their lives, I won't remove anything else. I'm keeping the girls here . . . and I'm going to fight any takeover of Bigham House, by anyone." Her voice trembled to silence. "This could get rather nasty. If you want to appoint someone else to represent me, I will understand."

Jacob chuckled. "Not on your life, child. Do you know how many imbroglios I was in with Cyrus? This is a mere nuisance. I'm standing with you, and we'll win." Jacob laughed. "Let them try anything with us."

"Up the rebels."

"Indeed." Jacob paused. "I think you should inform Tell of these new developments, my dear. As you know, he is now the CEO of Bigham Holdings and will have an interest in what is going on with anything that has that name."

"I thought I would talk to him later today. I just couldn't do it yesterday when Kathleen hit me with this."

"You needed time to get to your feet again. I understand and I'm very glad you called me."

"Thank you, Jacob. I do feel better."

"I understand that Tell spends a great deal of time out there."

"Well, yes, but many of Grandfather's business papers are still here in his library and Tell finds it easy to handle some things from here." Charity had heard the quizzical amusement in his voice and felt suddenly defensive with the man she'd known since childhood. Did all the thinking about Tell she did show on her face?

74

"I see, my child, no explanation necessary. Good-bye, Charity. Keep your chin up."

"Good-bye, Jacob and thank you."

After she replaced the receiver Charity sat back in her grandfather's chair in his library, lifting her feet and putting them on the worn oak desk just as he had often done. She had loved the quiet serenity of the room even as a child. Letting her eyes scan the floor-to-ceiling bookshelves, her glance rested on volumes that had been her favorites and her grandfather had read to her.

"If ever any of the Sherlock Holmes stories are out of the order that we placed them in, Charity, then you will know that something is amiss at Bigham House."

"And that's our secret, isn't it, Grandfather?" How she had loved having special secrets with Cyrus that just the two of them shared.

"Indeed it is. Now that we have finished Arthur Conan Doyle, let's try Melville to cleanse our palates. Go up the ladder and get *Moby Dick*, Charity."

She felt so close to her grandfather when she was in the library.

She had informed the Beeches several days ago that she didn't want anyone except Tell and herself in the library, since it was being used as their office. She could still visualize the encounter.

"You have your nerve, Charity. This is our home."

"Not any more, Amby. The will says it's mine."

"She's right, Amby," Jennifer Beech had interjected, earning her brother's glare and her mother's frown. "Well, it's true. And I for one hate all this unpleasantness. I would rather move. Lionel says that New York is very nice in the autumn and we could move there to the townhouse."

"You, young lady, are not to consort with those people from that place." Kathleen had an affronted, angry look on her face. "And I might remind you that you are showing very little loyalty to your family in this."

"Lionel Bevins is a warm and decent human being who happens to control a franchise of restaurants across this country that bear his name. The work he does at Promise House is strictly volunteer. He is a strong and gentle man." Charity had lashed out in defense of her friend.

"You will kindly not interfere in our family, Charity." Kathleen looked down her nose, her lips tightening. "And you will kindly not interfere in the running of this house." At that point Charity had turned and stalked from the sitting room, hearing the angry protests behind her.

Charity had developed an armor over the years she was on her own. She wasn't put off by the anger of the Beeches. When she felt the need, she spoke her mind. She admitted to herself that she wouldn't be as possessive about Bigham House if it hadn't involved the future of the girls. Determination to give them some measure of security and closeness became her driving force.

She sighed now as she thought of what Jacob had said. The Beeches were proving to be very tough adversaries and she would have to watch her step with them or risk losing everything.

Rising to her feet, she stretched, feeling a beading of moisture on her upper lip. It was the first week of September but the weather was even warmer than it had been in August. It would be heaven to swim in the lake. At that moment she wanted to bury her worries. Cool, refreshing exercise was the answer.

When she left the library, she carefully locked the door behind her. Only Macon and Tell had keys for the room and Charity knew that neither would give them up to anyone. She straightened with the key in her hand, a chill shivering up her spine. Something was not right. Why had she felt as though someone had walked on her grave as she locked the door? If she concentrated wouldn't what was bothering her surface so that she could deal with it?

"Careful, aren't we?"

Charity swung around to face Ambrose Beech, the elusive moment in time washed from her brain. "Yes, I am."

"We all are used to having free access to any room in this house that we choose to enter, Charity."

"Then unlearn the habit, because no one has carte blanche as far as this house is concerned any longer." Charity lifted her chin and stared at Ambrose when his hands curled into fists. "You have your rooms in this house and access to the living room, dining room, and kitchen. There is no need for a guest to have more." Charity strode past a sputtering Ambrose and hurried up the stairs to her bedroom. She wouldn't be sorry to see the Beeches out of her house.

Grabbing her bathing suit, nylon cap, goggles, and lightweight sailing jacket, she went to the back stairs that led to the kitchen. She knew that none of the Beeches ever used the back stairs and that was another inducement. She wanted privacy, peace and quiet.

"Hello, Rumrill." Charity greeted the plump, rosy-cheeked cook who beamed at her. The woman had been her staunch friend, just as Macon had been, since she'd been a child. Both retainers had been devoted to her mother, as well, neither one quite recovering from her mother's accidental death.

"Going swimming, Charity? Be careful when you're swimming alone. Maybe one of the boys at the stable will go with you."

"I want to be alone, Rum, really I do. Oh by the way, if you see Mr. Layton, tell him I would like to talk to him before dinner. Thank you."

"You be careful now, Charity. That lake is deep."

Charity nodded, blew the older woman a kiss and left the house, jogging across the well-manicured yard to the wood that was about a half-mile deep and acted as a natural barrier on the north side of Bigham House property. Because the house was on a knoll there was a view of the lake from it, but the woods still provided a measure of privacy.

The path to the lake wound its meandering way through the shady silence, the perfumed summer air filled with the cawing of crows, the singing of cardinals, the steady hammering of woodpeckers who sought their dinners in the dead trees dotted here and there throughout the mini-forest. Charity's grandfather had always insisted that the area maintain its wildness and as a result it was an almost untouched retreat. It had been her hideaway as a child and she felt at home in the woods.

She was halfway through when she heard the unusual but not unfamiliar sound of falling timber. Charity had often heard that certain roar when the men would split the dead trees to use as firewood in the huge fireplaces of Bigham House.

Turning and looking upward, she stared like an automaton at the huge oak that was falling toward her. Life went into slow motion as her brain told her to escape while her limbs were still paralyzed. When she began to move, the instructions hammered into her head by her grandfather dictated her action. Charity ran toward the danger, not away from it, angling from the fall line as she'd been drilled to do, time and time again. Getting scratched by branches from the tree was far preferable to being caught under its lethal weight. As she sped, dropping everything she carried, Charity could hear her grandfather's admonishments like a clarion in her mind.

"If you run at an angle toward the tree, child, you'll keep it in sight. Always watch the fall line. Don't ever turn your back. You'll be immediately disoriented and could easily take the wrong direction. Keep cool, use your head. Never panic."

A sixth sense told her she was not quite free of peril so Charity threw herself forward, feeling the searing tear of branches on her arms and legs as she tumbled to the ground a few feet from the now fallen oak, the thunder of sound reverberating like a fading drum roll in the woods. She was winded but not hurt, coughing from the dust that rose in a cloud around the fallen timber.

Some minutes later she moved, coming to a sitting position. Her hands shook as she wiped the sticks from her hair and touched her bloodied scratches gingerly. "Good God, that was too close."

Charity lifted a small branch from her legs, then brought them up to rest her chin on her knees, hugging herself, trying to still her trembling. Taking deep, shaky breaths, she stared at the oak. How the hell had such a fresh tree fallen? There wasn't even a breeze to give it impetus.

Pressing her hand to her forehead, she looked around her. Her things were scattered along the line of her flight. Bracing her hand on a limb of the oak she rose to her feet, feeling rocky, sweaty, off balance. Her wonderful, safe woods had just been a place of maximum danger and it shook her.

Gathering her things, one by one, she climbed over the hefty trunk and reached the path again, looking back once more at the tree. She would have to get the gardeners out here to clear away the path. It might be a good idea to have them check the rest of the trees at the same time. Instead of trotting the rest of the way, she walked slowly, the slight sprain she'd received in the garage aching in reaction to her running.

79

Charity was glad to see the sunshine glistening off the lake. She needed the light, the brightness, the safety.

Bigham Lake was a thirty-mile-long spring-fed body of water that was a recreation area for Bigham Park residents and some summer cottage owners at the far end. It wasn't too crowded with summer places near Bigham House because Cyrus Bigham had secured almost three thousand feet of frontage for himself, thus ensuring privacy on the house's side of Bigham Lake.

Charity had spent as much time as possible on the water during her summer vacations and she could swim like a seal, water ski, sail and do any other water sport like a veteran. Even now, as fatigued and shaken as she was, she looked forward to her swim and maybe a sail later.

Changing into her suit that was cut high on the thighs and low on the breast, the golden fabric like a second skin, silky and light, Charity walked out on the end of the dock, inhaling the fresh, soft air of a waning New York State summer. Kneeling down she reached into the water for handfuls to throw on herself, gasping at the sudden coldness, but laughing with joy of being in one of her favorite places.

Rising, she launched herself off the dock into what she knew was ten feet of water, thrusting herself outward in a long clean dive, staying underwater as long as she could to savor the freshness, the feverish feeling leaving her body in a rush.

Surfacing, she kicked outward, stroking strongly out to the middle of the lake. Caution dictated that she didn't try for the other side, two miles away, unless she had someone with her, so she turned when she was maybe halfway, not the least winded or out of control, and began stroking back the way she'd come.

Years of swimming in the lake had ingrained in her much knowledge about it. When she felt the roll of water about her she instinctively knew without looking that a powerful boat was headed her way. Realizing that she could be overlooked by the pilot of the boat and run over, she speedily doubled her body and shot downward in a strong dive that arrowed her into the depths of the clear lake. Lungs beginning to burn, she turned on her back and looked upward, seeing the froth of the engine right above her, churning the water.

Charity, with a last burst of air and strength, thrust her body sideways trying to get away from the path of the motor.

Dizzy with lack of oxygen, she shot to the surface. A sense of danger making her gulp air quickly and ready herself for another dive. What she saw almost made her lose the lungful of air she took. The boat, that she thought had gone over the top of her was being engaged by a sleeker and faster power boat, the two dueling not a hundred yards from her.

As one headed her way, Charity was mesmerized by the water battle taking place in front of her, the two boats charging her way at breakneck speed. Realizing that she was in imminent peril if she continued to watch, she took evasive action herself, sucking in gulps of air then jackknifing her body into another dive into the lake. This time she didn't waste energy and air by looking upward. Instead she angled her body toward the shore and pulled as hard as she could in the underwater breaststroke that took her out of the path of the boats.

Popping to the surface, totally out of breath and fatigued, she panted roughly and gazed at the shore as though it were leagues away instead of a few hundred feet. Charity didn't turn around when she heard the motor behind her, she just swam as hard as she could, though the breath labored from her body. In desperation she tried to go faster, knowing full well she didn't have the strength to dive again, nor the power to outrun a boat. When strong arms came around her, she gave a hoarse scream of fear.

"Darling, don't. It's all right. I have you."

"Tell," Charity breathed, her body going limp, stars whirling behind her eyes.

"It's all right. Let me take you. My boat's anchored back a ways. Come on."

Charity didn't have the strength to question him. She only knew she had faith in him, that he stood between her and the frightening moments of the past. Curling limp arms around his neck, she allowed him to tow then lift her up the wooden back platform of the boat and over onto the seats warmed by the sun.

She lay there looking up at him, not able to control the trembling of her limbs.

"What the hell is going on, Charity?" Tell's face was grim as he wrapped her in bath sheets, then lifted her in his arms as he sat down on the back bench seat. He cradled her close to him, the boat rocking gently beneath them.

"I almost had a bad accident in the lake," she told him shakily. The smile slipped from her face as she relived those harrowing moments, the boat like an evil specter in her memory.

"Some damn accident that was. Whoever the hell was driving that Formula looked like he was aiming his boat at you as if you were his target. Charity, tell me you're all right."

Charity was going to give him a flip answer until she saw the flicker of agony in his eyes, the tautness of his features. "I'm fine."

Tell tightened his grip on her as she continued to shiver. The only sounds in the summer stillness were the rasping of breaths and Charity's teeth chattering. "Charity, did you recognize the driver? I couldn't see anything but the back of him. He was dressed in white

82

clothes and was wearing a cap, but the damned wrap-around windscreen was black Plexiglas."

Charity shook her head. "I never even got a good look at the boat, let alone the driver." She looked up at Tell, noting his furrowed brow. Though his hand continued to massage her skin gently through the towel he'd wrapped around her, Charity knew his mind was elsewhere. "What are you thinking?"

"For someone who is one of the best coordinated persons I know you seem to be having a great many accidents, pet. You're already overshooting the law of averages and I don't like it." Tell gripped her upper arms. "Have you run afoul of a druggie at your work place, or a deranged person?"

"Promise House deals with children on drugs, but I have never felt threatened by any of them."

"How about the pusher or pimp who had one of the kids under his wing?"

Charity shook her head slowly. "No, ah, I don't know. No, I don't think there's anyone like that."

"But you're not sure, that's obvious."

"I don't know what you'll say when I tell you about the tree, then." Charity had every intention of smiling at him. When the tears bubbled out of her, she was shocked and dismayed.

Charity was not a crier. She was a doer, a chin-up person! Knowing that made fear swell in Tell. He felt threatened and infuriated by her vulnerability.

"I'm . . . I'm sorry." Charity gulped, trying to wipe her face with a loose end of the towel.

"Darling, darling, it's all right. I'm going to take care of you. I'm never letting you out of my sight." Tell bent his head and kissed her on the lips, his mouth covering hers gently, deepening the pressure as his hands held her closer. He lifted his head a fraction. "Tell me about the tree."

83

Dazed by his caresses but feeling calmer, she described in halting phrases the fall of the fresh oak tree.

"Oak trees don't usually tumble to the ground when there's no wind, and when the tree is very much alive."

"That's what I thought, Tell, but it must have been rotted in the core because it came down."

"Umm, I'll take a look at it when we return to the house." All at once he kissed her again, his hard mouth coaxing and tender on hers.

"Tell," Charity breathed into his mouth, her body going slack with joy when she felt his tongue touch hers then circle the inside of her mouth as though he had to explore, then mark her as his own. It was as though all her dreams of Tell as Romeo to her Juliet were being enacted. It was wonderful and incredible!

Tell lifted his head for a moment. He knew he couldn't make love to her in plain sight of any ogler passing by in another boat. With one strong motion of his body, Tell rose to his feet, carrying her with him. Then he lifted her, taking her down into the single forward cabin of his craft. Placing her on the wide bunk fastened to the bulkhead, he positioned himself at her side. "You're beautiful, Charity and I've waited for you a long time, darling."

"You have?" Charity couldn't seem to get air in her lungs.

'I have." He chuckled softly, leaning over her, his lips touching her eyelids, then slipping along her cheek to her ear, his tongue intruding there. "You must have known, pet."

"I didn't." Whenever she had been around Tell he had been satirical and cutting. She had spent her time lashing back at him, trying with all her might to wound the man who had been in her thoughts too often. Charity tried in every way she could to defend herself against her feelings for him. Now the planet had spun out of its

84

orbit and she was lying in Tell's arms. Was this only one of her dreams or was it real?

Charity's body began to quiver as Tell's strong fingers touched each pulse point. The shivering wasn't from reaction or fear, but from a wanting, a desire that seemed to have been lying dormant, deep in the core of her for so long, now blossoming to life at Tell's touch. A liquid heat permeated her that both enflamed and immobilized her. Never in her wildest imaginings had she conjured such sensations. She wanted nothing more than to embrace him, caress and kiss him.

"I don't want you to be cold," Tell said as he unwrapped the bathsheet from her body, his eyes not leaving her face.

"I'm not cold."

He smiled at her, the smile fading when his eyes washed slowly over her form, his face suddenly flushed, the glitter in his eyes like an electric charge that warmed her, taking away all chill, all foreboding.

Charity reached up and wrapped her bare arms around his neck, pulling him closer. She closed her eyes when she felt him slip the straps of her bathing suit off her shoulders, baring her breasts in slow, silky strokes.

"You are so beautiful, darling. I want to look in your green eyes, sweet one."

The hoarse words were like expletives torn from his mouth, as though he were afraid that somehow he was revealing too much of himself to her. Charity's eyes flew open, locking to his gaze.

"That's better, my pet," Tell said as he bent his head to her breast.

The tender pulling of her nipple with his mouth had Charity gasping and writhing beneath him. He was tearing her apart and rebuilding her in sweet, tortuous movements.

"I've wanted this for so long, Charity. I hated it when I knew I couldn't be your first."

At the harsh words, Charity stiffened. "Did you want to be?" Charity hardly recognized the rough sensuality of her own voice.

"Oh yes, I wanted that, but then I would never have let you go, so it couldn't have been." Tell grimaced at the thought.

Charity reached up and rubbed her hand against the slight growth of beard that was there even on his freshly shaven cheek. So many times she longed to rub her hand there. "You should have asked me what I thought of that."

Tell kissed the pulse in her throat. "You were so young, my pet. I was much older than you. I couldn't and wouldn't manacle you to me when you'd barely begun to test your wings at Columbia. You needed space, so I gave it to you and waited." His lips took hers in a hard kiss. "But if anyone had tried to tie you into a permanent relationship, darling, I would have kidnapped you and taken you away with me," he muttered, letting his mouth slide along her jawline, feeling the quiver there. "What's so funny?"

"You are. Most of the times when we met, we didn't even talk about the weather before we began arguing, let alone discuss a person either of us might have been seeing. Battling was the main thing we did. Besides, you wouldn't have known if I had decided to live with someone."

"I would have. I always knew where you were and what you were doing."

"Tell!" Charity cupped his face in both her hands, staring up into his face. All at sea, both excited and frightened by the torrent of passion between them, she felt confused. "You said you waited."

"Yes."

"Not without women." The words spurted from her mouth.

Tell looked down at her, his fingers combing through her hair. "Does that bother you?"

"Yes . . . no, I don't know. I . . ." He had been a man of varied tastes when it came to women. Blondes, brunettes, redheads had been brought to Bigham House at various times through the years. She had thought none of them attractive. "It was a stupid remark."

Before she could say anything else, his mouth closed over hers again. Then he lifted his head just a fraction. "No more talking. I want to love you."

Nothing could temper the passion he had for her. The longing had built over the years and now threatened to burst, but a deep sense of wanting to protect her filtered through the fire and he held back, still caressing her tenderly but masking his impatience, moving slowly.

"Tell?" He was wonderful, but why was he hesitating? "I'm not a virgin, you know."

"Dammit, I figured that. It's just that you're special, pet, and so is this moment. I never had any intention of making love to you on my boat the first time, anyway."

"I think it's beautiful here."

"Do you?" Tell's mouth moved down her body in slow exploration, his movements sure and sweet. He held her loosely, allowing her the decision of whether he should continue or stop. Then his hand began to tremble as the heat of the caresses penetrated him and his concentration intensified on her and became a hunger, an urgency that he couldn't control. "Darling?"

Charity muttered in protest when he pulled back from her, hating anything that intruded on the aura they'd created. Never had she felt such hot longing. "Don't leave me."

"Never." Tell's body thrust slowly into hers, luxuriating in the velvet hold of her body. When he heard her moan, he pulled back. "You're not ready, love." He scanned her face.

"I said I wasn't a virgin, I didn't say that I was actively involved with anyone."

"Damn you, Charity," he murmured huskily. "I could have hurt you."

"You didn't." She gasped when he ducked his head over her body, his mouth moving down her form. When his tongue touched her in an intimate way, a way that no one had ever touched her, her body arched in surprised delight. "Tell."

"Shhh. I'm loving you."

Torrid emotion cascaded through her body. Her limbs felt as heavy as lead, but she had the sensation of flying. Stars burst around her in a kaleidoscope of loving that she had never imagined, let alone felt. Her body melted under his ministrations. Digging her nails into him to keep him with her, she heard his low groan of satisfaction. Blood pumped through her body like a torrent, oxygen left her as she seemed to explode. Charity felt her body and mind break away and soar, as the rush of warmth suffused her. Heated and breathless, she stared up at him in wordless wonder, awed at the depth of feeling that had overcome her.

"We're just beginning, darling." Tell entered her moist cavern that his loveplay had created and began to move easily, his heart pounding as she began to move in rhythm with him in the age old joining of Adam and Eve.

In thunderous union they became one, neither able to hold back the flood of love that enveloped them.

Did hours pass? Or minutes?

"Tell? I'm wrung out, a dish rag," Charity told him, barely able to lift her lids to look at him. "Good heavens, does this happen to everyone? I had no idea. No wonder they write about it."

Tell hugged her, laughing into her hair, triumph a golden flood in him at her words. "I don't know if it happens to anyone else, but it's brand new and wonderful for me, lady."

With a doomsday joy, Charity accepted that Tell was the man of her dreams, even as she feared any union with him. It would be like diving off the cliffs at Acapulco . . . anyone's guess if you come out alive. Besides, if Tell was right and someone at Promise House was after her because of real or imagined grudge, then she couldn't draw him into it. It would tear her apart if anything happened to him. In one short moment on a hot late summer afternoon he had become the hub of her life and she was both elated and downhearted at the thought.

All the preconceived notions she'd had about never being able to get too excited about sensuous love had just gone up in smoke because of the touch of Griffith Tell Layton. Every passionate sensation on the planet was directed at the man who held her because he had introduced her to lovemaking. She realized that she had been waiting for this moment forever.

"I think we might be a little late for dinner this evening," Tell told her softly, cuddling her close to him.

"Good Lord," Charity cried, pushing away from him. "It's bad enough that Kathleen is threatening me with expulsion from Bigham House without giving her more ammunition."

"What? She'll do that over my dead body. I promise you that."

"They might just walk over both our bodies." Charity looked around for her things, swiping the damp hair from her forehead. "The Beeches think everything I do is insanity, now they'll be complaining about my tardiness at dinner."

"Again." Tell rose slowly, watching her creamy skin

turn peachy in the light that filtered through the small porthole, her nakedness turning him to fire again.

"Huh? What did you say? Oh, give me that, I have to get dressed."

"I reminded you that you were tardy for dinner the first night you stayed in Bigham House after your grandfather's death." Tell laughed out loud at the scathing look she gave him. "Don't look for something to throw at me. You said you're in a hurry."

"You had better get us back to the dock then. I'm not holding us up."

"You used to turn your nose up like that when you were a little girl." Tell grinned at her, then started the engine, gunning it toward the shore.

"You're certainly very cavalier about that expensive craft," she told him tartly, her heart cartwheeling at the hot look in his eyes.

"I'm more concerned that you are accompanied back to the house and anywhere else you may choose to go today and every day. C'mon, let's get out of here." Tell slipped to the dock then turned and lifted her down beside him, his arm around her waist keeping her close to his side.

Charity peeked over her shoulder at the boat they'd just left. The time with Tell would live in her always. It was a bitter moment of truth to realize it might be the only time together they would ever have. She wasn't about to draw him into the menacing web that seemed to be enclosing her. If she was in harm's way, she wanted to make sure that there would be no fallout on Tell.

CHAPTER FOUR

Charity's heart was in her shoes. What gremlin had ever made her open her mouth and offer Bigham House for the site of the annual fund-raising ball to benefit Promise House? It had been abysmally stupid on her part!

Father Desmond—the director and founder of Promise House—had been so depressed that they had been unable to find a suitable place to hold the gala, without which many of the education programs at Promise House would be impossible, that Charity hadn't been able to hold back. She had jumped to her feet and blurted that they could use the home that she'd just inherited. Father Desmond had been overjoyed, but Charity had had second thoughts that same day when she'd told the Beeches what she had planned.

"Again you show your thoughtlessness, Charity, and plunge ahead without any thought for anyone but yourself." Kathleen had walked away before Charity could formulate an answer.

And to compound the frost in the air, Tell made a very unpalatable suggestion to the Beeches: that they move to the townhouse in New York until after the party. This was met with a stony-faced veto. As the days progressed toward the gala, with the house taking on the look of an autumnal garden, the hostility had increased, augmenting the normal party blunders that were occurring. Charity was frazzled.

"I will certainly do my best to convince the family that they should change their minds and go to New York, Charity, but I doubt I will be successful," Lyle told her one afternoon when he entered the large solarium at the back of the house which would be used for dancing. "I think the leaves and bunting are sagging somewhat in that corner."

"Thank you, Lyle, I appreciate the input." Charity had all she could do to smile when what she wanted to do was bite through steel.

"I'm afraid it won't do too much good since the rest of the family seems so set against this venture."

"Speak for yourself, Lyle." Gareth entered the room, smiling wryly at his uncle and Charity. "I think the idea's great. I shall be there with bells on, Charity girl."

"I don't think you should be quite so open with your opinions, Gareth. You could hurt your mother's feelings." Lyle's voice was quiet but firm.

"Stuff it, uncle. My mother is as tough as tanned leather and you know it. Charity, put me to work."

Charity smiled at him, not missing the challenging look he shot his uncle. Lyle stared back enigmatically, inclined his head, and excused himself.

Now all the preparations were over, and the evening loomed disastrous in Charity's eyes. Only the family and a few select friends would be at dinner; the rest would be coming later to dance, offer contributions and feast on the midnight buffet. The good news was that the number of guests expected would fill not only Bigham House to capacity but also the coffers at Promise House.

"God, it will still be horrible," Charity moaned to her mirror image, oblivious to the clinging silk charmeuse dress that twisted around her body like a satin snake.

Its antique gold color enhanced the gold flecks in her emerald eyes, and her flamelike hair was swept up on top of her head. "Father Desmond, Jacob Henry and Lionel will be the only sane people at dinner."

"You look like a sunset goddess just risen from the sea."

Startled, Charity whirled around and saw Tell in the doorway of her bedroom, leaning in indolent grace. "I thought I locked that," she mumbled, staring at his sleek, tall build encased in black silk, the pristine white of his shirt seeming to intensify the black of his hair and the gold of his leonine eyes.

"You didn't darling, and I'm glad." He approached her. "Here. I've brought you something."

Charity eyed the green-gold orchid. "I don't have too many places to pin it, Tell."

"Mrs. Rumrill had told me you were going to wear you hair swept up on the top of your head. I thought it might look nice there." Tell noted how her fine cheekbones were accentuated by the severe style, how long and slender her neck looked with just the thin gold chain with the sapphire heart pendant suspended from it. "You look svelte, beautiful, cool, and competent to handle any situation that might arise . . . and I love it that you wore the heart I gave you."

"Silver-tongued devil, aren't you." Charity couldn't deny the feeling of calm that filled her as she was pulled into the warm aura of his smile. "You look fine as a fivepence, as Grandfather would have said."

"Thank you. You should be wearing earrings to match your pendant. Giving other jewelry to you would make me very happy."

"No thanks, just hand Father Desmond a big check. That's the gold I want from you," Charity told him pertly, grinning when he put back his head and laughed. Tell had the most beautiful strong jaw she'd ever seen, and his teeth were wonderful. It irked her that she couldn't find a flaw in him. Her skin quivered with the knowledge that he watched every move when she affixed the orchid to her hair. When he crooked his arm toward her, she moved foward as though pulled on a string.

"May I escort you downstairs?"

"History repeats itself tonight. The Christians and the lions will be together again in the arena!"

Tell chuckled, feeling his heart turn over when she leaned against him lightly. They walked down the wide stairway to the huge marbled foyer decorated with variegated maple leaves in shades of green, gold, russet, orange, and rust. "The house is an autumnal wonder. I think Cyrus would be pleased."

Charity smiled and looked around her at the brightness of the fall decorations.

"You can't put it off, you know."

Charity nodded at Tell's whisper in her ear, facing the closed drawing room doors where the others would be enjoying an aperitif. "It isn't fair to Father Desmond to leave him alone in there, with only Jacob Henry being decent to him."

"From what I've seen of Cormack Desmond, he's well able to handle himself in most situations. Besides, Gareth will be there and so will Lionel, so there are a few allies, but I repeat: I don't think your Father Desmond needs anyone to help him."

Charity smiled. "Grandfather would have called him a doer."

Tell reached around her and pushed open the double doors. He watched the faces turn toward Charity as she glided into the room, her unconscious grace belying the nervousness she was experiencing. It was wrenching pride and a desire to keep her all to himself that warred

94

within Tell as he noted the admiring glances turning her way.

"Good evening, everyone. I hope you have all met Father Desmond." Charity smiled at everyone, her warm glance lingering on Jacob Henry and her guest of honor.

"I performed the amenities for you, Charity." Lionel came up to her, a glowing Jennifer on his arm, a grin on his face. "He was especially delighted when I told him that Jennifer and I hoped he would officiate at our wedding."

Forgetting decorum, or the fact that she should have been the very circumspect hostess, Charity threw her arms around her friend, laughing and kissing him, then turned to hug Jennifer. "I'm so happy for the two of you."

"We are too." Jennifer's smile glowed up at her doting fiancé, then she looked back at Charity, grimacing. "But Mother is not thrilled."

"She'll get to like Lionel. How could she resist him?" At that moment the desultory conversation in the room faded for a moment and Charity's words caroled loud and clear to all.

Her face reddening even more when she heard Tell chuckle behind her, she lifted her chin, her demeanor stiffer than it had been. Moving forward rapidly, Charity put out her hand to her mentor and honored guest, smiling easily at the man who'd been her friend since she'd first set foot in Promise House. "Father, how are you? I'm sorry I'm tardy in greeting you. There were some last-minute details to be handled. Ready for the big bash?"

"Lionel told me you've been running all day. You shouldn't have done that, child, though I must say this house is a joy to see. It's a first with me to be entertained in anything half so grand." Father Desmond squeezed her hand and smiled at her. "And to answer your questions, I'm fine and yes, I am ready. I'm looking forward to it. And again I say this is a wonderful house, Charity. How kind you are to let us have use of it."

"You're most welcome, Father. I assume you've met everyone else in the room, but may I introduce Tell Layton to you."

"No need, Charity, we're old friends though I haven't seen much of him lately." Father Desmond shook Tell's hand and slapped him on the back, not noticing Charity's wide-eyed stare. "I thought that was you when you first came into the room, but I wasn't sure. These old eyes, you see, aren't what they once were. Are you a relative of Charity's?"

"Not exactly," Tell replied.

"No!" Heads turned at Charity's strong negative. Charity swallowed the words that rose in her throat and moved away from the two men, one watching her narrowly, the other puzzled.

"Charity." Gareth took her arm. "Pre-party nerves, stepniece?"

"You're absurd, Gareth. I'm not your stepniece." Charity could feel herself relaxing at his teasing. She smiled at him. "I guess I am uptight."

"Think how wracked up you'll be tomorrow if it's a success. Mother will be on your case for months if that happens. She considers herself the only hostess of merit for miles around."

"Oh, oh, then I'd better pray for failure."

"You'd better pray to become invisible; here comes the unholy three, my wimp of a brother, my apple-polishing uncle, and La Grande Dame."

Gareth's asides seemed a bit more acidic than usual but Charity didn't have time to question him as the three in question faced her.

"Charity, I do feel you have overstepped your boundaries in many areas but these latest faux pas are most annoying, first this foolish evening . . ." Kathleen began.

"Charity told you to stay at the townhouse, Mother." Gareth shot a tight grin at his brother Ambrose who glared at him. "You didn't want that."

"It was Tell who suggested that," Kathleen told her son frostily before looking back at Charity. "But the fostering of this liaison between that person and my daughter is the most outrageous thing you've done."

"I'm sorry that you don't approve of Lionel, Kathleen, but I didn't 'foster' anything." Charity shot a look at the couple standing next to the Steinway piano. "I doubt an earthquake could have kept them apart."

"They would not have met had you not brought those . . . those . . ."

"Unwed mothers." Charity supplied the words, her scanning eyes finding the girls clustered near Tell and Father Desmond, laughing and smiling. "Perhaps you're right, Kathleen, but I for one am happy for Jennifer and Lionel, especially Jennifer. I have never seen her look so happy."

Charity walked away before more could be said, determined to let nothing put her in a black mood. She touched the sapphire pendant to give herself courage. It had often worked for her in the past.

At that moment, Macon announced dinner and with a sigh of relief, Charity turned toward the door.

"Don't run away from me," Tell murmured behind her, taking her arm.

"Was I doing that? I thought I was running from the Beeches."

"Chin up, darling. You look beautiful and this is going to be a very successful evening."

"I hope you're right."

Charity was pleased that Father Desmond had been seated on her right and Tell on her left. She looked down the table at the Beeches and the girls, who were on opposite sides. She'd had the feeling up to that moment that Kathleen could have somehow changed the arrangement. Thanks to Rum, none of the antagonists was next to another. With a sigh of relief she watched Macon and an attendant serve the cauliflower soup, fragrant with herbs, and then place the crusty home-made finger rolls at each place. No one would be able to fault Rum's food.

Just as Charity lifted her spoon to her mouth, she heard Rum's "stop them!" In slow motion she turned to look at the swinging door leading into the kitchen.

"Oh no," Charity muttered, her spoon poised in front of her mouth, watching as the twin kittens spurted through the small opening. With the momentum of their rush they flung their bodies upward onto the table where the provocative smells were coming from, skidding across the surface, taking damask cloth, napkins, assorted cutlery in a tidal wave to the accompaniment of screeches, protests, muttered curses, and muffled amusement.

Dumbfounded, Charity saw Sweet Basil, who had followed right behind Oregano onto the table but in a lengthier jump, being carried beyond her tortoiseshell sister, only to do a tumble act right down the table as she struggled to right herself . . . finally coming to rest right in Kathleen's soup.

"Macon," Kathleen shrieked. "Do something at once. My God, this house is Bedlam."

At this doom-filled pronouncement, Sweet Basil purred and sat down in the best Haviland china side dish belonging to Bigham House to begin the delightful job of taking the cauliflower soup off her fur.

98

Rum dashed into the dining room, red-faced. "Lord a'mercy, and it's only the first course."

Father Desmond threw back his head and laughed. The young teenage girls watched him for a moment then followed suit.

"See, darling, your guests love the entertainment." Tell kissed the soft skin of Charity's wrist.

"How can you smile at this?" Charity breathed faintly.

"Because I'm beginning to understand how Milton coined the word pandemonium. He must have had Bigham House in mind."

"John Milton would never have written a coherent word in this house," Charity whispered crossly, trying to swallow the giggle that was bubbling up in her at the way Macon spoke stiffly to the cats in his most punctilious English while Rum and two helpers removed the tablecloth as the guests held their plates aloft to ease the procedure.

"Charity, my dear, this has been the most diverting dinner and I shall come again, make no mistake on that." Father Desmond beamed at her. "What do you think, Jacob?"

"Wouldn't have missed it."

Charity could feel the laughter bubble up inside her at the droll smile Jacob gave her. "I don't suppose you do get much chance to go to the circus."

"I will endeavor to change that and come out to visit you at least once a week, Charity my dear."

"Jacob, you're incorrigible." Charity blew him a kiss. "But you have the knack of making me feel better."

"Good, but don't be too affectionate with me. Tell is watching and gnashing his teeth and looking ready for a bit of bare knuckle. Does he bite?"

Charity turned slowly and looked at the man in question, experiencing a quickness of breath at the black emotion flitting over his features, at how the muscle jumped at the side of his mouth, and his eyebrows were like a tight bridge on his forehead. "I believe he does," she said mildly, winking at the angry man who'd been in and out of her dreams since she'd been a little girl. At that moment, for the first time, she felt a little of the power that had always been Tell's exclusively. "Who knows, we may have to cage him." Charity rose from her chair as a signal to the others to begin moving toward the foyer.

Putting her hand through Jacob's arm she smiled at him, turning her back on Tell. "Walk me out to the foyer, will you, Jacob. Our guests will be arriving soon and I should be at the door to greet them."

When they reached the foyer, Jacob rolled his eyes at her. "Why do I have the feeling that we are strolling to the guillotine, child? With Kathleen and her clique on one side and Tell on the other it's so much like running the gantlet or riding in the tumbril cart that I have a strong urge to gallop away and take you with me. *Courage, mon enfant.*"

"Up the rebels."

"You have tweaked a few tails, child, which I think is good, but exercise caution too. Kathleen's lawyer was in touch with me and she is very serious about regaining Bigham House . . . though I'll never know why for the life of me. She spent most of her time as Cyrus's wife begging him to sell the place."

"So I understand," Charity murmured, an elusive thought just bumping the surface of her mind, then melting away again.

"Why are you frowning, Charity?"

"I'm not sure. Something you said made me feel a bit uncomfortable for a moment, as though I had just located, then lost, a piece of important information." Charity looked away from Jacob as the front door was

100

opened by Macon. "Well, never mind, I imagine it will come to me. First we should greet the guests. Will you stand at my side, Jacob? Father Desmond will be joining us soon."

"I would be honored, child."

"If there is anything else you'd prefer doing, Jacob, I will be glad to take your place." Tell had come up on the other side of Charity, his face tight, the flecks in his golden eyes a glittering ebony.

"I'm fine where I am." Jacob smiled benignly at the younger man.

"Tell . . ." Charity's words died in her throat at the hot fury coming off him. "Ah, why don't you stay where you are and . . . and you can greet the guests with me. There might be some that you know that I don't."

"I had no intention of moving anyway."

"Here comes the first guest," Jacob told her brightly, his amusement growing when Charity scowled at him. "Ah, Father Desmond, just in time, take your place next to Charity. No, no I insist. I shall stand next to you." Jacob grinned at Tell again and moved to let the priest take his place."

Tell did all he could to stem his anger but he felt threatened, menaced in a most elemental way. At that moment he understood the ape who willingly dismembered any who would thwart him or stand between him and his chosen mate . . . and that included even kind old men such as Jacob Henry. Damn the man for baiting him! Charity was his and he was damn well going to convince her of that fact . . . and anyone else in the world who questioned it.

Since he was on Charity's right he was the first person to greet the guests who now came in thick and fast, laughing and admiring the decorations lacing their entry. Though many people were familiar to him and some he had invited himself, there were some of Charity's friends whom he did not know but who interested him greatly. Anything about her background or life-style had his attention.

"You invited the mayor of New York City?" Charity's surprised whisper reached Tell.

Tell nodded. "And the governor of this state, New Jersey, and Connecticut. Some of the throwaway kids come from their states and I was sure they'd be interested."

"My goodness. And Father Desmond invited television and film personalities . . . and look at the press coverage," Charity gasped, delight written over her face. "I'll bet you one dollar we make our financial quota for the year. Oh how do you do, Congresswoman. Thank you for coming."

"Why not make a wager? A night in my bed if I win, and a night on the town if you win?" Tell's left hand feathered at her waist, squeezing gently. "You're blushing, darling."

"What's new about that? Don't I always in your presence, Tell?" Her tart response elicited a low chuckle from him.

"Do you know how much I love getting your blood going, Charity, my sweet?"

"How do you do, governor. You honor us. Yes, I think we will reach our goal." Charity decided the best thing was to ignore Tell and since the line swelled to two abreast and was moving steadily, this was fairly simple to do.

After about an hour, her smile was plastic and her hand was numb but Charity was overjoyed at the crowd of people filing into Bigham House.

Just as Charity began to think that the line would never end, that the band had been playing for twenty minutes with no hostess to open the dancing, the doors

102

were closed by Macon who cocked his head at her and smiled.

"By my count, Miss Charity, I think we have a full house."

"Thank you, Macon."

"May I have the first dance? You should lead out the dancing very soon, Charity." Tell looked down at the creamy swell of breast that rose from the low-cut silk charmeuse and felt his heart lurch against his ribs. He didn't want anyone else looking at her lovely skin.

She took Tell's arm and nodded. "I hope everyone had something to eat and drink while waiting for the line to end." She turned to the older men beside her. "Jacob, Father, will you join us in the solarium?"

"Of course, child." The priest twinkled at her. "I have some checks to collect."

"Not only will I join you, but I shall ask Kathleen to dance as well." Jacob rolled his eyes making Charity laugh. "I hope she lets me lead."

"It's times like this when it's nice to be a priest." Father Desmond took Jacob's arm and led him toward the solarium.

"That should help smooth ruffled feathers, Jacob dancing with Kathleen, I mean." Charity looked at Tell. "Don't you think?"

He shrugged. "Who knows what would soften Kathleen? I can't say I've ever been able to figure out any of the Beeches except Gareth, and maybe Jennifer. Don't screw up your face. We're going to have a wonderful time this evening even if Ambrose and the rest of them pout all night."

"Right." Charity felt a tingling in her toes as she listened to the Big Band sound coming from the end of the spacious ballroom-sized area. "I'll bet Jacob selected that music."

"Actually Gareth and I did. We decided that we liked the danceable music."

Charity laughed. "Not a punk rock fan?"

"My tastes in music are varied, but they do not include anything unrhythmic."

"What a diplomatic answer." Charity's steps slowed before they reached the dance floor. "Doesn't the house look wonderful with all the downstairs rooms opened and lit?"

Tell looked around him. "This house was always beautiful. If Kathleen hadn't locked up so many of the rooms we might have been able to view its openness long ago. This wonderful design has been smothered by locking off suites. Kathleen always seemed to be more adept at handling pennies than dollars anyway, from what Cyrus used to tell me."

"I think Grandfather would be pleased at how Bigham House looks tonight." Charity nodded, looking up at the crystal chandeliers, the French wallpaper that looked new after its careful cleaning by the staff, the sconces lit by beeswax candles.

"Come along, lady, your guests are waiting for you to open up the dancing."

Charity felt her heart thud in anticipation. The last time she'd danced with Tell she'd been a senior in high school. He had accompanied her to a function at her school.

Tell felt her tremble when he turned her in his arms. "What are you thinking?"

"I recall the last time we danced together."

"At the senior parent and child get-together when you were in high school, Charity," Tell told her promptly.

"Yes, and I discovered that you could do all the new dances. Putting two and two together I deduced that you were a party animal."

Tell grinned down at her, sweeping her into his arms, the torrid beguine rhythm invading them like a voodoo chant. "What was I to do while waiting for you, pet? Don't glare at me. I was just marking time."

"Right," she murmured sarcastically.

"Such hostility, darling." Tell leaned down and breathed the words into her hair, inhaling the elusive fragrance wafting about her. "You're wearing Obsession. Trying to drive me mad?"

Ire curled through her. "You know far too much about women, Tell Layton, including their scents."

"More hostility, pet? It's time we were married so that you'll be able to develop a more confident air about my feelings toward you." Tell swung her away from his body, his eyes traveling over her.

"I think you're putting the cart before the horse." Charity's breath came quickly when he smiled at her. "You should be in love and confident of each other before taking such a big step."

"Don't speak in the abstract, love, we're talking about us. Would you rather we lived together for a while?"

"Yes . . . no . . . I don't want to discuss this now."

"Fine, but we will be talking about it. I don't want to wait too much longer to make you mine." Tell saw panic flash across her face for a second and it angered him.

Charity pushed back from him. "I love fast dancing." Relief filled her that the complicated steps of the hot beat allowed her to forget for a few seconds the provocative conversation.

Being Charity Bigham Layton, mothering Tell's children, seemed too mind-boggling to really happen.

Tell watched the play of emotions across her face as she twisted away from him, her body bending and swaying in sensuous accompaniment to the primal magnet of soft rock. "You're wonderful, darling."

Charity glanced at him and felt suddenly locked into a hot mystique that stunned her by its velvet, kinetic punch. She had the giddy feeling that she would have to jab and feint her way free. "And you damn well shouldn't be such a good dancer if you're a full-time tycoon," she blurted, coming out of her corner. "All that tripping the light fantastic from club to club wasn't wasted; you're letter-perfect." Charity pushed out her tongue at him in childish admonishment.

"Do that again when we're alone, will you?" Tell laughed out loud as her eyes widened, his one arm capturing her close to his body so that the thrumming rhythm collided their bodies in matching beat.

Tell's silky voice had coiled around her like a satin whip. "I think what we're doing is illegal; if not, it should be. You are a terrible man," Charity riposted, out of breath.

"May I cut in, Tell? I think Charity needs a younger partner for this." Gareth didn't look at Tell as he took his place in front of Charity.

Charity had been gazing at her partner and gasped at the black scowl that displaced Tell's smile. She didn't know where the giggle came from, but not even her hand covering her lips quite masked it and those glacial gold eyes swung back to fix on her. "Sorry, but you look so funny."

"Darling, your tally sheet of misdemeanors with me is growing longer." Tell inclined his head as he saw the tip of her tongue again as she looked at him over Gareth's shoulder. Then the gyrating couple moved away from him. Damn her! He was going to paddle her at the first opportunity. The thought of his hand on the satin texture of her backside made his whole body tingle. It was getting very hard to contain his want of her, his need to have her as his wife. He had desired her too long.

He turned his back on the dancing, nodding to those who spoke to him, but not stopping his forward motion until he reached one of the small bars placed strategically on the perimeter of the solarium. "Irish whiskey, please, straight up."

"Drowning your sorrows, Tell?" Ambrose Beech leaned against the oak bar, gesturing peremptorily to an attendant and ordering a Scotch and water. "It's pretty plain you have designs on the little heiress and you don't like Gareth cutting you out."

Tell turned to face him, smiling. "Ambrose, if you say one more provocative thing to me, I'll throw you through one of those priceless stained-glass windows." Tell sipped his drink, his smile widening when Ambrose took a step backward. "I see I needn't elaborate."

"You always were a primitive devil. That hasn't changed." Ambrose watched the other man warily. Tell Layton was unpredictable. No telling what he might do if the mood hit him. "But don't count your chickens yet, Tell. You may be running Bigham Holdings at this juncture, but that might not be true in the future. Our lawyer says that we have a good solid chance of getting our properties and our businesses back again."

"Your use of the possessive pronoun is laughable, Ambrose. Nothing that belonged to Cyrus Bigham should go to you. He despised you and would spin like a top in his grave if you were to have control of one telephone booth belonging to his estate."

Ambrose reddened, replacing his drink on the bar. "Really? Well, it seems as though Charity might feel the same about you if she ever discovers the heavy hand you've played in her life. My little stepniece is a very independent woman and wouldn't like knowing she'd been manipulated, that her way had been financially

107

greased by you. Maybe you won't get to keep everything you've coveted, including the elusive Miss Bigham . . ." Ambrose's words trailed away. "Damn you, Tell, don't you try anything here. I'll have you arrested." He backed three steps and turned to flee, looking over his shoulder. "You won't have it all your own way."

Tell placed the glass down so hard on the bar, the glass shattered, one tiny shard entering his thumb, a dot of blood rising there."

"Sir, here, let me help you." A bar attendant leaned forward with a clean napkin. Tell swiped at the bit of blood then tossed the paper back on the bar. "I'll get you another drink, sir."

"Please." Tell noticed Lyle Clausen coming up to him from the corner of his eye.

"You should put antiseptic on that, Tell. The smallest cuts can get infected. Something upset you?"

"You could say that."

Lyle saw that Tell wasn't going to be more forthcoming and looked around him at the dancing and laughing throng. "Very nice party. I can't get over the turnout of notables. A credit to you and Jacob, I imagine."

"And to Charity and Father Desmond. Promise House is very well known now and the work done there is highly respected."

"It doesn't hurt to have Jacob Henry in your corner either. I'm sure Charity knows that. Jacob has many influential friends just as you do, Tell."

"You seem to put a high level of importance on that, Lyle," Tell said mildly, his eyes sliding away from the other man and glancing toward a laughing Charity as she was swung in Gareth's arms.

"As you do with Charity," Lyle said just as mildly, turning Tell's gaze back to him. "I'm sure it doesn't surprise you that the whole family has always known of your interest in that direction. Excuse me. My sister insisted that we dance the first slow dance and this is it. I had better find her."

"Of course." Tell watched the other man move away, noting how his easy stride took him quickly out the door of the solarium. Tell couldn't remember ever noticing that the other man, though his frame was average in height and bone structure, had rather a muscular build and that he moved like an athlete. Sensing someone looking at him he turned and faced Jennifer. "How lovely you look. Love suits you, Jenny. Would you like to dance?"

"Yes." Jennifer laughed. "I fully intended to ask you if you hadn't asked me."

Tell led her out to the floor, chuckling. "You are certainly more outspoken than you once were. I like it. When do you plan on marrying the man of your dreams?"

"As soon as I can get him to the altar. Lionel is wonderful, isn't he? He says he wants to marry me as much and as soon as I do, but my mother and brother Ambrose are already throwing up barriers. Uncle Lyle says he supports me, but I can't see him defying Mother, can you?"

"I don't know about that. He might. Lyle doesn't reveal a lot about himself but I'm sure he can dig in his heels if he chooses."

"Mother says that when he was small he defied my grandfather all the time, but that he settled down nicely. To her that means he went along with what she said." The laughter that bubbled out of Jennifer elicited a smile from Tell.

"Yet you don't seem too worried."

"I'm not. Lionel says we're going to charge right through the line. That I believe."

Tell watched her laugh again and knew that the metamorphosis was complete. The shy, rather socially inept

Jennifer had indeed become the beautiful, self-confident swan. "Be happy."

"I intend to be . . . and I hope that you and Charity will be as happy one day. Don't look so surprised, Tell. You've been looking at her as though she were a prize cupcake for years."

"Have I?" Tell felt both irritation and amusement when she laughed again. "I won't ever think that I'm inscrutable again. People seem to see right through me."

"Only where Charity is concerned. Your business façade is impenetrable." Jennifer's smile died. "I know that Charity has no reason to trust me . . . any more than she does the rest of the Beeches, but I would like to be friends with her. Lionel says she is a wonderful person and that he loves her dearly, and I want to know her as he does."

"How kind of Lionel!"

"Don't be frosty and sarcastic, he means it in a friendly way. We all need friends, of the other sex as well as our own." Jennifer grinned. "I must say it's a treat to watch you scowling and pawing the ground."

"Thanks for the tutelage."

"Now you sound pompous. Jealousy does strange things to people . . ."

"Jealousy?"

"Yes. I was so jealous of Charity when I first met Lionel but now I understand degrees of love much better. So will you . . . after you're married to Charity."

"Damn you, Jenny."

"Your smile is very sexy when it's twisted like that, Tell, but you could never be as sexy as Lionel."

"I don't think my male ego will survive the evening."

The music ended and Tell led Jennifer to the side of the room aiming toward the spot where Lionel stood watching, his grin wide when it touched his fiancée."

"I'll take you back to your intended, Jenny. If I spend much more time in your company my opinion of myself will be permanently flattened."

"Impossible," Jenny said impudently, laughing then turning and walking into the arms of her beloved.

"You're a lucky man," Tell told the burly ex–football player who cuddled his fiancée."

"I know."

Charity was excited and elated. A rough count by two of the staff at Promise House, who were guests at the party but who had taken time to do a little tallying, showed that they had gone well over expectations. The gala was an unqualified financial success! "Thank you, William, Danny," she told the two, who had accompanied her down the hall with the bank bags. "I'll take the receipts and put them in the safe in the library until you two and Father Desmond are ready to leave."

"We can carry them into the room for you. When we leave here we're going to drop the two bags in the bank night deposit. It's on our way." William Morrison and his friend Danny Lee had been graduates of Promise House and had stayed on as counselors and trusted allies of the director.

"That's a good idea." Charity hefted the heavy bags delightedly, amused when the two men walked her to the library, watched her unlock the door and go to a table near the wall and indicate to them to place the bags there. "Thank you. Go back and do some dancing. I'll put these away, then join you. The combination is a little complicated and I'll have to consult a paper I have with the numbers on it." Charity watched the two of them leave, pulling the door behind them.

Turning back to the safe, she took the combination out of a book that was to one side of the safe, the combination written on the flyleaf almost as a dedication.

The deciphering had been in one of her grandfather's letters that he'd left with Jacob Henry to give to her.

TO MY *ONE* AND ONLY *ONE*
THREE PLUS *THREE* LIFETIMES IT WOULD TAKE TO PROVE IT *TO* YOU

Breaking it down the way her grandfather had shown her in his letter, the combination was 21–13–32.

Charity opened the safe, placed the bags inside, then was about to close the door of the safe which would automatically lock the money away. She thought she heard something behind her, but as she was turning, something struck her on the side of the head and all she saw was stars, the flashing pain receding into blackness.

Tell had been twice around the room looking for Charity. He'd even gone outside checking the grounds where the Chinese lanterns cast bizarre but colorful shadows among the trees. He scrutinized the many couples moving to the music which could be heard plainly on this side of the house where the band was situated and where the wide terrace made an ideal spot for outdoor dancing. Though there was a cool breeze, it was still very comfortable.

Gareth came up to him. "On the prowl, man?"

"Looking for Charity. Have you seen her?"

"Not since our dance. She was talking to some of her colleagues the last time I saw her and they were giving her a tally of the night's receipts."

"She might be in the library then. Thanks." Tell started to turn away when the other man's hand on his shoulder made him pause.

"She's very important to me too, but more as a sister than anything, Tell."

"Good, because if that weren't the case, I'd break your neck."

112

Gareth slapped him on the back. "C'mon, Tell, loosen up. I'll even help you find her."

Tell nodded, reentering the house in long strides, Gareth at his heels. Tell went right to the small group surrounding Father Desmond. "Father, have you seen Charity? This is our dance."

"We've seen her." Danny Lee sized up the larger man in front of him, his street smarts telling him that the man was on edge. "But that was a while ago. She was going to unlock the safe and put the receipts in it."

"Good, then she is in the library," Tell breathed, relief coursing through him. He should have looked there at once.

"Tell, you're not worried, are you?" Gareth glanced around him, aware that Danny Lee and his friend were listening intently to the exchange though most of what Tell said was muffled by the music from the dance band.

"Charity had a rather mysterious accident before she moved from her apartment to this house, on the day she brought the girls here for the first time."

"What are you talking about?"

In terse, clipped sentences Tell gave Gareth the barebones explanation of what had happened to Charity, beginning to move as he spoke, his own words acting as impetus to the motion.

Gareth followed behind Tell as he strode from the solarium, not looking right or left. "Easy, man, slow down." Gareth could feel a beading of cold sweat on his brow as he studied the other man.

Tell didn't answer him but instead broke into a run down the hall toward the library, twisting the handle, then shoving at the door when it resisted him. "Dammit, it's on automatic lock."

Gareth looked up at the heavy oak door. "Hercules would have trouble busting through this."

Tell didn't answer him, instead he whirled away loping toward the kitchen, not pausing when the cooks and servers made alarmed sounds and Macon asked if anything was wrong.

Breaking into a full run, icy sweat chilling his body, Tell bulled his way out of the rear entrance of the house, not breaking stride as he rounded the house and vaulted onto the stone terrace that surrounded the mansion on three sides. Not even hesitating long enough to look in the french doors, he threw his body at the triple windows, hearing the frame crack but not give.

Openmouthed, Gareth watched Tell for a heartbeat, then he too flung his body alongside Tell's, wincing at the jolting pain that ran through his body.

Then with the combined weight and strength of the two men there was a rending crash as the frame and leaded glass gave way, catapulting both men into the room, and sending them sprawling.

Tell was on his feet at once, his breathing heavy.

"How the hell we didn't cut ourselves to shreds, I'll never know," Gareth mumbled, staggering to his feet.

But Tell wasn't listening. Danger was there, he could smell it, taste it, every cell in his body on red alert. Vietnam had taught him to be wary. He looked around him quickly, spotting the huddled form, flinging himself across the room even as he saw her. He lifted Charity into his arms, feeling for a pulse and finding a strong but uneven one. "Darling? Open your eyes, Charity. You're all right. It's Tell."

"Jee-zus! What happened?" Gareth muttered, looking down at Charity.

Tell's words seemed to be coming through clouds to her, but Charity opened her eyes at the commanding tone, blinking at him. "I have a headache."

"All right, darling. Don't move. Gareth, call the medics." Gareth obeyed.

114

Charity nodded, the motion making her groan and close her eyes again.

Gareth replaced the receiver, glancing down at the desk as he did so, his eyes riveting on the heavy-gauge reinforced bags in front of him.

Tell turned his head when he heard the other man gasp. "What is it?"

"The bank bags are empty, Tell." Gareth waved the heavy canvas bag in front of him.

"Keep your voice down." Tell turned his body so that Gareth was shielded from Charity, cursing under his breath when he heard her hoarse groan, signaling she'd heard.

"No . . . oh no, we've been robbed." Charity started to cry.

"Stop it. Don't. I'll handle the money. Everything will be taken care of by me, I give you my word, darling. Please, don't cry, you have a bump on the side of your head and you should be very quiet until you're examined by a physician."

"But, Tell, all our work . . ."

"I'll take care of it, I swear to you. Promise House will get every nickel. I'll put Gareth on it tonight with a few of your staff people and it will be settled right away."

"But who would do it?" Charity lifted her hand to swipe away at the tears that slipped from her eyes. "I'm not really crying, I'm just being stupid."

Gareth knelt down on the other side of Charity, ignoring the banging on the library door by people trying to get into the room. "Tell's right, Charity. You couldn't be blamed for this. Who would ever think that someone was going to hit on a charity gala?"

"It's my fault, Gareth." Tears dripped from her eyes as Tell ran his hands over her head and neck. "It's so much money, and Father Desmond needs it right away. How will you get the money back, Tell?"

"That's not your problem." He kissed her forehead, then looked at the younger man. "Get the door, Gareth, before they take it down with an ax. And tell Macon he is to let only the medics into this room."

"Right. Damn my big mouth. I didn't mean to upset her more." Gareth grimaced, muttering imprecations under his breath as he crossed to the door.

The unmistakable sound of a cocking gun made Tell tent his body over Charity before he looked toward the smashed french doors leading to the terrace. Facing him through the shattered frame were the gardener and his son, the older man carrying a double-barreled shotgun, the son wielding a cudgel and a hand gun. "Hello, Davis, Johnny. Put away the weapons."

"Mr. Tell! What's happened here?"

"It looks like a robbery. We've called for the medics but I think you'd better call the police too, and get some extra people to patrol the grounds."

"Consider it done, Mr. Tell." Davis looked at Charity and shook his head. "Her grandfather would kill anyone who'd done this to her. Come along, Johnny."

"Yes, Father."

"Tell." Charity plucked at his sleeve. "I'm not going to the hospital. I can't go until this is settled and I must talk to Father Desmond."

"Yes, you are, darling, and I'm going with you. Gareth will take care of things here and talk to the police." He reached out and snatched a throw pillow from a nearby settee and put it under her head. "Did you see your assailant?"

"I didn't see or hear him, but he must have been in the room when I got here because it was then that I put on the automatic lock because we were putting the money in the safe and I didn't want anyone in here."

Charity was babbling but she couldn't seem to control her sentences.

"He must have been pretty slippery if he got by the patrols on the property."

"Couldn't he have gained access by coming in on one of the food trucks?"

"I suppose." Tell looked around the room, then back down at Charity, smiling at her. The commotion at the library door brought his head up again. "Open it up again and see what's going on but no one enters but the medics and police, Gareth."

"My mother is coming through, Tell." Gareth grimaced when Tell cursed steadily.

"How dare you try to keep me out of my own house?" Kathleen glared at her younger son who shook his head and waved her into the room.

"This is Charity's house, Mother, and at the moment she is not well. She was struck by an intruder who robbed the gala receipts."

Kathleen stared at Charity on the floor, her eyes flitting to the bank bags, the broken terrace door, then back to her son. "Impossible."

"Mother, I assure you it was not only possible, it happened." Gareth's face flashed irritation for a moment. "Now it might be better if you left."

Kathleen ignored the last statement Gareth made. "And tell me how a robber would get out of this room again, when the two of you had to break in here?" Kathleen pointed to the bent and broken frame of the french door.

"That's a good question, Kathleen, and one that has me wondering." Tell shot a glance at Charity, noting that her eyes were still closed.

Gareth looked puzzled as he stood with his back to the door, scowling at his mother and Tell. "Dammit, what the hell is going on?"

"That's what I would like to know. It would certainly be a disgrace for all of us if Charity has taken the money herself and faked this robbery," Kathleen muttered.

Tell stared at the woman for a long moment, noting the run of blood up her face when he continued to stare. "She didn't fake the lump on her head, and the position of the wound would make it damned difficult to self-inflict, Kathleen."

"Don't take that steely tone with me, Tell Layton."

"That was uncalled for, Mother, and you know it." Gareth's angry rejoinder overrode his mother's stiff tones.

Kathleen glared at her son but subsided into a chair. "You should take her to a hospital then."

"I think she shouldn't be moved until she has a preliminary examination by paramedics," Tell told her evenly, noting that though Charity's eyes were closed, her breathing was even.

In a flurry of arrival, the paramedics were let into the library; Gareth, with Macon's help, managed to keep the others out of the room. "No, no, Rita, she's fine. Jennifer, would you reassure the girls before they get hysterical. Tell Lionel to stop looking like a bear with a sore paw."

"Are you sure she'll be all right, Gareth?" Jennifer asked.

Gareth looked over his shoulder at the calm movements of the paramedics. "It looks good."

In minutes Tell was pushing through the throng that had gathered at the door, the paramedics behind him, guiding the gurney that carried Charity. All the while she kept murmuring that she didn't need to go to the hospital, but in the uproar of questions and musings, her voice was lost.

"Shh," Gareth whispered to her, smiling down at her.

"You want him to start up again. This time he won't bust down the french doors. He'll probably destroy the entire house." His smile faded when she nodded weakly. She really looked beaten.

Father Desmond pushed past the others going at once to Charity's side and stopping the progress of the gurney. "No, keep going, gentlemen, but I will be coming with you."

"Oh, Father, there's no need."

"Now, child, you mustn't cry like that." Father Desmond shot a glance at Tell, who nodded reassuringly.

"She'll be fine, Father, but it might be better if you wait here and talk to Gareth. He has my instructions."

Father Desmond nodded, his expression puzzled.

Kathleen stepped from the library into the wide hall that ran past the library and ended in the solarium in the back of the house. "Yes, I would think you had better go into the library and sit down, Father. It would seem that my stepgranddaughter has misappropriated the funds that were collected this evening for Promise House." Her clear voice stopped conversation, gasps arising as person turned to person, whispering.

"Mother!" Gareth roared.

"Did she really steal all of it, Mother?" Ambrose piped up.

Tell stopped and turned, letting the gurney precede him. "Amby, if you say another word, I'll break your damned neck for you."

"Not if I get him first." Lionel came up next to Gareth who put a restraining hand on his arm and gestured for him to follow him and the priest back into the library.

CHAPTER FIVE

Charity leaned back against the seat of the limousine that Tell had hired to return her from the hospital to Bigham House the next day.

"You're tired. You should have stayed in the hospital for a few more days."

Charity opened her eyes. "What did the police say?"

"They're being noncommittal and questioning everyone."

"You're being a little secretive yourself," Charity told him tartly.

"Darling, I told you not to worry. Gareth and members of my staff have gotten together with Father Desmond. He will get every penny of the money, I promise you. The wheels are already in motion."

"Will we ever know what happened, Tell?"

"We'll make every effort."

"Your face has that closed look that it gets when you're hiding things."

Tell lifted her hand, noting how fragile it seemed, seeing the bluish tinge of the veins just under the surface, yet knowing she was strong. He kissed her fingers one by one. "Why, love, do you accuse me of being a dissembler?"

"I know you well enough that when you're using very formal words you are throwing down red herrings."

Charity tried not to smile when he grinned at her but she couldn't resist the almost boyish beauty of him with his face relaxed in amusement.

Charity closed her eyes, pretending to rest. It was a sweet agony to look into Tell's face and she feared, not only what she would see there, but also what he might read in hers. More and more he filled her thoughts, cropping up at the most inopportune times. He was like a wraith in her mind, a ghost with a mind of its own, intruding when he chose. When she felt him take her hand, she stiffened then relaxed as the warm pressure comforted, yet excited her. He was her bête noire, even as he was her security blanket. It baffled her that he could be all things to her and still be the most sensually exciting person on the planet.

"We haven't discussed the day we would be marrying, Charity."

Her eyes flew open, fixing on him at once. "That's because it isn't settled that we should marry."

"I have no doubts. What are yours? We can settle them before we get to the house." Tell moved closer to her, scooping her into the curve of his shoulder, his mouth on her hair.

"Just like that."

"Yes."

"Tell, marriages are throwaway commodities today in the eyes of many people . . . but not in my view."

"So you've told me."

"Have you considered the fact that you might get bored with the forever concept very fast?"

"I've thought about being married to you for a long time . . . and boredom didn't come into it."

"What . . . what if I get bored?"

"You don't believe we'll bore each other any more than I do, darling."

"We might be the death of each other, though."

121

"True," he said, chuckling.

"Don't laugh, Tell."

"Then don't be so amusing."

"You sound irritated now."

"I am. Arranging our marriage might put me in a good mood."

"I thought that was the woman's job."

"In our case that would be stupid. I have no intention of marrying when I'm ninety."

"Now who's being funny."

"What's the matter, Rita?" Priscilla threw herself down on the other girl's bed. "You've been moping, at least that's what Father Den calls it."

Rita smiled at the other girl. She was closer to Priscilla than anyone, but she still couldn't quite open up all the way. "I don't know exactly; a lot of things, I suppose."

"Then it must be something about your family because otherwise you would talk about it."

Rita laughed and nodded ruefully. "That's true, I don't like to talk about my family . . . but right now I'm more worried about Charity than I am about them."

"Why? She'll be home today and Lional says she's fine." Priscilla frowned when she saw the other girl shrug again. "What's bothering you? You're making my skin goosebump."

"I don't know for sure, but I get a funny feeling every once in a while that she's in danger. I haven't seen anything wrong, it's just a cold shiver I get now and then." Rita gave her deprecatory smile. "Dumb, huh? But she never seemed to have that much trouble before she inherited this place, now every time we turn around, Charity's in some kind of danger . . ."

"Like the accident at her apartment, you mean? Things like that?"

Rita nodded. "I can't shake the feeling that someone's got it in for her. You know how when you're on the street and the back of your neck prickles it's time to watch yourself? Well, that's how I feel, but that we should be watching Charity's buns, not our own. Get my drift?"

Priscilla nodded. "If that's true, maybe we should look out for her. She's sure been careful about us."

Rita leaned back on the bed with a sigh, her hand going to her middle. "Should we talk to the others?"

"Yeah, but we should tell Liz to keep her trap shut. If someone is trying to make trouble for Charity we don't want her spilling to the wrong people."

"Right."

"Rita, do you think it could be her family?"

"No, but I heard Tell Layton talking and he said that maybe someone at the center could be angry at Charity. Remember the time that pimp Docky came after us and she whacked him with Father Desmond's cane?"

Priscilla nodded. "You think Docky or his boys could be after her?"

"Why not? Didn't he bust the jaw of one of his ladies for holding back five bucks once? Sure he did. And I'll bet he's still mad at Charity for what she did to him."

"Jeez, we need help with that rat."

"No!" Rita curled up her fingers. "We'll take care of him ourselves."

Father Desmond called Charity into his office the Thursday after the Promise House gala. "Ah, there you are, child. Sit down." He steepled his hands in front of him and gazed at the young woman across the desk from him. "You still have shadows under your eyes from your ordeal and I'm sorry for that, but if I see any signs

123

of recrimination on your features pertaining to that incident I will take you to task, Charity." He held up his hand when she would have spoken. "It didn't take Lionel to tell me that you've blamed yourself for what happened, and I'll have no more of it, and not just because Mr. Layton has already placed more than adequate funds at our disposal, but because you were not at fault. Do you understand me, Charity Bigham?"

Charity smiled at his stern question. "I do, Father. I'll put it behind me and get on with my work."

"Good. I have one more favor to ask of you."

"Of course."

"I would like to book Bigham House for our gala next year. What do you say?"

Charity nodded, feeling the sting of tears in her eyes. "I would love that. Consider it done for the second Saturday in October as usual . . . and this time I'll have an army of security in charge of receipts."

"Good idea. We'll get O'Neill and his boys on it. No one but a fool would mess with that bunch." Father Desmond was referring to a group of his graduates that had banded together and formed a fruit and vegetable wholesale business. They were doing well and were very loyal to Promise House. Father Desmond looked at his watch. "I have children to see to this morning. Quite a batch we have." He shook his head sadly at Charity and rose to his feet. "It would be a joyous day indeed if there was no more need for Promise House . . . but until then we'll do our job."

Charity stood in the well-worn hallway and watched the priest walk to the back of the building where the new members of Promise House were processed and interviewed. Charity knew it was both pain and joy for the elderly priest to talk to the young people because a percentage of them would be lost to him no matter what was done, and he agonized over this, but the work never stopped, so there was little time for repining.

The phone rang just as she reentered her office. "Promise House. Charity Bigham speaking. How may I help you?"

"Charity? It's Jennifer. I'm in town for today and tonight and I wondered if you would have lunch with me."

Charity hesitated, then thought of Lionel and how happy he was and how eagerly he looked forward to marrying Jennifer Beech, and knew that she would have to begin looking at the girl with new eyes. "All right. Why don't I meet you in Little Italy, if that's convenient for you?"

"It would be wonderful. Is Forlini's good for you?"

"Probably not for my waistline but I love the place. See you at twelve."

Charity stared at the phone when she replaced the receiver. She and Jennifer had never been close, and though Jennifer had never really said anything nasty to her, she seemed always to be aping her mother's moves and moods. Oh well, it was only a lunch and since Lionel was her friend, she would need to see Jennifer.

At eleven fifty-five, Charity walked into the well-known Italian restaurant, nodding to some of the staff who recognized her from other times she'd eaten there with Lionel and some of the others. It surprised her when she was led to a booth already occupied by Jennifer.

"Did you think I'd be late?" Jennifer smiled tentatively. "I suppose I would have been a year ago, but since Lionel prizes punctuality I've changed my ways." Her smile softened. "So much has changed in my life."

Charity slid into her seat, gazing at the girl across from her. "You are different in many ways. Your smile is quite lovely, but I don't remember you smiling very much when I was at Bigham House."

Jennifer grinned ruefully. "I didn't even have a personality then. I was mother's shadow and nothing else. Since Lionel . . . things have turned around. He's taught me to be myself, to speak for myself, to think for myself."

Charity laughed at the way Jennifer hit the table surface with her fist to emphasize each phrase. "You sound very definite."

Jennifer sighed, nodding. "I am. Lionel has done that too." She leaned on the table, staring at Charity. "May I say that it's nice to hear you laugh too. You've been sad lately."

"I talked to Father Desmond today and promised him no more long faces."

"Good. Lionel says that things look pretty bright what with the insurance on the money and Tell Layton covering the rest. Promise House will be all right." She grinned at Charity. "Mother had a cow when I told her that I was donating some of my inheritance to Promise House. Amby roared like a lion, but things like that don't bother me anymore."

"Good for you." Charity settled back, feeling less wary about the luncheon with Jennifer.

The two women ordered a pasta salad with tea and faced each other again.

"I know you have no reason to want to be my friend, Charity, but I want to be yours. When Lionel and I are married and settled here in New York, I'll want you to visit with us often and come to dine. Lionel has shown me many things and . . . Why are you smiling that way?"

"Do you know how many times the name Lionel peppers your conversation?" Charity chuckled when Jennifer rolled her eyes.

126

"Yes, I do. Amby and my mother have told me not to talk to them until I can learn to converse without dropping his name every other word."

Charity stopped smiling. "Don't let anyone try to dampen what you and Lionel have. It's too special. People live whole lifetimes and don't approach it, or even begin to understand it."

"Don't worry. I intend to fight anyone or anything that tries to come between us and Lionel is worse than I am . . . Oh Lord, there I go again."

"It's wonderful, Jennifer."

"Umm, yes, just like what you and Tell have."

"Pardon me." The waiter came to the table and replaced the fork that had slipped from Charity's fingers to the floor.

"Oh dear, does it make you nervous to talk about Tell? I thought sure you would be announcing your engagement soon."

"Ah, well, not right . . . that is, we have so many other things to worry about . . ."

"I won't say any more, but you should know by now how much he loves you. He certainly never tried to hide it, in fact he wears it like another coat."

Charity closed her mouth with a snap, aware that it had dropped open. "Does he?"

The luncheon seemed to fly and Charity was sorry when it was time to leave.

When the two of them parted at a corner, they both stated that they wanted to lunch together again.

Charity strolled toward the parking lot where she had left her car, pausing on the way to buy an Italian ice, which she loved. She mulled over the luncheon, pleased with how things had gone. Lionel had indeed exposed the true Jennifer under the frozen exterior that Charity had always known. His fiancée was truly very much in love with him.

Charity paused to observe some construction work going on at a site. She had not been watching very long when she sensed a commotion behind her. Like all good New Yorkers, she had carried her purse in front of her and as she turned, clutching it to her, she was crouched in a defensive position. But she saw at once that she had not been the one threatened. A fast peripheral glance caught a black-suited man running away from the scene.

In front of her a young man in his late teens or early twenties was bent over, holding his side, trying to point up the street where the man in the black jogging suit was running full tilt in the other direction. "Stop him! He tried to kill me . . . he stabbed me. Stop him! Aaagh!"

Appalled, Charity ran forward, trying to support the slightly built man. "Sit down, don't move. You must stay as still as possible." Charity stared at the onlookers gathering around her. "Someone call 911. Hurry. He's been hurt."

One of the workmen appeared through the fence with a plastic container. "Here, lady. It's water. Is your husband all right? We thought the guy was after you." He jerked his head upward. "Jack saw the guy behind you from up on the crane. He said he thought he saw him throw something just before your husband jumped in the way." The construction man looked up the street in the direction the black-suited man had run. "Damn, I wish we could have gotten him for you, lady."

"That man isn't my husband." Charity's mouth felt paralyzed, the words forced past her plastic lips. "I never saw him until he fell behind me. Will he live?"

"Looks like he's hurt bad but you never know." The man bent down next to Charity, putting pressure on the pad she'd made with her scarf. "That's the siren. Help will be here soon, buddy."

In minutes the man was being attended to by medics, then placed on a gurney and rushed to the ambulance.

Charity nodded at the construction man who helped her to her feet, watching the approach of the uniformed policeman, taking a deep shuddering breath, not knowing what she would say to the man.

"I'm Officer Clare, ma'am. If you could just tell me what you saw . . . and take your time."

His calming smile did a great deal for Charity and she was able to relax a bit, telling him, with many pauses, what had occurred since she'd left the ice cream place and Forlini's.

"And that's all you know?"

"Yes, Officer, except I feel very sorry for the man and hope he's going to be all right."

The policeman nodded. "There was quite a bit of blood but I think he'll make it." His smile twisted. "Don't be too sorry for Slippery Jim. He was probably getting ready to grab your purse."

Charity's hand went to her shoulder bag. "He was a thief?"

"Yes, ma'am, and a very good one. He's got a record as long as your arm." The policeman turned to the construction man. "Now, if I have my notes right a couple of your people saw the whole thing. Could you give me your statement then point out the others who witnessed the incident?"

"Sure."

Shortly afterward Charity gave her business card to the officer then was allowed to go. As she moved away from the throng around the construction site she glanced about her more carefully as she approached her car. Even though Slippery Jim was in custody, the feeling of foreboding didn't leave her until she'd started her car and pulled away for the short ride through traffic to

Promise House, parking her car in the usual spot, but checking twice to see that she'd locked her vehicle.

Lionel was standing in the hallway outside her office, his raincoat over his arm. "You two ladies must have done a great deal of talking, Charity. You're fifteen minutes late for the meeting with the hospital board and that isn't like you, but I filled in for you and covered pretty well, I think . . . Hey, what's the matter? You look pale." Lionel moved closer to her, taking her hand in his. "You and Jennifer didn't have words or . . ."

Charity smiled at her friend, squeezing his hand. "Nothing like that; in fact it was a great lunch. We talked and talked . . . about you much of the time. Stop preening, you conceited oaf." Charity hit his arm. "That girl loves you so much."

"The feeling is very mutual." Lionel released her hand and took hold of her shoulder, turning her fully to face him. "If you didn't have problems at lunch, what did get to you? Have a fender bender?"

"Come in the office after you hang up your coat and I'll tell you. It was bizarre." Charity watched Lionel go to his own cubbyhole of an office which he used to do his volunteer counseling. Despite the very full business life he had, Lionel was almost never missing from his post on Mondays, Wednesdays, and Fridays.

Charity hung up her own coat and glanced at the messages on her desk, noting that two of them were from Tell.

"Well? I'm here and I have ten minutes before my first clinic, so talk to me."

Charity faced her friend across her desk and recounted what had happened.

"What? Dammit, you were accosted? After what you went through at the gala? Run that by me again."

Charity repeated what she'd first told him, being interrupted repeatedly by Lionel, whose face became more mottled, thoughtful, and frowning by the minute.

"That does it." He jumped to his feet. "See you later."

Charity shook her head at his abrupt departure, then was quickly immersed in her own work, the happening of the lunch hour almost fading from her mind as she interviewed two new candidates for Promise House, their haunted, furtive eyes tugging at her heart as always.

It was well into late afternoon when she noticed her messages again and put a call into Tell's office. When she was told by his personal secretary that he'd left for the day, she was flooded with a disappointment that she couldn't contain. Blinking against the sting in her eyes, she replaced the receiver, staring at it as though it were the enemy. She wanted Tell so very much at that moment. Charity was so absorbed in her misery she didn't hear the flurry in the corridor outside her office. When the door was flung open and Tell stood there she could only stare. "You!"

"Yes, my darling." Tell watched her for a millisecond before striding into the room, slamming the door behind him, coming around her desk and lifting her from the chair into his arms. "We are getting married this afternoon . . . in less than an hour. Don't argue with me."

"You're crazy," she murmured just a moment before his hard mouth descended on hers with a ferocious gentleness that had her reeling. Her hands clutched him, never wanting to release him. "Tell . . . what . . ."

"I won't let you put it off anymore. Lionel called me and told me what happened to you today."

"But . . ."

"No! I won't allow you to be so vulnerable."

"But, Tell, it was an accident that had nothing to do with me . . ." Charity stared up at those chiseled features and what she saw had her shivering, the forebodings she'd felt after the incident coming back at her in black waves. "You think the attacker meant to stab me." The cold, flat words spewed forth from her mouth.

"I don't know, but I'm not taking chances. No more will we be apart. I've had a marriage license in my pocket for weeks. Now we're going to use it."

"Blood test." Charity managed weakly.

"Waived."

"You're not the governor of this state."

"No, nor do I want to be. Come along, darling. We're meeting with Father Desmond in the chapel."

"Does he know about this?"

"Of course, why else would he be meeting us in the chapel at Promise House?"

"Don't patronize me or I'll stamp on your instep."

"Good, you're fighting back again." Tell let his index finger course down her cheek. "You're a little off balance because this seems too fast for you . . ."

"It would be too fast for Wonder Woman," Charity said tautly, fighting the weakness in her bones at his touch, struggling against the need to throw herself in his arms and beg him to take her away from it all.

Tell kissed the corner of her mouth. "I've been waiting forever for you, darling. It doesn't seem too quick to me. Indulge me."

"We could live together . . ."

"We've been all through that. It wouldn't suit either one of us."

"Hey, you two, let's go." Lionel stuck his head in the door and grinned at them. "Jen is on her way from my apartment to witness this. Maybe we should get in line behind you and let Father marry us. Hurry up. You can cuddle later." He darted back out of the door again.

One tear rolled down Charity's cheek. "My skirt is wrinkled."

132

"You look perfect to me, love."

"Truly?"

Tell nodded, then bent to kiss her again, his mouth moving on hers in increasing pressure when he felt her tremulous response. He lifted his head a fraction. "Will you make me a happy man and be my wife? Please."

Charity nodded slowly, her heart beating out of rhythm when he lifted her from the floor and kissed her again, the passion coming through to her like an electric charge. In a wild response she coiled her arms around his neck, gripping him as though she could not let him go. "I believe in life-long commitments."

"So do I," Tell murmured into her neck.

"Ahem. I hope you will end that soon. I nearly broke every speed record in Lionel's car getting here and I would like to see a wedding." Jennifer beamed at them when they broke apart. "I just wish it were Lionel and I."

"That's what I said." Lionel came up behind his intended, his arms sliding around her. "Let's go, you two. Father is waiting plus almost all of the staff and some of our guests."

"I hope you intend to be our witnesses," Tell said coolly, not releasing Charity when she would have pulled back from him.

"Oh yes, please do." Charity smiled at Jennifer when the other girl sniffed into a hankie and nodded at the same time.

Tell and Charity followed behind Lionel and Jennifer, moving slowly down the hall to the main corridor that led to the chapel at the front of the house.

Tell tightened his grip and looked down at her when he felt her hand tremble. "I love you, darling."

"My goodness." Charity felt the earth hitch over a notch making her stumble, Tell's strong arm bracing her.

"That shouldn't surprise you." He told her as they stood in the open door of the chapel.

"Really? Then why do I feel so dizzy?"

"Happiness, I hope." Tell looked up to see many of the staff and guests looking back at him, Father Desmond standing at the small altar. "Here we go."

"Up the rebels," Charity pronounced faintly, the smile falling off her face as she moved slowly toward the crying Jennifer, the beaming Lionel, and the nodding priest.

Halfway down the aisle there was an angry yowl and the twin kittens tore over the top of the pews trying to get to Charity.

"Damn them," Tell muttered, catching the two of them easily while some of the young people guffawed and Father Desmond shook his head and tried to look stern. "I suppose these two will be living with us."

Charity nodded.

Tell shrugged, then looked down at the two kittens who stared at him unblinkingly and unafraid. "But not in our bed."

The laughter increased as Charity glared at Tell and tried to stem the blood she knew was rising in her face.

Tell handed the two kittens to one of the residents and turned to her. "Let's go, darling."

The words of the ancient ritual passed over Charity like rainwater, not clinging to her mind. She responded when Tell nudged her, but then her eyes went around the familiar room and she wondered if she hadn't been transported to another planet, as Dorothy had been transported to Oz.

When she looked up and saw Tell's head descending, she smiled. "Now you're mine, Tell Layton, and I won't let go easily." She grinned when she saw his face whiten, his mouth go slack. "It's nice to put you off the mark for a change."

134

"Darling," Tell murmured, his mouth taking hold of hers and clinging.

Charity turned and faced the small congregation after giving Father Desmond a kiss, grinning at all the smiling faces that looked back at her.

When applause broke out Father Desmond joined in, giving Charity a little pat on the shoulder. "Time to walk down the aisle with your spouse, child."

"That's right," she whispered, looking up at him. Clutching Tell's arm Charity could feel tears sting her eyes when many of her girls reached out to touch her as she passed, their own eyes moist.

"I should have supplied a ton of tissue, I see," Tell told her huskily, at the end of the aisle when he turned her toward him, his lips coursing over her face in a gentle caress.

"We're a teary bunch at Promise House, I guess."

"And yet I never saw you cry once when you were a child, not even the time you took a fence that was too much for your mare and you broke your arm. Why is that, wife?"

Charity's heart jerked at the word "wife," breath shuddering from her body. "I was happy with Grandfather . . . most of the time. But there were so many times when I missed my mother, when I tried to imagine who my father was and if he ever thought of me, but I knew if I talked to Grandfather about that it could hurt him, so I hid my feelings. When I wasn't pleased with life I tried to cover up, bury it. I learned very early not to cry." She stared up at him. "But I don't think I've ever been able to bamboozle you."

Tell's finger captured a tear at the corner of her eye. "I remember a little girl with her trembling chin held high telling me that she wasn't scared and that she didn't cry and that as soon as her cast was removed she would try the fence again."

"And I did and went over easily." Charity nodded, so caught in Tell's wonderful aura that Jennifer and Lionel had to speak twice before she noticed them.

"I know marriage is pretty spellbinding, lady, but you shouldn't ignore your friends." Lionel plucked her away from Tell and gave her a bear hug and loud smack on the mouth that had the girls giggling and Jennifer laughing.

"He's only being friendly, Tell," Jennifer joked.

He shook his head, his smile like steel. "I know but it doesn't seem to matter even knowing that he's very much in love with you."

"And he is that." Jennifer was smug and smiling.

"And you have never been so beautiful, Jen." Tell grinned when Jennifer turned fiery red.

"Whatever did you say to her, Tell?" Charity looked from Jen to the satiric smile on her husband's face.

Lionel's one eyebrow arched in inquiry while his other hand hooked his fiancée closer to him.

"Don't plot my murder, my friend. I just told your fiancée that I had never seen her look as beautiful as she has since her engagement."

Charity nodded. "That's true."

"Thank you." Lionel grinned down at Jennifer then kissed her soundly.

"I never saw so much kissing, Father." One of the very pregnant girls rolled her eyes.

"That's true, my child, but there's much happiness at Promise House today, so a bit of cuddling is not amiss."

"I'd rather eat, Father."

"All right, Madeleine, I think we could scare up something in celebration."

"No need, Father." Tell smiled at the elderly clergyman who looked puzzled for a moment. "Caterers should be coming through your service entrance soon bringing everything we'll need for a lovely midday feast." Tell smiled at the cluster of girls. "Lots of good-ies."

"Is that true?" One of the girls squealed. "God, I'm going to die . . . but first I'll tell the ones who were in class."

"Oh Tell, I hope there'll be enough." Charity glanced around at the horde of young people who were spreading the message about the food, then looked back at her spouse. "How did you organize the caterers so fast?"

"I didn't. I left orders with my secretary when I left the office."

"And the world snaps to do your bidding."

He grinned down at her lazily. "Something like that, wife." Tell kissed her leisurely, holding her fast when she would have wriggled free.

"Stop that," Charity gasped when she could move a fraction back from him. "I don't want my young people to see me carrying on in the hallway."

"All right, love, we'll wait until we get home until we carry on."

Charity was prevented from replying by the peremptory ringing of the service bell. "Good Lord," she whispered, after strolling down the main hall to the huge dining room and watching the many workers scurrying about, putting up silky-looking decorations, covering the rough wood tables with linen covers and silverware. "There must be a hundred people working in here."

"And there will be help in the kitchen, too, but they will have been instructed not to upset the regular help."

"How could they not! Our cooks make soups and stews, we rarely have Beluga caviar."

"And you won't have it today, darling, but I think you'll approve of the choices and so will the guests."

Charity swung around to face him. "I didn't mean to sound ungrateful."

"You didn't. You sounded concerned about those under your care and your coworkers and I love you for that. Now, why does that make you blush, love?"

"I'm not used to it, I suppose."

"Well, get used to it, you'll be hearing it all the time." Tell led her to a table indicated by the man who seemed to be in charge.

"I hope this will be suitable, sir. I would have preferred to have had a head table for you but it didn't seem feasible with the number of persons we'll be serving."

"This is fine," Tell told him. "My wife prefers to be close to her guests." Tell nodded. "Everything looks wonderful."

The man inclined his head in acknowledgment, signaled to one of his underlings, and the guests were quickly seated and the serving begun.

"When we tell Priscilla and the others what they missed, they'll choke," one of the girls said with a benign smile, tasting some of the Caesar salad and closing her eyes in glee.

"Oh dear, Louise is right." Charity looked at Lionel and laughed. "And how the others will enjoy telling them every detail."

"That's all right, love. We'll have another small party for them at Bigham House. Won't that smooth the ruffled feathers?"

"Yes." Charity put her hand on Tell's hand, looking down at the wide band that fit her third finger so snugly. "And how did you manage a ring so fast?"

"That I've had for a while."

Tell's face had a closed look. Charity knew that it would be useless to question him further.

The audible signs and groans at the second course—tender prawns broiled in lemon with tiny parsley boiled potatoes—had Charity smiling at a rueful Father Desmond. "It will be tough selling them on stew tomorrow."

"Impossible, Charity, but today is such a treat for them, I don't care." Father Desmond smiled at Tell. "It was a nice thing you did. They will love you for it."

"Thank you, Father." When the priest turned away to speak to the person next to him, Tell looked at Charity. "I'm hoping it will have the same effect on my wife," Tell whispered to her.

She looked around at him. "Bribery? You?"

"Bribery, usury, kidnapping, any of the capital crimes it takes to get you, love."

Behind his grin she saw steely determination. "You're not easily turned from a purpose."

"True, even if it takes twenty lifetimes."

Charity turned back to her plate, pondering the moment, eating the food without tasting it and smiling blindly at the ice sculptures and the lovely three-tiered cake with white pilasters.

A little later she turned to Tell again. "I should finish up my work before I leave today."

"Even on your wedding day?"

"Yes." She didn't tell him that she needed space from him, that her breathing was impaired by his nearness and she had to think about that. More and more she was uneasy about her reactions to him and to the marriage. It delighted her! So did the man! Insanity must be in the Bigham family.

"We'll do it your way. Incidentally, I want you to tell me more about that accident you had after you left Jennifer today. Lionel gave me the details he had."

"Why did Lionel call you?"

"Let's say that we had an understanding about that."

"I know you think that there's something sinister . . ."

"I didn't use that word."

139

"But you still feel that there is more involved in the accidents I've had. Even if that were true, Tell, this couldn't be one of them because I wasn't really part of it, just close to what happened. It was some other poor soul and now he's in the hospital." Charity pondered for a moment. "Though the policeman did say the man had a record."

"So I understand."

At the finish of the meal, both Father Desmond and Lionel made toasts and short speeches. There was much applauding and laughter, especially from the guests at Promise House, who fully enjoyed the treat of having a party in the middle of the day.

In a few minutes Tell looked around him, noting how most of the people had dispersed to whatever chore or job called them as soon as they finished eating. Then he leaned down and rubbed his mouth across hers. "No one's around now." His mouth pressed hers, scalding and caressing. He lifted her off her chair to his lap with his strong arms, his heart beating out of rhythm when he felt her arms coil around him. For an eternity he held her, then he lowered her to her chair again. "Tonight we'll be alone," he told her thickly. "And I look forward to that, wife. I had better see to a few things myself this afternoon." He kissed her nose, rose, turned and strode down the hall, not noticing when she followed him to watch him go out the front door because he never looked back.

Charity leaned against the wall, feeling as though she'd been hit in the solar plexus. "It will be like living with a cyclone. I'll be hit hard and fast and never know when I'll be drawn into the eye. Damn that man, he draws and repels me."

The afternoon went swiftly if not smoothly. Charity had all she could do to keep the minds of her interviewees on the subject at hand . . . their pregnancies.

"So where did you meet your husband, Mrs. Layton?" Gladys, an interviewee, asked.

Charity was so taken aback by being addressed by her married name that she could only stare for several heartbeats. "Ah, I've known my . . . Mr. Layton for many years. He was a friend of my family's. Now to get back to . . ."

"Jeez, there sure was nobody like that who was a friend of my family."

"I know that, Gladys, and that's why we should . . ."

"Wow, he was really something coming storming in here and sweeping you off your feet that way. Just like Prince Charming, isn't he?"

"Well, I never thought him quite that way, but . . ." Prince Charming! Tell! What a crazy comparison that was . . . yet, there had been something wonderful about those moments when he first arrived in the house and then when they went to the chapel. "But that's getting us nowhere, Gladys, so let's settle on this for now, shall we?"

"Okay, but it won't be as much fun."

Later, when Charity was cleaning off her desk preparing to close down for the night, she was surprised when she heard a knock on her door and the girls burst in giggling. "What's this?"

"We brought you something, Mrs. Layton." The girls displayed a lovely piece of fabric that she had seen them embroidering on from time to time. Many of the girls delighted in the craft that a volunteer had shown them how to execute and some of them showed a strong artistic bent. "It isn't done yet, so you can't take it home, but when we finish it, you'll have it."

Charity fingered the fine cloth, then looked at each girl in turn. "Nothing could be more perfect than this

141

and I thank you so much. My . . . Mr. Layton will be so pleased."

After Charity parted from the girls she realized that the autumn evening was getting dark, so she hurried on, not really caring to walk out to her car in the darkness even though it was parked in a lot belonging to Promise House. She opened the front door of the brownstone and saw Tell leaning against a Rolls Royce, a uniformed chauffeur at the wheel. "Aren't you afraid that someone in this neighborhood would steal that?"

Tell shook his head, his eyes running over her. "The only thing I fear losing is you, wife, and I intend to do everything I can to see that that doesn't happen."

"Oh." Charity went down the steps and past Tell into the car, feeling him right at her heels, tensing when she saw him push a button that put up the window between the front and back seats. "Disclosing secrets?"

"Maybe that too, but mostly I just wanted to be alone with you. It seems to be the most difficult thing in the world."

"Are we going to Bigham House?"

"No, to my apartment."

"Oh."

"Stop being nervous. You call the shots, wife. It's going to be what you want all the way."

Charity grinned up at him. "And how long will that last, I wonder? You not calling the shots? It doesn't compute, o great one."

With one strong motion, Tell swept her onto his lap, tucking her into his shoulder and staring down at her. "It doesn't?" Tell chucked her under the chin so that she had to look up at him. "Well, lady mine, you ain't seen nothin' yet. I have you now and we are going to have a wonderful time, a great life and it starts now . . . and I will never let you go."

"I'm . . . I'm beginning to believe you." The thought of losing him was a stab of agony.

"Oh? Then why did you look as though you suddenly had a stitch in your side?"

"My life passing in front of my eyes, I guess." It was easier to dissemble than to disclose to this man how vulnerable she was to him. It was incomprehensible to her that she was now his wife. This was the man who'd haunted her dreams since childhood and now he was her husband. Do fantasies come to life?

When they pulled up in front of the fashionable blond brick apartment building overlooking Central Park, Charity looked up at the top penthouse, Tell's.

"Do you remember visiting here when you were a little girl?"

"Mother brought me in to see *Peter Pan* and we were going to meet Grandfather that evening. We came here for high tea." Charity laughed. "I thought I had forgotten that. How Mother loved to keep some of the English customs she'd learned when she went to school there."

"Julia was a *grande dame* in the nicest sense of the words. She was the sister I never had." Tell touched her cheek again.

"Doesn't that make you my uncle?" Charity laughed up at him, surprised at the run of blood up those hard cheekbones.

"Never," he told her harshly, leading her over to the one elevator that just had a *P* over the closed doors and inserting a key.

"Ruffled your feathers, have I?"

"Yes. I lost my avuncular feeling toward you a long time ago."

"Well, it's nice to know I can upset you. You're always knocking me off my perch."

The elevator door closed and Tell swept her into his

143

arms, his mouth fierce and gentle on hers, feelings igniting like dry tinder touched by lightning.

Charity had the sensation of flying through a fire storm, of all her defenses melting in the torrid aura of Tell Layton. Her head fell back against his arm. "I hope you know that we can be arrested for putting on such a display."

"Not true, darling. This is our own elevator opening into our foyer and nowhere else."

"I can see why you need it if you put on this passionate performance every time you take a female up here."

"You are not any female, you're my wife, and I've never used this as my passion pit anyway." Tell laughed when she shot a narrow, suspicious look his way. "I've sold all my . . . er . . . other properties that were for those special situations."

"Damned roué." Charity tried to pull away from him but he held her fast.

"Trust me, love, you can, you know." Tell spoke into her hair, his mouth caressing the silky surface.

He was still holding her when the doors opened into the foyer, the pale caramel marble floor reflecting the color of the silk wallpaper that covered the two-story entrance. The place had a soft golden glow, a homey warmth. "Welcome home, my sweet."

' Charity looked about her, up the curving stairway that hugged the far wall and led upward to the second-floor suite that she knew was Tell's private area. There were other bedrooms on the first floor of the apartment plus a living room, dining room, library, kitchen, and staff quarters. Her mother had taken her on a tour of the place when she'd been young—with Tell's permission, of course. "It's a lovely apartment, spacious and with all the colors that I have always liked."

"I know."

Charity turned at the peculiar inflection in his voice

but his face was bland, so she continued to move forward and look over her surroundings. "I'll have to get some clothes from . . ."

"No need. Charine, the dressmaker, will be sending things over for you, if they're not here already." Tell held up his hand, palm outward. "Now, don't read me a lecture on economizing."

"I wasn't going to," Charity said loftily. "It's just that I have perfectly good clothes . . ."

"You have very good taste, love, and know how to dress."

She swung to face him.

"You have a let's-go-four-rounds look on your face, darling."

"And why wouldn't I have? I just married a man who constantly interrupts me."

Tell spread his hands apologetically. "I'll do better. Come and give me a kiss and tell me you forgive me."

Charity knew by the look on his face that he didn't expect her to do it. She glided forward and reached up, seeing his slight flinch as though he expected her to slap him rather than kiss him. Letting her fingers slip gently down the slightly roughened face that needed shaving twice a day, she lifted herself upward and placed her parted lips on his, her tongue touching the inside of his mouth. Charity felt the quake that ran through his body as she teased his tongue with hers and emboldened by his response she increased the pressure, exerting all the sensuous power she had. It stunned her when her own control started to slide away, her own body shivering with the old-new sensation of sexual emotion. When she tried to take a deep breath it was Tell's oxygen she took. His arms came around her and lifted her up to fit her more comfortably into his body. Dizziness assailed her as she clutched him more tightly, groaning audibly when he lifted his head.

"I will not take you the first time after our marriage in our foyer, darling," he told her shakily, bending to catch her behind the knees and lift her into his arms. "That's not to say it might not happen in the future, though."

"Spoilsport," Charity murmured lazily, her finger touching his ear, probing, rubbing there.

"You are definitely not getting out of the bedroom for a while."

"I'll scream," she whispered, her arms tightening around his neck.

"If you breathe in my ear much longer, I'll be the one screaming," Tell said grimly, grimacing at her when she chuckled. "I wonder if you realize the forest fire you've started in me."

"I think I'm beginning to get an inkling." Charity smiled up at him when he placed her on the bed, the hard features above her own etched black and gold in the shadows of the one small lamp that was lit. "Won't your housekeeper wonder what's going on?"

"No! My staff knows better than to interfere with me."

"Big man." Charity ran her fingernail down his nose. When he opened his mouth and snapped the finger into it she laughed, feeling carefree and more unafraid than she'd ever been.

Tell nuzzled his face into her neck, his fingers busy on her clothes. "I've waited far too long to get you into my bed, sweet one . . . and now I'm as clumsy as a jackass."

"Are jackasses clumsy?" Charity crooned to him, her hands threading through ebony crispness of his hair. "Your hair has a little curl to it, doesn't it?"

"Does it?" Tell's voice was muffled against her now bared breasts.

"When we have children, their hair will be dark and curling, I like that."

Tell's head whipped up, his hot eyes fixing on her. "Children, my love? Are we having them?"

Charity touched his face, feeling warm and relaxed. "I have always thought of marriage and children as inseparable. Wouldn't you like some?"

. "Some? Maybe one or two would be fine, but you're still very young and I would like some time alone with you first . . . unless you object to that."

"No. It's a good idea to get to know the people you marry."

"No more talking." Tell's mouth moved down her body in slow, exquisite exploration, eliciting groans from Charity. Tell had to struggle to keep his own libido from crashing through the top of his head but he made every effort, wanting her ecstasy more than his own.

"No one's ever kissed my toes before," Charity gasped, delight rivering through her at the tousled look of Tell when he gazed at her, his eyes glazed with his own passion.

"I thought we weren't talking, my love."

"I like to when you're loving me."

Tell laughed out loud, delighted at how open she was being with him, how giving. "Then we must talk all the time."

Whatever else Charity was going to say faded from her mind when she felt him divest her of the last of her clothing, his hands and mouth turning her to flame. "Tell . . . Tell . . ."

"I'm with you all the way." He felt the thrust of passion stiffen her body with pleasure and surprise. In gentle abrasion he moved up her body, entering her with a wild serenity that had her calling out to him again and again.

The questing rhythm of the ages was on them and all

147

control left except the primeval need to become one with the stars.

In desperate joy Charity hugged him, legs and arms joining him to her as her husband took her over the brink of sensual love, making her soar, then disappear into the beauty that only lovers ever know.

CHAPTER SIX

The weeks following her marriage to Tell were happier than any Charity had ever known or even imagined. She alternately felt shy and bold with her new spouse, finding joy in the discovery that whenever she turned to look at him most of the time he was looking at her as well. The lovemaking between them was both explosive and serene and she felt caught in a whirlpool of love that grew stronger each time they were together.

They lunched together often, and they always ate dinner together, juggling their schedules so that this was possible. Some evenings they went out to Bigham House, sometimes they stayed in town at either the apartment her grandfather had left her or at Tell's. As much as Charity loved Bigham House she was happier when they could stay in Manhattan and be alone. Sometimes they would talk all evening, discussing things that were dear to them, or finding out more about each other.

More and more Charity was beginning to realize that her husband knew far more about her than she did about him.

One day, she was hurrying to the ladies' room at Promise House before meeting Tell for lunch. She glanced at her watch as she walked; being late was anathema to her since she wanted to spend every mo-

149

ment she could with her husband. She was about to step through the door when she heard voices.

". . . and I think we should tell Charity what Docky did to Priscilla when she came to town last week. What if she'd been hurt? Or if he'd hidden her someplace?"

"Priscilla is tough. She got away, didn't she? We shouldn't tell Charity, she just got married and besides she might not let the girls stay out at that house she owns."

"Yeah, I guess so."

Charity pushed open the door walking up to the open-mouthed girls, Lily and Madeleine, who faced her. "All right. I want all of it right now and I mean it. What has been going on?"

"Ah, Charity, you won't be mad at Priscilla, will you?"

"Start talking."

The two girls looked at one another, their faces conveying both their instinctive need to be secretive and their desire to share their burden with another person. The ambivalence of the life they'd led on the street caused them to tread the high wire most of the time. Charity knew those looks. Time after time she'd seen them on the faces of the ones she'd counseled at Promise House and as often on the faces of youngsters she'd seen on the street.

"Don't be mad at Priscilla or Rita or any of the others out at Bigham House, Charity. Promise?"

Charity nodded, staring at Madeleine grimly. She almost didn't want to hear what was coming. Docky was a well-known pimp in the rough, tough area around Promise House; he'd had a few of her girls on his pimp's string at one time. Charity had warned him off more than once when he'd come around trying to coerce the girls to come with him, and the last time Docky had shown his face Lionel had thrown him down the front steps of Promise House into the street. Docky was a nasty man with a long memory. If he was coming after any of her girls again, Charity wouldn't have hesitated to call the police. "Tell me."

"You remember when Rita and Priscilla came into town with you to take those preliminary equivalency tests for their high school degree?"

"Yes, yes, last Thursday, get on with it, Madeleine. Lily, you stay right where you are."

"Okay," Lily muttered, smiling sheepishly. Running and hiding were second nature to street kids.

"Well, they told us that they'd overheard your husband and Lionel talking about how your accidents could have been caused by a drug pusher of one of the street people that hang around this neighborhood . . ."

Charity stiffened, but nodded to the girl to continue.

"Well, when they finished their exams they told Father Desmond that they would stay overnight in the dorm and go back to Bigham House the next day . . ."

"But instead they sought out Docky and talked to him," Charity finished, her voice rising, her eyes closing for a moment in painful fear of what could have happened to them. "Do any of you realize how really dangerous he is, how quickly he would take your life and not even bat an eye?"

Madeleine spread her hands, her glance sliding to Lily then back to Charity. "We knew you'd kick up a storm about this, Charity."

Charity took several deep breaths and put her hand out to the very pregnant girl. "All right, I'm sorry I barked at you, but it frightens me to death that any of you could be near that devil. Tell me what he did to Priscilla."

"Damn! Look at her, Madeleine, she's all white."

"It wasn't that bad, honest, Charity. He grabbed her and told her he was having a party for her that night that he had a few friends that liked to play with pregnant ladies . . . so Priscilla drop kicked him in the you-know-where and she got away . . . Gee, Charity, are you laughing or crying?"

"Both." Charity put her arms around the two girls and hugged them to her. "I want you to promise me that there will be no more vigilante forays by any of you . . . and I want to see the rest of the girls in . . ." Charity looked at her watch. "Five minutes . . . all of them before I go to lunch. Got that?"

"Yessir, general."

The two girls left the ladies' room and Charity leaned on the sink looking at herself in the mirror, shaking her head. If anything had happened to Priscilla . . . she could have disappeared and not all their efforts would have turned her up. Charity put her hand over her eyes. Damn that Docky! She would kill him if he ever came near her girls again. She hurried to her office to call Tell and say she'd be a little late. "Yes, I'll be there, but I have a few things I want to hammer home to my girls, about safety mostly."

That night when Tell showed up to follow her home as he always did, she blew him a kiss in her rearview mirror when she saw him frowning. It bothered him mightily that she wouldn't let him buy her a new car, or that she insisted on driving herself to work because she might have to go out on a call during the day. She couldn't help but smile at his scowling face, knowing exactly what was going through his mind. What a man her husband was! And how she loved him. It was ridiculous of her to try and deny it now. He had woven himself into the fabric of her being so he was blood of her blood, skin to skin with her. Losing him now would be unthinkable! All those deathless writings of the Bard and his contemporaries about undying devotion had not been mere poetic and lyrical literature. Instead it was bonafide fact, rock-hard certainty that couldn't be denied. Charity wanted to hug the strong emotion to her for an eternity and tie Tell to her even longer than that.

All at once her talk that day to the girls at Promise House came into her mind and all amusement left her. She had called them in and read the riot act to them, but it hadn't banished the pimp from her mind. Docky! There was no need to discuss that vile procurer with Tell. Nothing that dirty should intrude on their moments alone. Besides he'd hit the ceiling and she certainly didn't want him . . . or Lionel . . . or Gareth looking for that obscenity, especially on his own turf. They might find him and that could be their undoing. Docky was a devious vengeful rat who had wreaked his own special vindictiveness on more than one member of Promise House and two of them had been young people that Charity had worked with, both of whom had had good chances for a straight life before Docky had decided to pay them back for deserting him.

It wasn't often that Charity thought of the past but she could still recall Terry Radcliffe and Linda Wills. Terry was a fine young man now who'd made it back from a life of drugs and petty crime to support his habit and was living in the Midwest, a partner in a paint store and doing well. Linda bucked Docky and wound up dead in an alley. Everyone on the street knew Docky had had Linda killed, but he was never even questioned about it, let alone charged. There was no way she was going to involve Tell and the other two men in the latest brush with Docky. Now that she had talked with the girls and she would call the ones in Bigham House in the morning, she could handle the rest herself. Tomorrow she would put out the word that Docky was to stay away from Promise House or she would set the Vice Squad on his tail, insisting that action be taken against him. Even though he could weasel out of most anything, he was no different from most criminal pariahs. He hated the heat turned on him full force and would go out of his way to avoid it.

That evening after dinner Tell sat as he always did when they had coffee, in the front room with his wife in the crook of his arm. His pose was relaxed, although all his senses were on full alert. "What's making you so tense, darling, so brooding?" Tell felt his bride stiffen.

"Ah, it's just work. It looks as though we'll be getting a new contingent of young people soon and Father has really been searching for more quarters nearby," she replied.

"Yes, so you told me last night," Tell mused, irritation rising in him that she was being evasive with him, that something she refused to share with him was eating away at her. "Nothing else on your mind?"

Charity didn't look up at him, but instead stared into the fire. "I was thinking that we should probably go out to Bigham House tomorrow night and commute for the rest of the week."

"Oh? I thought we were going to stay here until Friday and then go out then."

"Oh. Right, but you wouldn't mind if we upped the time a little, would you?"

"Not at all . . . Shall we go to bed?"

"Bed? Now? Tell, it's only nine o'clock."

"I know, but I feel like communicating with my wife and I'm not doing it here." Tell placed his cup on the table in front of him. "And please don't tell me to take my cup to the kitchen, I really don't feel like doing that right now."

"Oooh, we are petulant. Why are you so angry?" Charity asked him when he rose and pulled her to her feet and into his arms.

"Think about it, darling, you'll come up with the answer." He could tell by the weak smile she gave him that she was aware that he knew she was hiding something from him.

"Would you like me to sleep in the guest bedroom?" she asked.

"If you would like that, I'll join you there."

"I meant that maybe you don't want to sleep with me because you're miffed with me."

"Miffed? I would say more than that, but the day won't come that I don't want to share your bed, Charity, nor will we ever sleep apart unless it is impossible to be together."

"Sounds good to me." She started to laugh, even as he swept her up in his arms. "You're a scowling Romeo, I must say."

Tell gave her a hard smile. "And you're a secretive Juliet, my darling."

"Tell, don't be mad."

"I can't help being angry when you don't share your problems with me. Stop blowing in my ear. That drives me crazy."

"I know."

"Dammit, Charity, what am I going to do with you?"

"Oh, I think you're doing pretty well now," she told him when he pushed open their bedroom door and carried her to the bed. When he lowered himself beside her, she ran her hands over that strong-planed face. "I know all problems are not solved in the bedroom, but you must admit we do very well here."

"I agree, but I would still like you to be open with me, Charity. Did you have another accident today?"

"No. I promise you that I would tell you if something went wrong that way. Trust me."

"I do, and I want you to trust me."

"What I'm not telling you has nothing to do with our

155

belief in each other. It's just something I have to mull over by myself. Please."

"I'll give you your space, darling, but I don't like it."

"Thank you." Charity pulled him down to her and began kissing him slowly and deeply.

Tell lifted his head, his hair tousled, his eyes heavy with passion. "And don't think you can put me off that way . . . Stop that. God, I want you, Charity."

"And I want you, Tell darling."

Tell groaned as though she'd pained him, then slowly he began the rhythm of love that delighted them both, that had the world exploding around them.

It struck Tell like a velvet fist that he not only enjoyed making love to his wife, he wanted and needed it more each time she was with him. He couldn't get enough of her and it rocked him. "I love you, Charity," he muttered against her skin, the body that entrapped his exciting him more than he'd ever thought was possible.

"Me too," Charity mumbled as the passionate gale took them and tossed them out beyond the stars and planets into the turbulent world of love.

The next day Tell and Charity were later than usual, grabbing juice and vitamins and toast, barely sitting in their chairs before they were up again.

"I don't know what Mrs. Hunstable thinks of us," Charity whispered as she and Tell left the table in a hurry and rushed upstairs to brush their teeth.

"I could always tell her that we were up all night making love and we didn't fall asleep until dawn. Don't glower, darling, it's true."

"Shh."

Despite having two bathrooms in their suite, more often than not Tell would come into hers and brush his

156

teeth when she was doing hers. "If ever I'm encroaching just say so and I'll get out of your way."

Charity smiled at him, her lathered mouth looking silly to her in the mirror. "I don't know why you'd want to see me like this."

"I like ladies with white mustaches all around their mouths." He leaned around and kissed her, some of her toothpaste lather clinging to him. "Now we look like a vaudeville act."

Charity laughed all the way to work. Tell had that effect on her. Every time there was a free moment in traffic she would look in her rearview mirror and wave, overjoyed when her man, who followed her to work each day, waved back and gave her that hot smile that made her flesh tingle.

As usual Tell got out of his car after she parked hers. "Why do you look so surprised? Don't I always kiss you good-bye?"

"Not when you're twenty minutes late for a conference and you've kissed me a dozen times already this morning." Charity lifted her chin and closed her eyes, savoring his strong mouth on hers.

"If only you'd let me buy you a new car," Tell said against her lips.

"Mine is perfect for this neighborhood and it has several thousand miles to go before trade-in."

"It should be junked. Kiss me again."

The person in the black jumpsuit with the fitted hood stared at the two of them embracing in the parking lot and felt a blinding fury, as always when she was around. She would pay, just as the others had! And Judgment Day was not far off!

It was amusing to note that there was someone else spying on the couple. The other person, who was not

157

important anyway, was oblivious to all but Charity and Tell, and it was just as well.

How wonderful it was to plan the annihilation of the enemy when the enemy had no knowledge it was being done!

Charity walked around the front of the building to the front door of Promise House, her thoughts on her wonderful husband.

"Miss Charity Bigham, it has come to my attention that you wish to speak with me."

Startled, Charity spun around at the sound of the rasping voice right behind her. "Docky! Where did you come from?"

"I was watching the little show you were putting on in the parking lot. I could put you to work making my customers happy in any parking lot you choose if that's your thing."

"How would you like a kick in the groin, Docky?" Charity asked him conversationally, relaxing and bending her body, aware that the street-smart, slightly built man with the face like a sewer rat would do what he could to kill her if she showed the slightest weakness. "Incidentally, you look terrible in black: your skin looks yellow." Charity sidled quickly toward him, her hand shooting out quickly and missing him purposefully.

Docky took a step backward, his both hands held in front of him, palm outward, his smile belied by the flashing venom in his brown eyes. "Hey! Charity Bigham, take it easy. I heard you wanted to talk to me so I came and I find you ready to work karate on me. Cool out, chick. Forget the talk and I'm outta here."

"Wait. You heard right. I wanted to tell you to stay away from my girls. You threatened one of them and tried to get her into your stable. If you ever even look at my girls again I'll raise a uproar that will carry right

158

to the mayor and you and your sleaze bags will burn, Docky. You know I mean it. I won't stop until they put you away until you're a doddering old man."

The weasel eyes fixed on her unblinkingly. "And you might have an accident yourself one of these fine days, Miss Almighty Bigham."

"Are you saying that you're the one who tried to run me down with a car? Or a boat?" Charity saw his opaque eyes flutter and felt a dance of fear up and down her spine.

"I don't know what the hell you're talkin' about, Miss Charity Bigham, but just don't try to threaten me or you won't like it."

"And you just stay away from my girls, or you won't like it." Charity faced him down, wondering if her thudding heart was showing through her blouse. She felt as though it were coming through her breastbone. "Get out of here." For a moment she thought he was going to strike her.

"This is my turf, Miss godalmighty Bigham, and don't you go ordering me around."

Neither one of the antagonists was aware of anything but each other. When the rough voice intruded both Charity and Docky whirled around.

"What the hell are you doing here, Docky?" Lionel approached them warily like a fighter looking for an opening, his rough-hewn face etched in anger, his fingers curled into fists. With one sweep he moved himself between Charity and the smaller man.

"Wait, Lionel . . ."

"Hold on, Bevins, you got no call stickin' your nose in this . . ."

"I'm going to tear your ears off, then bite off your nose," Lionel told him cheerfully. "I need the recreation."

"You're nuts, man." Docky whirled and ran up the

street, his high-heeled boots beating a staccato rhythm on the sidewalk.

"How did you know I was through talking to him?" Charity stared up at her big friend, arms akimbo, glaring at him.

"Why would you speak to that slime? Were you through talking to him?"

"Yes. I found out that he tried to force one of my girls back into his stable and I warned him off."

"You should have let me give him a brain implant . . . Bevins style." Lionel ground his teeth in frustration. "It isn't only the girls he pimps for."

"I know." Charity took his arm and walked with him up the flight of cement steps into the brownstone. Charity looked around her. "I think we should get a crew together and give this place a coat of paint. It's getting seedy-looking."

"Charity, what else did Docky say to you? You have a funny look on your face."

"I asked him if he'd had anything to do with the accident that I'd had with my car in the underground garage, or with the boat."

"Tell told me about those. So? What did he say?"

"He denied it but there was a strange, arrested look to him all at once that makes me wonder."

"Damn him! If I ever find out that he's had anything to do with something like that, I'll break him in half."

Charity patted her friend's arm. "Jennifer would never forgive me if anything interfered with your wedding in three weeks, and that includes you being arrested for mayhem."

"She would understand," Lionel said grimly, his features lightening at the mention of his fiancée. "I can't wait for that wedding and to get Jen out of that house and into my own." He took hold of Charity's hand. "Not that I don't think it's wonderful that we're having our wedding reception at Bigham House, because I do. It's just that . . ."

"You want to be together, away from her family. I think she's pretty anxious too."

"I expect you to dance at my wedding, sister that I never had."

"How would we not be there? Tell and I practically live there, and besides, I wouldn't let you get married without me!"

Jacob Henry called Gareth into his office, his glasses sliding down his nose when he looked at the younger man. "Sit down, Gareth."

"Yessir." Gareth was very fond of the man who'd been his stepfather's close business associate, and he had enjoyed working for the firm. It never ceased to amaze the younger man how shrewd and able Jacob was in a courtroom.

"Tell Layton talks to you quite freely of his worries about Charity, I understand."

Gareth nodded, puzzled and wary by the older man's cool manner.

"Would it surprise you if I told you, that from the few license numbers Tell was able to get when the boat almost ran Charity down, that the only craft in the immediate vicinity that fits the bill belongs to you?"

"What?" Gareth leaped to his feet, his hands clenching. "That's not true. It can't be. My boat was only taken out a few times this summer because of the bad weather. It's been in dry dock since early September in the old storage barn on Bigham House property."

"I see. Could someone have borrowed your boat to do the deed?"

"Yes, but it would be a tough job getting it into the water unless there were more than one person doing it."

161

"I think you'd better check the status of your boat, Gareth."

"I'll do better than that. I'll raise hell if I find that anyone has used my property to go after Charity."

"Good." The older man stood as a signal that the interview was ended.

Three days later when Jacob was leaving the Manhattan apartment he'd had for years on Riverside Drive someone fired at him, but the aim was off because an alert doorman pulled the elderly gentleman out of the way.

That afternoon, Tell went to Jacob's office, well aware that the older man was in the law library, and buzzed for Gareth.

Tell didn't smile when the younger man came in, mouth agape at who was sitting in Jacob's chair.

"What's going on, Tell?"

"Jacob was shot at today. The doorman says the shot came from a black Eldorado . . ."

"Just like the car that went after Charity."

Gareth's twisted smile had a coldness to it, but Tell pressed on. "Are you saying you don't know anything about it?"

"That's what I'm saying, Tell. And you should know that Jacob questioned me about my boat being the one that went after Charity."

"I knew he talked to you . . . and three days after that someone shot at him."

"I had nothing to do with any of it," Gareth told him, his tones clipped.

Tell steepled his hands. "I never believed that you did and neither did Jacob."

Gareth's taut face relaxed at once. "Thank you. Then what do you believe?"

"I think you or Jacob must have mentioned the conversation between you to the wrong someone, and that's why he was put in jeopardy. I've talked to Jacob and he can't recall discussing it."

Gareth shook his head slowly. "That doesn't compute for me either. Oh I raised hell about it, but with the maintenance man at Bigham House, no one else."

"Davis's boy?"

"Right."

Tell looked thoughtful. "I have to talk to him again . . . and while I'm at it I'll question his father again too."

"But they didn't tell you anything the first time you questioned them?"

"No, Gareth, they didn't, but someone knows something about this and I intend to get some answers." Tell stood, striding toward the tall windows looking down on the busy New York avenue, his fist beating a tattoo on the expanse of glass.

The door opened and Jacob came through going to the large conference table in his office and putting down a large estate folder. "These are all the old wills that Cyrus wrote over the years and the papers of instructions he left before and after his marriage to Kathleen." Jacob looked over his pincenez and shook his head at Tell. "I don't know how these could aid you. I helped draft most of them and I don't recall anything that would be germane to the problem."

Tell shrugged, his jaw hardening. "I feel otherwise, Jacob. I knew Cyrus in a very close business and personal way for many years. He was complex, often unpredictable and changeable. His fiery personality made him hard to figure and often gave him the edge in the marketplace. The one absolute about the man was his love for his daughter and granddaughter. His great passion for business went second to them, even though nothing else did. Cyrus was very in tune with both Julia and Charity, and they with him. I have a suspicion that he would know, consciously or subconsciously, if his granddaughter was in potential jeopardy and take elaborate and complicated steps to prevent it." Tell inhaled, staring at each man in turn. "He was a wealthy man, he always knew how to guard his businesses and I see him as being even more careful about the two women he loved more than anything in the world."

Gareth nodded his head. "But searching through this mountain of paper for an elusive answer is, at best, a long shot, Tell."

"The longest," Jacob concurred dryly.

"If you two are tied up, I'll take these home with me and go over them in my leisure time."

Gareth laughed. "Don't get edgy, friend. You have my help."

"And mine, but I think I have a better idea, Tell. Why don't we split them up, each take a third with us and we'll go over them when we can."

"Jacob's got a good idea there, Tell. Rather than try to fit this into a workday we could go over them later in the day or even at home." Gareth felt a dart of sympathy when the other man looked at him, his eyes burning with a cold fever, as though he had a race to run and no more time to train.

Gareth thought back to the conversation he'd had with Lionel that morning when the other man had called him on the phone and asked if he would consider being his best man. "Not that you have much to fear with that spunky wife of yours. If she could stand up to that resident pimp on Forty-first Street, she could face anything." Gareth was looking at the folders in his hand as he finished so he wasn't watching Tell's face, but the stillness had the reverberation of a cathedral bell, bringing up his head. "Tell! For God's sakes, man, I thought you knew."

"Tell me."

The husky pain in Layton's voice brought Jacob's understanding glance his way.

"Lionel said he found Charity on the sidewalk in front of Promise House reading the riot act to Docky because it seemed he tried to coerce one of her girls back into his stable." Gareth laughed. "Lionel said she was shaking her finger in his face, obviously threatening him about something."

"Little devil." Tell's smile had a sting in it.

"She was the spunkiest child I ever knew outside of my own Jake." Jacob shook his head. "I don't think I'll ever forget the day she was out in the paddock when Cyrus and I were looking at some yearlings he'd just purchased and that were in the south pasture. I'll never know what ever possessed her but she jumped onto the back of Cyrus's big stallion and went roaring down the meadow, taking the high gate like a master in dressage." Jacob shook his head. "She was like the wind that day."

"I told Cyrus more than once that she shouldn't ride anything she chose in the stable, but he was so damned proud of her prowess," Tell said grimly.

"That was the only time you and Cyrus argued when you disagreed with the way he was raising Charity," Jacob mused, a faraway look in his eyes. "Quite frankly, Tell, I disagreed with my old friend that day." Jacob shook his head. "Cyrus let her take the wildest chances but at the same time he was fiercely protective of her."

"That hell-for-leather method of his should have been kept in the boardroom. It wasn't for a girl like Charity." Tell's head shot Gareth's way when the other man laughed.

"You were always standing between her and something, Tell. You've always loved her too much."

Jacob sucked in a deep breath at the look of demonic fury that crossed Tell's face and was as quickly gone.

* * *

Charity was glad that they had decided to go out to Bigham House right from work that evening. "I wanted to take a look at the house and see what we could do to decorate it for the wedding. There will be two hundred guests, Jennifer tells me, which isn't many when you think of the number of friends and relatives on her mother's side that will not be invited to this." Charity shook her head. "I think Kathleen is making a tactical mistake with Jennifer, throwing up barriers at every turn, manifesting all this disapproval of the nuptials by not inviting her close friends or some of the family. Don't you? Tell?"

"What? Oh sorry, darling, I was thinking of something else."

He had been distracted since he'd come to work that afternoon and then followed her back to their apartment. Even when they'd packed the few things they needed for the trip to Bigham House he'd been in a dream world. "What's bothering you, Tell?"

"Ah, nothing really." He shot her a twisted smile. "It will be a nice ride. Even though the days are getting shorter we'll still get a glimpse of the beautiful autumn colors."

What was it that he didn't want to discuss with her, but that seemed to be riveted in his mind to the exclusion of all other thoughts?

When he hit the steering wheel hard with the flat of his hand, Charity's head swiveled his way. "Why did I have to hear about you and a pimp having a brouhaha from Gareth?"

Charity sighed. "I've had conversations like that with others of Docky's ilk, Tell, and I will again. It wasn't that important."

"You're my wife and I happen to think it is, Charity."

166

"I was doing my job, Tell, that's all."

"Damn your job."

The rest of the journey consisted of sporadic observations and long silences.

As soon as they reached Bigham House and Macon took the small amount of baggage they had, Charity headed for the library, her chin in the air. "Going to check a few things."

Tell was right at her heels. "I'll join you."

When the heavy door closed behind them, he caught hold of her. "You're angry with me because I was upset about your confrontation with a known criminal. That's stupid, Charity."

"Stuff it," his bride said inelegantly, turning her face when he tried to kiss her.

"I love you, pet, but I have things on my mind, the primary one being you."

"You want to know everything about me, Tell, but how often do you share your work with me? I realize that I don't have a business brain but I'm not the dolt you seem to think."

Tell held her close, his chin resting on the top of her head. "Gareth made the observation the other day that I've always loved you too much. It set me thinking that maybe I have been monopolizing you, crowding you, that I'm possessive. I didn't like looking at the picture of myself that has been emerging."

Relief and delight coursed through her, lighting her blood, firing her laughter. "That's what's bothering you?"

"Yes, that . . . the fact that my wife faced a dangerous person on her own."

Charity touched his nose with one finger. "You tell Gareth that your wife insists on you monopolizing her time, crowding her, loving her and even worrying when I talk to scum like Docky. Will you do that?"

167

"Yes, my pet, I will." Scooping her higher up his chest until their mouths were level and a centimeter apart, he stared at her. "I do love you too much, but I guess that's a problem I'll have to wrestle with, not you. Right?"

Charity sagged against him, hardly able to credit the acidic amusement on his features, his words making her wary but at the same time warmer and safer than she ever believed she could. "You keep throwing these curves at me," she told him breathlessly. "I think you just like to keep me off balance." She touched his nose with one finger. "Is it love we feel? I will never know how that happened, but I can tell you that I have never felt smothered by you and would hate it if you pulled back from me." She blinked at him. "How did we ever get to that plateau?"

"Written in the stars, my sweet, written in the stars." Tell carried her over to the large leather chair behind the desk, sitting down and cuddling her in his lap. "Let's forget about work."

Charity laughed, her head thrown back, her gaze glancing off the floor-to-ceiling bookshelves. All at once she sat straight up in his lap, eyes riveting on the bookshelf. "That's it. That's what's bothered me all this time but I couldn't put my finger on it."

"What are you talking about?" Tell tried to pull her down to his lap again, his glance following hers to the bookshelf.

"Grandfather gave me a message," Charity said in hushed tones, her eyes never leaving the oak-braced bookshelves.

"He did?" Tell's eyes went from her enrapt expression to the books and back again. "What was the message?" The back of his neck prickled and he had an insane sensation that he'd just heard Cyrus laugh.

"I don't know the words exactly . . . but . . . but Grandfather has given me a warning."

"What?" Tell straightened from his lounging position, his hands tightening on her instinctively, his body tenting over hers as he cuddled her closer to him. "What do you mean, Charity?" Fear filled him like a poison, making breathing difficult, the sense of jeopardy firing his temper. "Tell me."

Coming out of her concentration, Charity looked at him, blinking as though she needed time to organize her thoughts. Then, taking note of his tight features, the pinched look around his lips, she put her hands on either side of his face. "Tell, it's all right. Let me explain."

"Please. I had a bad moment there, a feeling that your grandfather was in the room."

"Did you?" Charity looked pleased rather than alarmed. "I have always been able to communicate with him best in this room. It wouldn't surprise me to see him here one day."

"Really? I can't say I'd look forward to that. Cyrus was formidable enough in life," Tell informed her dryly.

Though she chuckled, his husky undertones telegraphed to Charity just how tense her words had made him and she knew that he didn't fear an apparition. Settling back in his arms, she wriggled around so that she was leaning against his shoulder and both of them were facing the bookcase.

"If you were seeking a way to distract me by moving that lovely tush of yours, you have succeeded, wife," Tell breathed into her hair.

Looking up at him, laughing, she nibbled at his chin. "Later, o lecherous one, later."

"I'll remember that."

"Do. Now, to the books. Follow my pointing finger to the second shelf from the top. Do you see what's there?"

Tell let his eyes wander along the designated area, then he nodded, trying to fight down the trepidation that was building in him. "It looks like the complete *Sherlock Holmes* all individually bound and from the looks of them, the collection is very old."

"Indeed it is. In fact most of them are the original bindings, the set was a rare collection that Grandfather was able to purchase when my mother was a young girl. That's why the entire grouping plus the other antique books are in the glassed-in section of the shelves."

Tell watched her eyes flash with memory, color come into her cheeks as though she were marching through a wonderful vision. "Go on, darling."

"What? Oh, yes. Well, when I was old enough to begin taking the books from here and reading them myself . . . Mother and Grandfather read to me every night, you see." Charity swallowed a sheen of tears in her eyes when she smiled up at her husband. "Well, Grandfather suggested that he and I read Sherlock Holmes together, a little every day, or every other day if he was busy." Charity laughed. "Some of those stories were really scary and I was glad that we read them in the daytime and not at night." She pointed upward. *"A Study in Scarlet"* was the beginning of it all, when Sherlock Holmes met Dr. Watson. See, that volume is first. After that was *The Sign of Four.* That one made you look over your shoulder for days afterward. Then you'll notice that there's a section of very narrow books. Those are the ones that were in short newspaper form, completed in one issue and not serialized, if I remember Grandfather correctly . . ."

"There are other larger volumes and then more smaller ones, put into a prescribed order, I suppose."

"Yes, yes, that's it. Grandfather and I only read the stories in the order they were in on the shelf, that never changed . . . and he told me that I would know if there was ever trouble at Bigham House if the books were out of order."

"And are they, darling?" Tell shot a quick look at the volumes.

"Yes, yes they are, but only Grandfather and I would know, I think because it was our secret and because he was so very fussy about his collection that was in the glass case only Macon and a prescribed helper were allowed to clean them. Don't you see, Tell? Grandfather was so persnickety that he wouldn't let anyone touch them unless it was under his eye." Charity looked back at the bookshelf. "In the section marked as The Adventures of Sherlock Holmes with the twelve narrow volumes, you'll notice one called *The Man with the Twisted Lip.*"

"Yes, the one that is not quite tight to its neighbor and leans a little." Still holding her Tell rose from the chair, letting her slide down his body as he moved toward the shelves, still with his arm around her.

"That's it. Well, that volume should be standing straight and be in front of *The Adventure of the Blue Carbuncle* and *The Adventure of the Speckled Band,* not following them on the shelf as it does now."

"You're sure?"

"As sure as I am that we're standing in the library at Bigham House." Charity turned and went to the desk, taking a key from her key chain that she'd removed from her purse and fitting it into the middle drawer and unlocking it.

"Darling, did you know that Gareth and I were looking for that key? We needed to get in the desk."

"Why? Grandfather left it to me and it just has a few papers in it, nothing valuable." She shot a look at Tell, then pulled open the drawer, fumbling through the papers and assorted minutiae until she found a small black notebook. "Ah, here it is. Grandfather and I wrote

down the sequence in here just in case one of us forgot."
Charity grinned at her husband. "I think he was more
worried I would than he might."

"He was a very sharp man."

Tell's offhand voice brought Charity's focus on him.
"You don't think it means anything."

"No, sweetheart, I'm not saying that. It's just if your
grandfather was trying to give you a message . . ." Tell
shrugged. "What was it?" If only she were wrong about
this.

Charity inhaled a deep breath, nodding. "You're
right, I don't know what it would be, but he did tell me
that if ever the books weren't right, out of order, I
should look for the reason because something was wrong
at Bigham House."

Panic rippled down Tell's spine as he recalled the
times that Cyrus told him that he knew how to protect
his granddaughter. Damn the man for being so enigmatic! "Think, Charity. What would Cryus be trying to
say to you with the disorder of the books . . . other
than that there was trouble at Bigham House?"

Charity frowned at her husband, noting the perspira-
tion on his upper lip. He wasn't as unconcerned as he
seemed to be. Her gaze slipped past him to the bookcase, a slant of sun touching the books, giving them an
aura they hadn't had until that moment. "He . . . he
could be telling me about a man with a . . ." Charity
stared at the disordered volume. "A man with the
twisted lip," she said slowly. "But I don't know anyone
who fits that description."

Tell stared at her, seeing her eyes narrow, knowing
that she was searching her brain, being able to tell that
though his wife might not think she knew anything her
subconscious was nudging her about something. "Don't
concentrate on it, just let it tumble around your mind
for a time, maybe something will hit home."

"I'll do that." Tell seemed more agitated than he had when she had first told him. What had set off this fever in him?

"Maybe we should go up and get changed for dinner, darling. It's in fifteen minutes and Kathleen will have something to say if we're late."

"Since when has what she says ever bothered you, Tell?"

Tell shrugged, taking the notebook from her hand and flipping through it. "She doesn't bother me but it would be nice to have a dinner free from strife. I'm sure the girls would agree with me.".

Contrite, Charity nodded, holding out her hand. "Shouldn't you give me back the notebook so I can lock it in the drawer again?"

"Uh, all right." Tell tried to mask his disappointment. It would have been nice to peruse the book in private.

Charity noted his reluctance to return it. "Do you want to study it?"

"No, you keep it in the desk. If I want it, I'll ask you for the key."

Charity walked up the stairs to their suite, her arm around her husband as his was around her. She felt warm and safe with him as she always did but she couldn't shake the suspicion that there was something that Tell was keeping from her, and it had to do with how upset he'd been when she'd been telling him about the books.

It had been their habit to shower together whenever they could and Tell could discern that his bride was very surprised when he told her that he would use the other bathroom in the suite.

Tell needed to think, to ponder what had happened that afternoon. He had been rocked to his shoes when

Charity had dropped her bomb that her grandfather had left her a message and that it had been very clear to her from what she'd seen that he'd told her that something was not right at Bigham House. What had he meant? Coupled with the information that he had about Cyrus being able to take care of his granddaughter and the fact that she felt she'd been warned by her relative, added up to a very serious situation that he neither trusted nor wanted.

Tell had been almost relieved when he'd thought that her enemy had been a man named Docky. That foe was real, could be touched. Now, after today, they were back to square one . . . the elusive unknown. Whatever was out there and after his wife, neither Charity nor he had a clue.

Tell smacked his hand against the tiling of the bathroom as he stared at his wet image in the mirror.

Who was stalking Charity?

Why was the stalker after her?

What secret did Bigham House hold?

Damn, damn, damn! He would find out or die in the attempt because it had been hammered home to him most painfully by the "accidents" she'd had that somebody meant to carry through with the threats and attempts until Charity was hurt badly, or worse.

Pondering life without Charity was something he couldn't do, facing a world without her presence was an impossibility. He had the fatalistic sureness in order to protect her the best he could that he would have to remain with her as much as possible here at Bigham House, perhaps the focus of danger to her, in order to discover the terror and wipe it away.

The galling fear that in order to free her from danger, he would have to put her in harm's way tore him apart.

When Tell returned to the main suite Charity could

174

see that he was still distracted. "I thought I was the one holding up going down to dinner, not you."

Tell focused on her, then glanced at his watch, an expletive firing from his mouth. "Sorry, I was thinking about something else."

"Obviously."

Tell took her arm. "What does that mean? By the way, you look wonderful in that shade of aqua and that knit shows your great body to perfection." He kissed her nose. "Take it off and put on a kimono."

Charity relaxed a little. He was more like the Tell she was used to living with as he ran his hands over the silky knit that clung to her body all the way to midcalf. Tell had been such a stranger after they'd talked in the library, but the mood seemed to have left him. "I'm going to tell Kathleen that it was all your fault we're late," Charity told him at the foot of the winding staircase as they paused for a moment in the large foyer. Her heart rolled over and thudded into new rhythm at the lazy heat in his gaze.

"Are you, my darling?" His head lowered, but instead of taking her mouth fully, he pressed tiny kisses around it, finally nipping at the soft skin of her upper lip. "And I'm going to tell her that I couldn't resist my wife with her red hair swept up with turquoise combs, dangling turquoise in her ears and a dress that would tempt a saint to madness . . . and I'm no saint." He nipped at her again.

"You're right about that."

Tell bit gently on her lower lip.

"Cannibal," Charity breathed.

"Oh there you are, Charity. You're always fooling around with your main man," Priscilla said, studying them clinically, grinning when Charity tried to pull free and Tell wouldn't release her. "Kathleen is having a cow in the dining room because the lettuce is going limp, I

175

guess. I don't think she should complain. It's not as though the twin kittens are in her soup again, or anything like that. She freaks at the littlest things." Priscilla shook her head.

Tell laughed when his wife groaned. "Don't worry, darling, we can always throw her out on her ear."

"Yeah, and I could help." Priscilla laughed out loud when Tell offered her his other arm. "Not that she's so bad all the time. She helped Marybeth and me make fudge and it was real good, even though she said we should only have three pieces because it might be too rich for the baby." Priscilla rolled her eyes.

The trio entered the wide doorway leading to the dining room still laughing, though the room looked back at them in silence.

"Gosh, it's nice to hear someone laugh." Marybeth shrugged when Kathleen looked down her nose at her. "I'm not trying to insult you, ma'am, it's just that I've seen bag women of New York get more fun out of life than anyone around here."

"Good Lord," Charity murmured faintly.

Macon's sudden rattle of amusement, quickly masked by a cough was the only sound for the few moments it took for Tell to shepherd both Priscilla and Charity to chairs at the table.

"I think you'd better watch your mouth around my mother."

"And you'd better watch yours around us, Beechy boy." Priscilla defended her friend fiercely.

"Relax, Ambrose, or I might be tempted to escort you from this house permanently. Frankly, I think it's time you were out of here, even if your mother chooses to stay."

"I agree," Charity said quietly. "In either case I don't want you censuring my girls. They are none of your business, Ambrose . . . after all, they were in-

176

vited here by me." Charity stared at her step-grandmother's son. "Though I expect the girls to be well behaved too." Charity's glance slid over her charges.

"Ambrose talks out of turn at times, Charity, but I assure you no one in this house would elect to interfere with the girls." Lyle smiled from Charity to the unwed mothers. "In fact there have been many projects we joined in together. Right?"

The girls nodded and the bad moment passed, though Kathleen's tight features showed that she had been irked by the exchange of words.

Dinner was not the strained time it could have been because between Lyle and Tell they were able to draw out the girls about what they had been doing at Bigham House . . . which to Charity's ears sounded fulfilling.

"You mean besides your school work, you're exercising the horses and helping with the farm?"

"But Rita doesn't do much because she's getting so big, so she drives the jeep that pulls the haywagon. It's fun and even when it's cold, the sun shines most of the time." Priscilla grinned at the most reserved member of the group who smiled back, her voice full of wonder at the sun and fresh air.

Charity stared at Rita too, her experienced eye telling her that the seventeen-year-old was getting near term. Charity decided she would be working out of Bigham House for the next few weeks.

When they'd finished dining they left the oak-paneled room with its priceless antique crystal chandelier and went through the double doors that opened directly into the living room to have their coffee.

Charity ignored Kathleen when the other woman usurped her place by pouring the hot fragrant liquid. "Tell." Charity took hold of her husband's sleeve and urged him toward the grand piano where they were by

177

themselves. "I think I have to remain at Bigham House for the immediate future. Rita looks as though she might go into labor at any time." To Charity's surprise, Tell not only acquiesced, he seemed relieved that she'd made the decision. "It will be harder for you to get into work so if you . . ."

"Living out here at Bigham House will suit me just fine."

Before Charity could ask him what he meant Macon entered the room and approached her. "Telephone, Miss Charity."

"Thank you, Macon." Charity ran a quick eye around the room, noting that most of the coffee drinkers were watching her and had heard what the butler said to her. "I'll take the call in the library."

Tell had a fierce desire to go with her, letting her out of his sight bothered him, but he steeled himself against it, not wanting to smother her. It was a nightmare to Tell that Charity could have an enemy who could get to her on the job and at home.

In the library Charity picked up the phone and identified herself.

"Mrs. Layton, you don't know me. My name's Jeremy Williams and I have had detectives on the trail of my stepdaughter for many, many months. They found her at Promise House and they now inform me that you, her custodian at Promise House, have taken her to your place in the country. Her name is Margarite Collins and you know her as Rita Smith."

Charity sat down in the big leather chair, sighing, her gaze going to the bookshelf containing the Sherlock Holmes collection. "Are you trying to make a point, Mr. Williams?" Charity sparred, trying to get her breath.

"Yes. I love my stepdaughter as much as I loved her

mother and I know what took her from my home and I want her back and I want her to know that she will be safe, and that I have removed the source of fear from our household. May I come and see her, Mrs. Layton? I'm in Bigham Park at this moment and I long to see her."

Charity's first response was an unqualified negative, knowing full well that Rita was frightened of her past, but she bit back the no because of the palpable grief she heard in the man's voice. "Do you realize that you cannot legally remove the girl from my protection if she does not wish to go?"

"Yes," Mr. Williams whispered. "My lawyers have been very clear on that, Mrs. Layton. I know you might find this hard to believe, but it is not I whom my stepdaughter fears . . . and I think once she realizes that I have taken steps to remove her nemesis . . . forever, she will have second thoughts."

"You may come out to Bigham House, Mr. Williams, but in the meantime I will talk to Rita. If she says she doesn't choose to see you, I will have you marched off the premises, I promise you that."

"Agreed."

Charity broke the connection and rang for Macon to bring Rita to the library.

When the young girl appeared in the doorway and traversed the room to take the chair across the desk from her, Charity could see the wariness on her face, the opaque, hidden look to her eyes. "Rita, I hope you know you can count on us at Promise House and that we will stand your friend."

"What's wrong, Charity?" Rita sat on the edge of her chair, her one hand going to her distended middle.

"Nothing, but I've just had a call from a man named Jeremy Williams . . ."

179

"Oh no." Rita went to rise, then fell back into the chair, biting her lip.

Charity was around the desk in an instant, on her knees next to the girl. "Pain?"

"Just a bit."

"Does this man frighten you, Rita, because if he does, the Davises will waltz him off the property and you need never see him. You will be protected by us and there will be no one to bother you."

"I love my stepfather, Charity." Tears flowed from the girl's eyes in the first real emotion she'd shown Charity since her arrival at Promise House many months back. "But I didn't want him to know. He was always wonderful to me."

Charity embraced the girl, shushing her. "He told me he knows all about what happened to you and that he has removed what terrorized you."

"What?" Rita pulled back. "He knows about Aaron? Oh, Charity, Aaron is his nephew and they were close, but . . ."

"He seduced you."

"He raped me, more than once. I tried to fight him . . . he told me that if I ever said anything it would kill Jeremy because he would know the kind of slut I am. I'm not a slut, Charity." The girl leaned on Charity, sobbing.

"You're a wonderful, kind person who has been very, very supportive to the others. Don't you ever think anything else." Charity kissed the girl's hair. "Will you see him?"

"Will you stay with me?"

As Charity nodded they both heard the sound of someone at the front door. Charity shook her head when Rita tried to rise, then turned her swivel chair so that both of them faced the door. Charity squeezed her hand.

It was Tell who opened the door and accompanied the gray-haired man into the room. "I thought you might need me," Tell said cryptically.

Jeremy Williams took little notice of Tell or Charity as he hurried across the room and went to his knees in front of the girl, tears in his eyes. "My child, my dearest child, are you all right? Come home, Margarite, and let me care for you. We'll solve our problems together, as a family, child. You needn't worry that you will ever be bothered by Aaron again. He's gone and won't be back . . . ever."

"I didn't want you to know, Daddy." Rita cried great gulping sobs.

"Shh, mustn't do that. It can't be good for you, and I want to take care of you."

"I think we can leave them alone, don't you, wife?" Tell put his arm around her, urging her toward the door.

Charity nodded, too emotion-filled to speak.

Out in the corridor, she took a hankie from her husband. "And I'll bet Rita's is the best story of all the ones those girls could tell."

Tell nodded, pulling her into his arms. "It's too tough a world for too many young people, darling, I know that, but at least you are making a difference for some of them."

Charity nodded her face pushed into the warmth of his evening suit, the citrony smell of Tell's aftershave like a balm to her spirit. She looked up at him at last. "It's really too bad I can't clone you and pass you out to the women of the world. What a boon that would be." Charity started to smile. "Why, Griffith Tell Layton, you're blushing."

"What did you expect? I haven't learned to expect kudos from you, sweetheart . . . but, of course, I welcome them."

181

"Glad to oblige." Charity coiled her arms around his neck, lifting her face eagerly to his descending mouth.

Tell kissed her gently. "How emotional you are when one of your chicks is finding her way free of life's chains."

Charity closed her eyes, nodding, savoring the warm caresses that he placed all over her face. "In many ways they are so innocent, despite their street smarts, Tell. They need a hand so desperately, but not once in the years I've been doing this has there been one of them without personal courage. I think that says a great deal."

"And there's a little tear in one corner of your eye." Tell let his lips glide over the spot. "I can see that our home will always be spilling over with young people in trouble."

"You have to admit there is a need, and we sure do have the room."

"True."

Charity leaned back from him, her hands cupping his face, her eyes locked with his. "No matter how many twists and turns our lives take, I can't picture me giving up my work completely."

"I don't think you should, love, not when it's so important to you." They paused in front of the wide entryway leading into the living room, Tell faced her, grimacing. "I wish we didn't have to go in there. Why don't we skip upstairs and be alone?" He kissed her ear. "Shall I tell you what I'd like to do?"

Charity felt a quickening of her pulse beat, but shook her head ruefully. "It's probably the same thing I'd like but I have to wait until I see how things go with Rita."

"I need a stiff brandy to face this crew," Tell said, ushering her ahead of him into the room and to a chair near the girls. "Join me."

"Not now. I think I'll have some lemon tea." She

smiled at her husband when he grimaced, feeling the frustration emanating from him. It would be so much better up in their room . . . just the two of them.

"Sit here, Charity." Priscilla bit her lip. "Is Rita in labor? Is that why she left?" Charity saw the palpable angst, and it struck her forcibly, as it had so many times, that these girls, having babies, were not much more than babies themselves, that they were venturing into a frightening unknown.

"Rita's fine. She isn't in labor, but she has been visited by a member of her family."

"What?" Marybeth looked alarmed, straightening from her lounging position too fast and getting a stitch in her side. "But Charity, you shouldn't have left her alone with anyone from her family. She doesn't like them."

"Marybeth's right, Charity." Priscilla looked toward the door to the foyer. "Maybe I should go . . ."

"No, no it's all right. I wouldn't have left her alone with Mr. Williams if I wasn't sure she was safe and comfortable."

Charity was questioned over and over by the girls and it cheered her that they were so loyal and protective of one another.

Every once in a while she would look over to the small bar in the corner where her husband was carrying on a desultory conversation with Lyle Clausen. Each time he saluted her with his brandy snifter, the liquid sloshing against the sides of the glass.

Kathleen wandered over, her manner diffident and a little unsure.

"I'll get you a chair, Mrs. Beech."

"No, Marybeth, I have a side chair right here and I don't want you girls moving furniture, ever. I think I've said that before, have I not?"

"Yes, ma'am," the girls chorused, laughing.

To Charity's surprise, her stepgrandmother's cheeks turned pink and she laughed with the girls. Some things had changed at Bigham House!

In a few minutes, the girls, who were often restless, rose as a group and went to the piano. Though Priscilla didn't play as well as Rita she could knock out a tune that the others would sing to, and they did it often, especially after dinner.

The lack of something to say between the two left sitting was awkward for a moment.

"Ah, Charity, I have been trying for some time to say something to you . . . and I find it hard, to say the least."

Bracing herself, Charity nodded, not able to find the words to tell the older woman that she had had just about enough of Beech sayings.

"Charity, I have regretted very much what I said at the gala about you taking the money. I was wrong to do that because I know that you have always been an honest girl." Kathleen stared at a point over Charity's shoulder. "I suppose I always resented you because Cyrus loved you so much."

Charity was so taken aback she could only stare.

"Yes, I see that I've startled you, but he did love you so much, everyone knew that." The color in Kathleen's face turned a mottled red. "I am not a monster, Charity, however much you may think that is true."

"Kathleen, I don't think that, but I have never been comfortable with the Beeches because I always felt so disliked by you." Charity took a deep breath and plunged ahead. "I always resented that you kept me from my grandfather when he was so ill."

It was Kathleen's turn to look surprised. "But I didn't do that. Cyrus refused to allow you at the house and he gave me firm orders that you were to be kept off the grounds. Not even Jacob could convince him to change his mind."

Stunned, Charity just blinked, shaking her head in disbelief. "But Grandfather loved me. Why would he do such a thing?"

"No one, least of all me, could doubt that, Charity. You were the one who made him the happiest." Kathleen smiled, a lacing of bitterness on those lips. "Maybe it was knowing that that convinced me you weren't good for the family."

"Why, Kathleen? Why wouldn't he want me with him when he knew he was dying?"

Kathleen saw the sheen of tears in Charity's eyes and leaned forward and put her hand on her knee. "Don't look like that. I really don't know why, but it wasn't because he didn't love you, Charity."

Charity shook her head. "This isn't getting us anywhere, so why don't we talk of something else? It's too painful to dwell on." Charity swallowed. "Will Lyle and Ambrose be moving with you when you go to Florida, Kathleen?"

Kathleen's lips tightened. "That is all up in the air now, due in great part to the . . . coming nuptials."

Charity nodded, her glance sliding away from the other woman's.

"I know you heartily approve of this venture and of Jennifer's young man, but I must tell you that I have misgivings."

"Kathleen, you can't have missed how much they love each other."

"He does seem devoted," Kathleen said grudgingly, unbending just a hair.

Charity leaned forward in her chair, her tea forgotten on the table beside her. "Jennifer will want for nothing in her life and she will have all his love. I've known Lionel a long time and have met some of his girlfriends, but there has been no one who has captured his devotion as Jen has."

Kathleen nodded once, looking a bit mollified.

The two women talked of other things but there were long moments of silence too. More than once the girls sang some sweet songs but one or two bawdy songs had Charity cringing.

When Rita appeared in the doorway, the girls ran toward her, their suspicious glances touching on the man who had his arm around her.

"This is my stepfather. Daddy, these are my friends who have been so close to me all this time."

Charity watched with no small sense of pride when Rita took her stepfather to each person and introduced him, finishing up in front of her. "It looks as though a few things have been resolved."

"Yes, Charity. Daddy is going to move to a place close to Bigham House so that we can see each other every day until the baby is born."

"Then we'll take it from there." Jeremy Williams kissed his stepdaughter on the hair. "I'm just staying in Bigham Park, so I'll be back tomorrow."

Charity shook hands with him and nodded. "You're welcome here, sir, at any time of the day, though the girls have lessons in the morning."

"I'll be here at noon."

After Rita and her stepfather went to the door to say good night, some of the girls yawned and made their way to the elevator that would take them to the third floor. Others drifted to their rooms in small groups.

Finally Tell came over to Charity and held out his arms. "Bedtime, darling."

Charity said good night to the few left in the room, including Ambrose and Lyle, and preceded him out to the hall. When she felt his hand feather her backside as they were climbing the stairs, she looked back, startled.

When she saw the lopsided grin, the glassy cast to his eyes, she chuckled. "Tell Layton, you are drunk. How many brandies did you have?"

"How could you blame a man? I wanted to be alone with my wife, instead I exchanged useless prattle with a man I do not hold in high esteem."

Charity didn't fail to notice his practiced wording, how punctilious he was with each syllable he uttered. "You are really shot down, aren't you?"

Tell encircled his wife's waist, staggering a bit. "You malign me, wife."

"I've never seen you this way. It must have hit you wrong or something. Grandfather said you had a hard head for drinking."

"I used to." Tell paused on one of the steps looking puzzled, then he shrugged.

When they reached the second floor, Charity steered him to their suite of rooms and closed the door behind them. Before she could flick the light switch on, she was swept into a hard embrace.

"Damn them all. They were chattering like blackbirds and I couldn't think of anything but getting my wife into bed."

Charity laughed. "Let me turn on the lights or we'll bump into something."

"Don't be silly. I have the eyes of a bat." Tell fell against something, cursing roundly. He almost regained his balance but the brandy made the difference and down he went, with Charity on top of him. "What the bloody hell . . ."

"Shh. You'll have the whole house on us." Charity couldn't smother her amusement. She had never seen Tell rocky, let alone off balance and it tickled her as nothing else could have. "Someday I'll be telling our children about the night their father had a bout with brandy and lost."

"Very unkind of you. No, don't move, I like you lying on top of me."

"Tell, you fool, let me go, so that I can turn on a light."

"I'll never let you go, Charity. You're mine."

Charity chuckled, relaxing. She knew that the brandies were working through him and dictating a great deal of his speech. "All right, we'll make love right here." What did it matter? They had often loved each other any place they happened to be in the apartment. Why not here, at Bigham House?

"That's what I said." Tell's voice had a slurred huskiness to it.

The triumph in his voice made Charity laugh. She caught the sweet, not unpleasant aroma of brandy on his breath when he leaned closer, nibbling at her ear.

"Don't think I don't know you're laughing at me, wife."

Charity let the amusement break from her. "I can't help it. You've never been like a little boy before . . . I think you're cute."

"You do." Again there was a pleased note in his voice. "Good. I want you to think I'm cute . . . as a . . . as a cuff link."

"Button."

"That's what I said." His lips slid to her chest. "Even through your clothing you have the most beautiful breasts, pet. I love them. I want to kiss them forever," he told her solemnly.

"Tell," Charity said breathily, half laughing.

"But there's a lot you don't know about me, Charity." Tell gave an exaggerated sigh, his hands lifting her dress from her, then tossing it aside. "Do you remember that day when I was swimming naked in the lake and you joined me?"

188

"How could I forget? You chewed my ear off and threatened me if I ever did it again."

"I know, but you see, I was ashamed of loving you, even then. I wanted you and you were a baby and I hated myself. It was awful." He buried his face in her neck, his tongue making lazy forays over her skin. "There were so many beautiful women and I wanted some of them pretty badly, but always you were there, in the back corner of my mind. It was damnable waiting for you and I would have killed anyone who tried to take you from me . . . or who stood in the way of our getting married."

Shock rendered Charity weak for a moment, then her arms that had fallen away from him lifted to him tentatively. "No one wanted to part us, Tell."

"No?"

When his head came up she saw the demonic golden glitter of his eyes. "But we're married, aren't we?"

"Now we are, but there were those that didn't want it. Your grandfather knew that I wanted you. As much as he trusted me fiscally, he told me flat out to steer clear of you. I hated that. Lyle Clausen reminded me of that tonight. Even he used to tell me that I was obsessed with you, to back off. Kathleen told me I was a fool more than once and often I agreed with her."

Charity's total surprise had a lacing of trepidation to it. There were depths to her husband that she hadn't suspected. Never in this world would she have surmised that her grandfather would think that Tell wasn't right for her, or for any woman. It had been Charity's understanding that her grandfather thought Tell perfect, her grandfather had trusted Tell fully . . . or at least that was the way it seemed. Her mind tumbled with the ramifications of what she'd just heard, until Tell's hands became urgent on her again. "Tell, what are you doing?"

"Removing your clothes, darling. Shh, I don't want you to say any more. I just want to love you."

"But, Tell . . ."

"Kiss me, wife."

Charity heard the slight thickness in his voice but his hands and mouth on her were very sure. To hell with it! Why bother to tell him that she hadn't taken birth control pills in a while because she'd been feeling headachy? She was going to get a new prescription from the doctor tomorrow anyway. The other anxieties that had surfaced at his words she managed to bury just as effectively.

Reaching up she took his face between her hands, letting her mouth run over those tough features, the velvet abrasion an erotic spur to her own libido, even as she heard his breathing become labored.

Pushing at his shoulders she was able to convince him without words to lie on his side so that she could continue the love quest she had begun, Charity felt a rush of love through her being. He was a very special man . . . even if there were facets about him unknown and alien to her. Tell was so very beautiful, and as she moved her lips down his strong throat, her hands feathering over his taut body, she was most aware of how wonderfully nature had packaged him.

When she pressed her mouth to those firm chest nipples, it delighted her when he groaned loudly and his hands clutched her convulsively. All her emotion was in her heart when she made the silent covenant to love him, to take him as he had so often taken her . . . in sweet ferocity. If all was not perfect with them on every level, there could be no fault found in their passion.

"No, no, Charity . . ."

Charity lifted her head from his body. "I'm only loving you as you have loved me, husband. Shh, no more talking." Her tone was husky because she was also in

190

the grip of the great passion that had been between them since the first moment they had made love. In great tenderness and awe she loved him, feeling his body jerk and tremble under her in response.

"No more," Tell gasped, lifting her up his body and turning her on her back, entering her quickly but with a love and sweetness that had her moaning and grasping at him.

Holding each other against the world they crested the mountain where only lovers go, exploding in their own love with all the fiery serenity in them.

Bodies still tremoring they embraced one another for a long moment.

"Let's go to bed, wife. I'm either very drunk or we did soar out of this house, around the grounds and back again. What do you think?"

"I think you're right."

Fumbling to reach their clothing and rise from the floor together, laughing and giggling like children, they found the light, then stared into each other's eyes.

"You are an incredible lover, Charity Bigham Layton."

"Thank you. You're not half bad either."

"Half bad, she says. We'll see about that."

That night they made love again . . . and again, and if there was something in the back of Charity's mind that nagged at her much like the time she wasn't sure about what was out of whack in the library, she was able to bury the prickling annoyance in the welling emotion that she and her husband engendered, then surrendered to over and over again.

The next day Charity awakened first. Being very quiet so as not to waken her husband, she crept into the bathroom, showered and washed her hair. She had decided not to go into Manhattan that morning. If she could arrange it she was going to take Rita and her stepfather to Olivet Hospital to confer with Rita's obstetrician. Dr. Converse was a wise person and Charity wanted her opinion on the new happening in Rita's life; at the same time she would ask her about a prescription for birth control pills for herself. Since she had married she had begun seeing Dr. Converse herself.

Charity frowned as she let the water sluice her body. Rita had had more visits than the other girls and though the obstetrician had been noncommittal, Charity had had the feeling that all had not been perfect in the last few examinations.

"Hi."

Charity felt the movement of air even as Tell opened the cubicle and stared at her. "Hi, yourself. How do you feel?" Charity bit her lip to keep back a smile at how he was frowning, the palm of one hand pressed to his forehead.

"Wonderful," Tell said tightly, stepping under the shower and closing the door behind him so that the two of them were crowded into the enclosure. "You're laughing at me."

"Because you're hung over."

"Dammit, I haven't had a hangover since college." His eyes slid away from hers, though he didn't stop soaping her body. "I have the vague memory that I talked too much last night."

"Oh, we did more than talk."

"Don't be evasive, Charity. You know what I mean. Did I say all those things to you last night or was it a nightmare?"

"Maybe both."

"The soul of discretion, that's you."

"Now, you're being sardonic again."

"And was I before?"

"Often, but especially when you feel a bit off center." Charity nodded. "I love this shower, but I do have to go. I'm going to stay here today and try to make an appointment to see Dr. Converse."

"The obstetrician at Olivet? Is it for the girls? Are you feeling all right?"

It always amazed Charity how he was able to store whatever information was given him, no matter how minute, and call it up from that computer brain whenever he chose. "Yes to all three questions. I want Rita and her stepfather to confer with her since she'll be coming to term soon."

Tell frowned. "Unless you object I'm going to run a check on Jeremy Williams."

"I was going to ask you to do that. Rita loves him and that means a lot but I would like to double-check that she is going back to a safe environment. I don't want anything else detouring that girl's chance at a productive, happy life."

"You're a good mama." Tell kissed her on the nose, then opened the door so that she could leave the cubicle, his one hand patting her gently on the backside.

Charity noticed how, though he smiled at her, he wouldn't meet her gaze.

Tell cursed fluently all the while he showered. If his memory was only nominally accurate, he had shown a side of himself to Charity that he would never have wanted her to see. He had never been a heavy drinker by choice but he had also had a high tolerance for alcohol, not being affected by it too much. What the hell had happened last night? His stomach felt queasy and that was a new sensation and his head pounded like a jungle drum out of control. If he didn't know that Cyrus kept the best Napoleon brandy in the world, he would have questioned whether it had been tainted.

Worse was that he said things to Charity that he had wanted hidden from her.

193

"Damned soppy fool, telling her that you'd loved her since she'd been a baby almost. She'll be damned disgusted with you if she ever dwells on that." Tell slapped the palm of his hand against the tile wall hard enough to send pain shooting to his shoulder before he turned off the water and stepped from the cubicle.

He had made a fool of himself and he didn't like the feeling.

All the while he dressed he tried to piece together last evening and most of what he recalled had him grinding his teeth together in frustration.

Why the hell did he let Lyle Clausen fill his damned glass so much? Tell blinked at the sudden pain behind his eyes. Clausen had asked a great many questions, but he couldn't seem to recall any at the moment.

Pulling on a pair of sweat pants, he went to the phone in the bedroom and dialed his office. "David? Yes, it's Tell, cancel my meetings today, will you, and get a messenger to send me the file on the merger. I'm going to work out here today. What? Damn, I forgot about the conference. Yes, I know I should be there." Tell knew his tones were cutting and angry but he couldn't stem his frustration. He had wanted to stay at Bigham House whenever Charity was going to be in residence and now a damned conference . . . and his voting presence was crucial, in order to kick a little verbal ass. "All right, all right, I'll be there." Tell slammed down the phone, then winced as the sound seemed to rattle through his head. "What the hell was in that brandy anyway?"

Charity felt buoyed in her estimation of Mr. Williams when he arrived at the house as she and Rita were getting ready to leave. Charity saw the tight look Rita's stepfather gave her car and had to mask a smile. "She's safe with me, Mr. Williams."

Jeremy Williams shut the rusted door, flinching at the

squeaking, scraping sound. Then he looked over the top of the car, his voice lowered. "But she looks so pale to me. Rita always had good color."

Charity tried to smile as the man voiced her own concerns. "The doctor has not said anything was wrong, Mr. Williams. Why don't you follow us and perhaps we can both question Dr. Converse more closely? I think your concern is very normal."

"Thank you." Mr. Williams leaned down and blew a kiss to Rita and then went back to the car he'd driven to Bigham House.

During the few miles to Bigham Park and Olivet Memorial, which was situated some distance from the town proper, Charity was given new insight into Rita. It was as though a damn had burst in the girl and she couldn't contain the rush of words as she struggled to tell Charity all about her childhood, about her stepfather, who had been the only father she had ever known, having married her mother when she'd been two years old, and how happy the three of them had been until her mother died when she was fourteen and her stepfather's nephew had begun coming around the house all the time.

"At first I wasn't afraid of him. He was always kissing and hugging me, but Daddy did that too and so it didn't seem . . . strange."

"Of course, it wouldn't." Charity reached over and patted the girl's arm.

"But then he tried things that I knew were wrong, so I hit him and told him to leave me alone . . ."

"All right, Rita, you're fine now." Charity tried to soothe the girl as the whole sordid tale of intimidation and rape rolled from her lips. "I don't think your stepfather will ever allow that person or anyone like him near you again."

"Daddy said he would hang Aaron or anyone like him by his heels if he approached me." Rita laughed through

195

her tears. "He was grinding his teeth so much when he told me." Rita's laugh was cut off in the middle. "Oooh."

"Pain?" Instinctively Charity increased her speed, noting that Mr. Williams was right at her heels.

"Yes. Oooh, Charity, it hurts so much . . . and it doesn't stop the way it's supposed to do." Rita breathed through her mouth as she had been trained to do.

Charity glanced at the girl, seeing the panic building there. When she passed a state police car going the other way she laid on the horn getting the officer's attention, then gestured with her hand that she required aid.

In minutes the official car was at her side and Charity mouthed the word "hospital." The trooper nodded, spoke into his radio, then turned on his strobe, pulling in front of her in one smooth move.

"Charity, help me."

"Hang on, honey, hang on, just a mile or so to go. Breathe, breathe, thatta girl." Charity tried to keep calm but when her quick glance showed a gray-faced girl next to her, bitter gall rose in her throat. Rita needed help right away.

Charity bent over the wheel, following the policeman and not taking her eyes from him.

As she pulled into the emergency entrance at Olivet, attendants, whom Charity assumed were alerted by the trooper, were already there with a gurney, getting Rita out and moving her through the double doors into the hospital.

Mr. Williams came up to Charity, his face creased in concern. "My daughter, Mrs. Layton, what is it? How is she?"

"Come on, Mr. Williams, we'll find out together. Dr. Converse's office is in this building so they'll be able to have her here in minutes if she isn't already here."

Charity and Williams followed the gurney right into the treatment section, but they were only allowed to look through the window as the attendants worked over the girl. They saw Dr. Converse, masked and gowned, enter the area, work with the personnel, then step back while the gurney was moved again.

When the doctor came out to speak with them she was grim-faced and terse. "We're going after the baby now. I can't get a heartbeat."

"Save my daughter, Doctor."

Dr. Converse opened her mouth to say something but she only stared at the tear-stained face of the man who faced her in mute misery and entreaty and nodded.

While they waited, Charity went to the phone and dialed into New York and Promise House. "No, Father, I don't know all the details, but the birth has gone sour somehow. I'm sure that Rita will be all right or the doctor would have said so, but I'm waiting here with her father until we know more. Yes, I know I have a great deal to tell you. Of course, I'll keep you informed. Would you call Bigham House and tell them? Thank you, Father."

Minutes turned into hours before the doctor rejoined them, looking tired and drawn. "I'm sorry, Charity, sir, but we couldn't save the child, a genetic flaw in the heart we think but we'll know more later. Rita is weak but fine. I expect with rest and care she will be herself in no time."

"Thank you, thank you." Mr. Williams wrung the doctor's hand. "May I see my little girl?"

The doctor gestured to an attendant who shot one look at Mr. Williams and took his arm, leading him along the hall, speaking soothingly to him.

"He loves her very much, I think, Charity."

Charity nodded. "He's a good man. I'll tell you the story some time. Was it a little boy or girl?"

197

"The baby was a boy, beautiful, unmarked . . . but not strong enough for this world." The doctor rubbed her face. "I hate that."

Charity nodded and the two women walked toward the doctor's office. "I'll see Rita later; I think she and her father need to be alone now." Charity glanced at the doctor. "I was going to ask you about the new prescription for birth control pills you were going to get for me."

Dr. Converse stopped at an unmarked door in the corridor and unlocked it. It led into her private office. "Sit down, Charity, I wanted to speak to you about that. I have studied your records and the medication that you've taken and I would rather, unless it's an emergency, not put you on these new pills for a week or so. I want to see if there is any change in the headaches first. Suit you?"

Charity shrugged. "Well, I might get pregnant . . . maybe even have, if that's possible, unless you're saying that I could have some residual protection from the last ones I took."

Dr. Converse shook her head. "I don't think so, but you never know. Would a baby be a bad thing in your life at the moment?"

"Not in mine, but my husband didn't want children for a while."

"Well, I still would like you to hold off on using anything just so I can get a better picture."

Charity rose to her feet, nodding. "The gamble could be fun."

Dr. Converse laughed and stretched. "See Rita if you like, Charity, but don't encourage the girls to come here right away. It could be . . ." The doctor shrugged.

"I know, I'll tell them she needs to rest, which is true."

* * *

When Charity was on her way back to Bigham House, her mind wandered a bit as she went past the many familiar places of her young years. It was when she came to the old dirt road that led into the back of Bigham House property that the impulse came on her to venture back in time to her girlhood.

The old car squeaked and protested at the potholes and ruts along the way, but Charity felt such a surge of déjà vu that she wouldn't have gone back even if she'd known she'd get a blowout. Coming to the old gate that was rarely used that blocked off the road that led down past the boathouse, then up again to meander through the woods, to finish at the side of the big ten-car garage at the back of Bigham House, Charity was cheered at the fine condition of the macadam on the other side of the gate.

It was when she tried to open the gate that she had trouble. Oh, the lock seemed to be oiled and in excellent order but the old key she had on her chain was not as in good shape and she had a difficult time turning it. Finally, with a rasping screech it turned the lock and she was able to swing back the metal barrier that led to Bigham House property.

After she drove through she went back and closed it and it was then that she saw the marks on the lock as though someone had tried to force it with a sharp instrument that had scratched the surface. At the same time she noted the many hoofprints around the area as though several horsemen had been in the area or one horseman several times. Charity stared at the prints for several minutes then shrugged and went back to her car. Why would someone be trying to get out of Bigham House property? It made more sense if someone were trying to get inside.

Charity drove along the macadam road, feeling a

199

sense of pride that the property was hers. At the crest of the hill where she could look down on the lake and the boathouse, she stopped the car to gaze at the beautiful autumnal scene of the sun dappling through the russet, red, and gold trees and casting the hues on the water.

When the man in the black jogging suit came out of the boathouse, looked up the hill at her as though startled, then disappeared at once around the boathouse, she didn't react at once. Then the memory of the man running away in Manhattan assailed her and fearful recollection filled her.

Charity turned on the ignition and drove away, her speed beyond what was safe on the twisting road leading to the big house but she had to get away from the man in the black jogging suit.

He was danger! And he had come to Bigham House to threaten her just as he had done in Manhattan.

200

CHAPTER SEVEN

Lionel's and Jennifer's wedding day dawned bright, clear, and cold. There were still a few golden and russet leaves clinging to the trees but the cold wind that blew down from the Adirondack Mountains telegraphed that winter was coming.

"Jennifer, stop fidgeting." Charity laughed at the other woman as she tried to arrange the cobwebby silk train that fell in soft folds behind the bride as an exquisite accompaniment to the candlelight satin gown.

"I can't believe I'll be Lionel's wife in less than an hour," Jennifer breathed, clasping her hands together, her eyes alight.

"Believe it, believe it." Charity grinned at the ecstatic girl. "I understand from Gareth that Lionel is a basket case."

"Charity, how can you laugh about that!"

It had been decided that the bride should dress in Charity and Tell's suite since the second floor cluster of rooms was by far the biggest area for dressing and could easily accommodate the bride and her attendants.

"Don't the girls look beautiful."

"Jennifer, if you dare to cry again and spoil your makeup, I'll go downstairs this minute and cancel everything," Kathleen told her daughter spiritedly, even though her eyes were suspiciously moist. "You do look beautiful, my child, and so do the girls."

"Thank you, Mother . . . and thank you for being such a help with them, ordering their dresses and getting them fitted, and helping with their hair and all that."

Kathleen looked through the door to the sitting room of the suite where the girls were giggling and admiring themselves. "That group will have to rank with the strangest gathering of bridesmaids in the world. All but Rita and Charity are expecting." Kathleen's lips quivered. "Rona Klem's mouth will fall to the floor."

Charity had an almost overpowering urge to mention that she was two weeks late but she said nothing.

"Why, Mother, I think you'll enjoy shocking your friends." Jennifer laughed joyously.

"I think I will too." Kathleen chuckled.

Charity thought she had never seen mother and daughter so in tune with one another and it had surprised her when Kathleen had done an aboutface and invited her friends to her daughter's nuptials and had insisted on taking the girls for their attendant's dresses, since Jennifer would not be talked out of having the girls in her wedding.

With a last twitch of the skirt, Charity left mother and daughter alone for a few minutes and went to the sitting room off the bedroom to confer with the girls.

"Oh, Charity, you look smashing . . . but so do I." Marybeth beamed at her. "Kathleen says that we can have these dresses made to fit us . . . afterward."

"Of course you can and you do look wonderful." Charity looked at each girl in turn, thinking that the silky gowns did much to disguise their round shapes and that Kathleen had gone to great pains to choose colors that suited the girls. "Oops, be careful, Liz, you almost sat on your flowers. Are you ready?" Charity smiled at

Rita, noting that though the girl was still too thin and pale, she was better each day and would soon be leaving the protective arms of Promise House. Though she had suffered the trauma of losing her child, with the help of her stepfather who had been at her side and had taken her to a home he had rented nearby when she'd come from the hospital, Rita was making good progress.

Things had turned around in so many ways for Rita and her stepfather, so much so that Mr. Williams had decided to move the central office of his business from Buffalo to Albany.

"I can't thank you enough, Mrs. Layton," Jeremy Williams had told Charity a day before the wedding when he had brought Rita to Bigham House so that she could take part in the wedding. "It's my daughter's and my wish to help the girls at Promise House and we intend to take an active part in doing so." He had smiled at Charity. "Rita has applied to Russell Sage College and I have found a home in the Albany suburbs. The future looks bright for us, thanks to you and Father Desmond."

Now, as Charity recalled that conversation and studied her girls she felt more cheered about their future than she had in a long time.

Tell was using the smaller bedroom of the second-floor suite, his eyes thoughtful as he studied his own reflection in the mirror while arranging the neckcloth that went with the morning suit that all the men would be wearing.

He had a doomsday feeling that he couldn't shake as though he had come to a crossroads and hadn't recognized it and gone past into quicksand.

It made his neck prickle with wariness when he dwelt on how pensive his wife had been for the last few days. Oh, she had been responsive enough when they'd talked and made love, but there had been other times when she might as well been on another planet. Just thinking of their time together in bed made his blood percolate. But there had been other odd moments when he'd caught her frowning out a window, or sitting with her chin in her hand staring at the bookshelves in the library, almost always at the Sherlock Holmes collection. Somehow, some way, knowledge was getting past him and into her and no matter how many questions he asked her nothing seemed to shed light on how she was learning things and what they were.

Poring over the files that he'd taken from Jacob Henry's office had elicted no information . . . another blind alley. Frustration was building in him because he had a gut feeling that whoever was stalking Charity meant to do her harm, that whatever was holding him back would no longer do so, and at that moment his beloved wife would be in maximum jeopardy.

There was no doubt in his mind that something else had occurred that had affected Charity. He could read her so well . . . but he knew if he pushed her she was just as likely to retreat into a shell as confide in him. It was a galling frustration that his wife felt she was protecting him by not sharing some of the happenings in her life. Of course, he had been able to glean knowledge by the way she clammed up when he talked about various subjects, more or less backing into discovering facts. It was this method that showed him that whatever new happening there had been, it had been very recent and had happened in the area of Bigham House.

When the door opened behind him and he saw the object of his thoughts appear in the doorway, he stared. How lovely she was with the gold silk swathed around her body, making her eyes glitter with the same lustrous hue, her hair gleam with reddish highlights, catching the sunlight that beamed in one window. He turned to face her. "You're too beautiful." He smiled when he saw the run of blood up her face. She never seemed to get used to his compliments. "I don't think matrons of honor are supposed to outshine the bride."

Charity laughed. "I don't, and when you see Jennifer you'll agree."

"No, I won't. There is no one lovelier than you anywhere."

"Tell." Charity laughed, her heart fluttering her chest like a trapped bird at the twist of smile that went over her from head to foot. "It's time for you to take your place with Gareth supporting Lionel."

"Is Ambrose with the bride?"

"Yes, but he hasn't smiled much, even though Kathleen told him to lighten up."

"She didn't say it like that."

"Yes, she did. Jen and I nearly collapsed, but the girls didn't turn a hair. It seems that Kathleen works with them quite a bit and has picked up some of their vernacular."

Tell laughed out loud, the sound running through his wife like warm wine. "Let's go, darling."

The wedding ceremony was a beautiful simple service held in the solarium where there was ample room for the guests to sit.

Father Desmond instructed the couple to cling to each other, forsaking all others.

Charity's glance was pulled to her husband who was watching her, his sardonic smile softened. When he blew her a kiss, her heart turned over in her chest and her breathing became constricted.

After the wedding the guests were shepherded out to the hall and down to the sitting room and dining room that opened onto each other. There Lionel and his new wife greeted their guests for the first time as man and wife standing in front of the ornate marble fireplace while the caterers hired for the occasion arranged the solarium for the sit-down dinner.

Gareth came up next to Tell, who was watching the guests through narrowed eyes. "Have you any news on the person who might have used my boat?"

Tell shook his head, taking his eyes off the throng long enough to scrutinize the other man. "Shouldn't you be in the receiving line?"

Gareth shrugged. "I was getting jumpy. Since that incident with the boat I can't relax at this house anymore. I used to think that Bigham House was one of the safest, most insular places on earth. I don't feel that way anymore." Gareth followed Tell's gaze as it circled the room. "You certainly don't think the culprit is among the guests, do you?"

"I don't know, but I'm not leaving anything to chance. By the way, did you have any luck with the files you took home from the office?"

"I went through them once with no luck, now I'm going through them in a more thorough way, but I'm not encouraged."

"I didn't have any luck either, but I'm not giving up. Somewhere in Cyrus's papers there must be something that would clue us in on the person we need. I feel damned sure that Cyrus knew who would have threatened his daughter. He was a damned canny man." Tell glanced around the room again. "Ah, there's Jacob. Maybe he had better luck with the files than we had."

"Good day, gentlemen. Lovely wedding, isn't it?" Jacob looked from one to the other. "I see you're impatient. Well, I don't think I had any luck, but I do have a few things that I want to show you. Cyrus was such an enigmatic man. He would sometimes hide things behind other things and on and on, so that more than once when searching for something I have to go through reams of so-called unrelated material to find what was needed."

"You're pretty mysterious yourself, Jacob," Tell said abruptly.

"Patience, my boy, patience. All will be explained to you. I thought we'd wait until the guests went in to dinner and then we might gather in the library and talk about this."

Gareth pressed Tell's shoulder with a strong hand. "Jacob's right, Tell. Take it easy. It's better we don't give away what we're doing by hightailing it out of here now."

Tell nodded curtly, his eyes returning to his wife, who was greeting a guest and smiling.

All at once the beautifully decorated room had a nether-world chill to it that made his blood run cold.

When the receiving line was finished, Jennifer assembled the girls in a prearranged plan that she and Charity formulated so that when she threw her bouquet, Priscilla caught it, rendering the girls ecstatic.

After the bride and groom began the dancing, Tell went right to Charity's side, seeing Gareth there before him, smiling down at Charity. "Forget it, Beech. Husbands have priority."

"Jealous bastard," Gareth said mildly, his eyes running over the guests and quickly homing in on a vivacious blonde.

"Wait just a moment, the two of you." Charity took an arm of each, then winked at Jennifer who was at that moment urging her brand-new husband toward them. "Jen and I decided that you three and anyone else we could rustle up would lead out the dancing with the girls."

"Only if you guarantee that nothing will happen, like having a baby at my feet, for instance." Gareth looked around him uneasily.

"Don't be silly. Oh, there's Jacob, Tell. Collar him."

"Collar Jacob Henry? Darling, that would be like lassoing the Chief Justice of the United States. Not done."

"You know what I mean, oh, and get Mr. Williams too." Charity laughed at her husband when his well-chiseled face twitched once in annoyance. "Come on, lover, do your thing. We have all night to dance together."

"All right, pet, but I'll talk to you later."

"I'm counting on it."

"Sexy little devil," Tell whispered in her ear, giving her a quick kiss, then moving away from her.

One by one the girls were solicited for the dance, their beaming faces telling of their pleasure.

Jennifer and Charity chuckled when the men led the girls out to the floor to the tune of a rather sedate ballad.

"I think the girls like it even though I'm sure they consider the music written by dinosaurs." Jennifer laughed again.

"If it were any faster your brother and my husband would be white as ghosts."

"Even Lionel who is most relaxed with them would be a little shaky if anything happened."

"You have never looked more beautiful, Jen."

"I feel it, too."

Other guests drifted toward them to make comments to Jen and Charity moved away from them, wandering toward the french doors, looking out into the crisp, darkening November afternoon.

The light from the library could be seen dancing on the terrace that skirted most of the lower part of the house. Lights? From the library? No one should be in there. A quivering awareness ran over her skin as she remembered when she had been struck on the head after the gala.

Shaking herself from her dark thoughts she stared at the right angle jut of the library that she could see clearly though autumn darkness would soon be on them. At first she thought the flickering light was her imagination, but then when she fixed her gaze on it she saw that she was not mistaken. It looked as though someone were in the library with a flashlight or some sort of torch. Turning away from the window, Charity saw that the girls were still dancing with the men, that her husband was not available to her at the moment.

Moving quickly around the perimeter of the room, Charity barely glanced at the dancers but she was aware that the laughing girls were receiving a good deal of atttention from the other guests. Walking more rapidly now, she went through the dining room smiling distractedly to anyone who spoke to her, but not pausing until she reached the hallway leading to the library.

Stopping in front of the tall ornate oak door that led to her grandfather's sanctum sanctorum, she studied the woodworking while taking in great gulps of air, the memory of what had happened to her after the gala coming back to her mind, in clear black pictures. It took all her courage to contain her fear, to banish it to the back of her mind.

Reaching for the keys that were always in her possession, she inserted the library one and turned it, the well-oiled works making no telltale squeak or protest. Pushing open the door with great caution she tried to look around her before stepping inside, then her eyes settled on the desk lamp and the tree branches that slapped at the windows. Laughing with relief she moved fully into the room. "Fool. You're the one who left the light on, it cast shadows through the tree branches making it look as though the light was moving." Charity spoke out loud, castigating herself. Feeling silly at being so spooked, Charity moved toward the desk, the pinch of

209

the new peau de soie slippers she wore aiming her toward the large overstuffed leather chair. She would take advantage of the solitary state to relax a little.

Slipping off the shoes she put her feet on the desk and sighed. It had been a wonderful day . . . but a tiring one. She bent her leg toward her to rub her instep and at the same time gaze about her. This room was the most important in the house for her. She and her grandfather had shared so much in here.

Getting to her feet, sans shoes, she wandered over to the bookshelves, staring up at old, familiar friends. She pressed the button, bringing the sliding ladder along on its track so that she could climb up and look at the leather-bound collection behind the glass.

On impulse, she retreated down the ladder and returned to the desk, unlocking the drawer with a key from her key ring and removing the smaller key for the glass case from the center drawer. Retracing her steps back up the ladder she opened the sliding glass doors and reached up and straightened the books so that *The Man with the Twisted Lip* no longer leaned but stood straight like its companions.

Charity was about to pull back and relock the glass front of the collection when a bizarre cool wind seemed to swirl around her, making her pause in the act of closing the cabinet. She found herself taking out the volume, closing the door and climbing back down the ladder. She winced at the slight soreness on the bottom of her feet from the ladder rungs, and wriggled her toes on the thick Aubusson carpet.

Sighing with delight when she sank back in the comfortable chair, she elevated her feet once more.

Flipping open the very slender volume she perused it carefully, as she had been taught to do, keeping in mind the age and delicacy of the binding.

It was when she had gone through the book twice

that she had another strange sensation, a tingling on her skin. In slow motion she turned the pages again. Yes, the fifth page into the story was different than the others, it seemed thicker somehow. When Charity ran her hands over the surface it had a weird consistency as though two of the pages were stuck together. But that couldn't be since the numbering was correct and there was no skipping of pages or anything missing. Still there was a sponginess to it that the other pages didn't seem to have.

Leaning forward she took the miniature gold saber that her grandfather used as a letter opener and touched the edge of the page, being very careful not to tear or puncture the fine parchment. When an opening appeared, Charity caught her breath and just stared.

Beginning again and in easy stages she ran the opener up the sharp edge and as though by magic the page separated like an envelope opening. Inside was a very thin piece of white fabric like paper, soft, malleable, but not crinkly or crackly.

Pulling out the small folded sheet, Charity opened it and recognized her grandfather's writing at once.

My Darling Charity,
    When you read this, if you ever do, I will be gone. My child, I have been murdered.

"No! That's impossible!" The sound of her own voice reverberated around the room like an echoing rejection. The words danced in front of her eyes. Grandfather! Murdered? How could that be?

    You mustn't try to do anything about it. I fear that the monster has us all in his power . . . because you see I'm not sure who it is. I have tried so

211

very hard to discover the identity, but he or she seems to be one step ahead of me all the time.

Dearest Charity, I told you more than once that I grieved for your mother because she died so young. What you didn't know was that I had always thought her death suspicious, even though that seemed silly since everyone loved your mother. But it nagged at me so much that I had an investigation instituted only hours after I lost her and I insisted that experts from private medical teams examine the remains.

I used every bit of prestige and money I had to get an answer to my questions about Julia. She had been too good and careful a swimmer to have lost her life in the lake.

In the final analysis it was a crack Interpol pathological team who discovered the puncture mark in her neck and with their special chemical team they also found the "untraceable" poison that killed her. None of this was ever released to the public because I thought that under a veil of secrecy there would be a better chance for investigators to track the culprit, but to no avail. Except this, my child. It seems the enemy is closer than even I suspected and I know that the foe stalks me now.

I'm writing this letter to you, Charity, because I sense that the killer is aware of the investigation and will soon kill me as well. How I fear leaving you, my child, with the job undone, but I fear to confide my trepidation to anyone. Whom can I trust?

That is why my remains are not in the crypt as everyone is supposed to think but in a medical examiner's vault in Paris as I secretly ordered. With a little help we should be able to discover if I was killed just as my darling Julia was. If that is so, then we will be closer to a solution.

Take care, my beloved child. You have the same

enemy. It tears my heart out that I can't be sure who it is . . . and I die knowing that you could be a victim one day too. What bitter gall I leave you as a legacy, child of my heart!

Perhaps before I'm taken I will have the proof I need to show you who your father was. That has been a tandem investigation that has gotten all mixed up in this one.

Guard yourself, Charity. I love you, Grandfather.

Charity stared at the crabbed script of her grandfather's writing, at how hurried he must have been when he wrote it and she could feel the urgency of that moment. She looked at the date at the top. It was dated three weeks before his death. He had still been moving around then, with the aid of a walker but still mobile.

All at once Charity became aware of her surroundings and how she had left the door unlocked to the library. With quick moves she replaced the soft writing material in the pocket and pressed the ends together. To her amazement they stuck together. Her grandfather must have had one of his chemists come up with the ingenious method he'd used to hide the note.

"Grandfather, how frightened you must have been, knowing that someone was stalking you, perhaps poisoning you." Charity looked around the room as she spoke, quite sure she could feel his beloved presence. "Is this why you wouldn't let me visit you those last days? Why didn't you tell me so that I could have helped you?"

Angry tears filled her eyes as she crossed the room, climbed the ladder, and replaced the book in its proper slot, making sure that everything was in order before she closed the sliding glass doors, locked them, and climbed down, pushing the ladder on its track toward the corner of the room.

A covenant to herself firmed inside her. She, Charity Bigham Layton, granddaughter of Cyrus Publius Bigham, would find the person who killed the two people she'd loved so dearly.

As she was standing there, motionless, the doorknob to the hallway turned silently and the door came open a fraction, then was pushed wider.

Charity reached out, grasping a heavy metal sculpture wrought by the great Cellini centuries ago, a prized possession of Bigham House, and part of a collection of the notorious artist that included one of his well-known enamel and gold salt cellars. Charity had a moment of hysterical humor when picturing herself using the priceless sculpture as a weapon. The great Cellini who had boasted of his murders would have been delighted with her, she was sure.

When Tell stepped through the partially opened door, she sagged with relief, watching his relaxed smile tighten, his golden eyes darken with wariness when he saw how she gripped the piece of art, then shoot around the room as though to find the marauder.

"What happened in here? Why the weapon?"

Charity replaced the statuette on the reading table in front of the bookshelves, shaking her head. "Nothing happened."

Tell stiffened when he saw the way her features flickered with tension, the way her gaze slid away from his. "Something seems to have upset you."

Charity tried to smile at him. "It's your imagination. I was just leaving. Since I am an attendant I should get back and dance with the guests. I'm sure Lionel and Jennifer will wonder where I am."

Charity was hiding something! And she had no intention of confiding in him. Nothing was more glaringly obvious to him than that. The hurt that knowledge engendered was a knife wound to him. "By all means let's get back to the guests."

Tell was angry with her! He'd known she was dissembling, just as he always seemed to know what she was thinking. But what could she tell him? Showing him what her grandfather had written somehow seemed a breach of confidence at the moment. Grandfather had revealed things to her that rocked her to her very soul. Her beloved mother had been murdered! She had been injected with something that had rendered her incapable of saving herself, that had caused her to drown. Nothing had ever shocked her as much as reading that. Her gentle, always laughing mother had been the victim of a killer. And her grandfather had suffered the same fate. What a vicious coil she was entrapped in. Did her husband know anything about the contents of the hidden letter? She didn't distrust Tell . . . but she couldn't talk to him about what she'd discovered until she'd had a chance to mull it over, until she dealt with the very sharp grief of knowing that someone had deliberately deprived her of the people she'd loved most in the world in her formative years.

"Charity? Answer me."

"Ah, what did you say?"

"I asked if you'd talked to anyone in the library."

"No. No, I was alone."

Anger at her restraint and evasiveness crackled through Tell like an electric charge. At that moment he almost hated her. Something had happened to her in the library. Either someone or something had been there. Admittedly she was more on edge since the many "accidents" that had happened to her, but there was a facet to her now that was unknown to him before she'd entered the library, and it covered up something.

When they entered the solarium with its laughing

throng, Charity avoided looking at her husband when he swept her into his arms and moved about the floor. The strong arms holding her were stiff and inflexible, not the warm bands they had always been when they'd been around her. Though their bodies touched and moved in rhythm, they were miles apart.

More than once, Charity wanted to tell him what had occurred, but something held her back.

Lionel tapped Tell on the shoulder, his beaming smile touching both of them, seemingly unaware of how grim-faced Charity's husband was, how unsmiling she was.

Though not as graceful as Tell, Lionel made up for his lack of rhythm with energy and enthusiasm.

Charity welcomed the distraction that dancing with her friend brought and she had to smile at the shining happiness that seemed to come out of every pore. "You could put the sun to shame."

"I know. I'm afraid I'll burst with it all." Lionel laughed. "Jennifer's my wife now and that makes me wild just to think about it." He gave Charity a smacking kiss on the cheek. "My wonderful wife has already announced that when we come back from our honeymoon she is signing on as a full-time volunteer at Promise House."

"Lionel! That's wonderful. Jennifer has been very good with the girls here, I know that."

"Yes, she has, and believe it or not so has her mother."

Charity laughed and nodded. "I wouldn't have believed it of Kathleen but she has actually been helpful and instructive with the girls, generous with her time and quite understanding."

"Are you going to continue with the experiment of bringing some of them out here?"

"Yes, Tell and I feel that it's been a good experience for the girls. They seem to thrive on the care and fresh air." Just mentioning her husband's name made her wince inwardly, the rift between them causing her a great deal of pain. "We've been working a new job training program for them that will help smooth the transition for some of them when they get back into the mainstream."

Lionel outlined a program he initiated for the boys in his care.

Charity tried to concentrate on what he was saying but her mind kept going back to the library, what had happened there and afterward.

Since their marriage she and Tell had had differences, some of them strong-worded and angry, but they had always been able to patch up things quickly because of the love between them. Charity had the feeling that the moments in the library had begun a fissure that would be hard to mend. The rejection would not be forgotten nor would it be so easily dissipated.

Gareth came up and cut in, grinning at Lionel. "That damned smile of yours is downright sickening, man."

"I don't care." Lionel kissed Charity's cheek. "Maybe Gareth can make you smile, friend, I sure couldn't."

Startled by his observation, Charity felt the blood rise in her face. "Sorry about that."

"Don't be sorry, let a friend help you, Charity."

"Just be happy with Jennifer. I'm fine."

"What did he mean?" Gareth swung her away from his body, his eyes going over her admiringly as she didn't miss a step of the intricate movement.

Charity shrugged. "I guess this old house is getting to me."

"Ah, you're remembering all the old tales about the secret passages that Amby and I used to tell you."

"And scare me witless so that I had to sleep with my

217

light on at night. Do you know I had forgotten your horror stories? Was there any truth to them?"

"You know there could have been because I recall once when Amby and I were talking about it in Cyrus's hearing and how startled he'd looked, as though we'd opened his safe or something. His usual polite mask settled into place almost at once though."

"You sound a little wry. I thought you liked my grandfather, Gareth."

"I did . . . but I never really knew him . . . and I admit that he intimidated us more than a little." Gareth looked pensive. "There was a side of Cyrus that was shadowed from everyone."

"But you give credence to the tale that there are secret passages?"

"Hey, lady, wait a minute. Are you serious?" Gareth's gaze sharpened on her. "Why all the questions? Have you had problems?"

Charity smiled into his eyes, shaking her head. She couldn't confide in anyone for the moment. Besides, she had the feeling that if she ever voiced out loud that her mother and maybe her grandfather had been murdered, she would fly apart like a bad watch. She had to keep her own counsel, trust in her own moves and keep to herself anything she might glean or discover. "Just a morbid fascination about living in a house that could have secret passages, I suppose."

Gareth studied her for a second before the steps of the dance moved her away from him again. "Well, I suppose if Cyrus did do such a thing, the main passageway would lead from his bedroom, or from the library. Those were his special rooms."

"True." Charity smiled again, hoping that agitation she felt at his words didn't show in her face. Would her grandfather have installed such a tunnel in his house? It didn't fit the open, laughing man she remembered, though he had become more reserved in his last years. He had supervised the building of this house personally, she could recall her mother telling her that.

The wedding reception went on well into the evening with neither the guests nor the bride and groom seeming anxious to leave, but finally the celebration ended and the wedding couple left in a flurry of laughter and good-byes, rice showering all about them.

"Macon will have a job cleaning this up in the morning," Kathleen said sternly, though a smile trembled over her face.

"We'll have him get extra help tomorrow," Charity told her.

"Yes, that would be best." Kathleen faced her. "Thank you for what you did for my daughter today, Charity. She is very happy."

"I had the wedding here because I wanted that for both of them, Kathleen."

"I know. Thank you."

Little by little guests drifted away and soon the house was empty.

Tell approached Charity. "I'm going for a walk on the grounds." Though he was polite his face was closed to her.

"Fine." It hurt her that he didn't invite her to join him.

Charity went upstairs blindly, her mind in turmoil with the events that had transpired that evening. Myriad emotions warred in her. Grief at her grandfather's revelations, sadness that she was being secretive with Tell, fear that someone could have killed her grandfather and was still in or near Bigham House.

She readied herself for bed, donning a light-as-air cashmere robe that Tell had bought her, taking a book with her into bed, but unable to focus on it.

Restless and irritated, both with Tell and with herself,

she rose from the bed and prowled the room. When she began touching the wainscoted walls and pressing certain areas, she had no clear plan of action but once started she worked her way around the octagonal room. The rose centers of the scrolled oak drew her more and more and she tried to turn and press each one.

When she had gone over the perimeter of the room and found nothing she was still edgy. Walking over to the huge closets that took up one wall of the room she opened them, pushing aside her clothes to study the walls, then moving farther down toward Tell's clothes and looking behind. As she flattened her hand against one panel, she heard a click as though a lock had released. Pressing harder she felt the strong oak give way and swing sideways like a narrow door opening.

Charity saw the stairs leading downward but not much else with the little light that was able to penetrate from the bedroom. She was about to switch on the closet light when she heard the door to their bedroom being opened. With a speed she didn't know she had, she shut the passage entrance and closed the closet door in one swift motion, turning to face the door as Tell came through it, spotting her at once.

Tell's skin crawled with the awareness that his wife was hiding something. The closed look on her face told him more than anything could that something else had occurred and she wasn't going to share it with him any more than she had been open with him when they had been together in the library.

It firmed his resolve to dig away at her until he was able to discover what it was that had built a wall around her, what it was that was keeping her away from him. Charity had found another message, perhaps this from her grandfather too, but anyway she had gone into the library during the festivities and had found out some-

thing else that had made her cautious and suspicious
. . . even of him, her husband.

All the wonderful weeks they'd had together since
their marriage seemed to have evaporated in one evening. Tell didn't deal well with the frustration he was
experiencing at the moment. He was used to being in
command, running a situation his way, directing the
fire. It had been a great joy to him that he and Charity
had become closer each day they'd been married, then
out of the blue, a phantom happening had pulled down
everything and he was standing in the middle of the
wreckage.

"Cleaning the closet?" He noticed that Charity's chin
tilted upward, her green eyes flashing emerald. His eyes
scanned the clothing and the disarrayed shoes on the
floor.

"And if I was?"

"Save it for another day; I'm tired."

"If I disturb you, sleep in the other bedroom."

Tell felt his temper erupt, hot steel poking through
the top of his head. He ripped the tie from his neck and
threw it, striding toward her.

Charity put up her fists. "Don't think I won't go
back at you if you hit me."

Tell stopped as though she'd already struck him.
"And when have I done that since our marriage?"

"Never." Charity watched the muscle jump at the
side of his jaw. "But you look mad enough to wrestle a
bear."

"I am."

"I can't help that."

"Oh yes you can, and you know it. It's your damned
evasions that are causing the problems."

"Stop grinding your teeth like that. It will cost a
fortune for root canals." Charity had always loved that
strong mouth and purposeful jaw.

"Charity!" Tell's roar banged off the walls in angry reverberations.

She jumped backward. "What? For heaven's sake! You'll bring the house down if you don't cool off." Charity stared as his face turned granite hard, his eyes like shiny flint as they went over her. "If you'll be patient with me things will work out, I know. I have to sort things in my mind," she whispered.

"I won't be shut out of your life. You're my wife, and I won't stand for it."

"Did Grandfather ever tell you that I was in danger?" The blurted words spilled into the room.

Wariness washed away his anger, his mind computing her tone and the words, filling in the spaces of what she was not telling him, before fear began to mount in him. "What are you saying? Are you speaking of the bookshelves again?"

Charity felt his searching questions like ice on her spirit, aware that he had not answered hers. "He did say something to you, didn't he?"

"What brought you to that conclusion?" The memory of Cyrus telling him in taut anger that he could watch over his granddaughter came back like a forceful specter to his mind.

"My grandfather didn't trust everyone living here, Tell."

"Don't be enigmatic, Charity. I want to know what has put you on edge. How do you know what your grandfather thought?"

"What do you know about my mother's death?"

"What? Your mother?" His eyes studied her for long moments, the tangent she was on shaking him to his shoes, then he spoke more slowly. "She drowned in the lake. Julia loved to swim and had gone alone to the water," Tell recited, his eyes still going over her, his mind trying to pierce the barrier that her brain had thrown up, attempting to delve into the meaning behind her words. "She never should have been by herself and both Cyrus and I had warned her about doing it . . . even though she was one of the best swimmers I've ever seen."

"Was there an investigation?" Charity watched his face change as his mind tried to recapture the time and sort the information into a useful tool for him.

"Yes, naturally there would be when there's an accident. Death by drowning was the coroner's finding and the case was closed."

"Grandfather had other investigations."

Tell gasped as though he'd taken a blow to the solar plexus. "What are you saying? How would you know that?"

"Are you saying you didn't know about them?" Charity felt as though the jousting between Tell and herself was not doing them any good; on the contrary it seemed to be driving a wedge between them, but she had to keep chipping away. Someone knew a great deal about her mother and her death and Charity was sure that the person had not left the area.

"Charity, if you know anything at all, please tell me."

Charity inhaled deeply, shaking her head slowly. "It's something I have to work out by myself, Tell." His face went gray. "Right now it's really nebulous rather than concrete."

"What are you saying?" His whisper cut through the air like a whip.

"Nothing. And I want you to accept that. I won't tell you any more until . . . until I can."

"Damn your twisted soul! You're driving me crazy." Tell spun away from her, striding back the way he'd come, yanking open the door and going through it, slamming it behind him with enough force to knock a picture askew.

223

"Oh Tell, I do love you." Her shaken voice echoed back to her. "But I'm afraid this specter might go after you, my darling."

Turning she looked toward the closet, but rejected doing anything about it until the next day when there would be ample daylight and she could arm herself with what she would need. Then she would get a flashlight and some rope and anything else she might need to explore the stairs that led downward into the bowels of Bigham House.

Charity hurried through a quick shower, her eyelids feeling leaden, the shock she'd sustained at what she'd seen in the library like an anchor to her spirit.

She climbed between the silken sheets feeling bereft and cold without Tell's warm presence. Her hands and feet felt as though she'd sustained a frostbite and she was sure that sleep would elude her. Charity knew that she needed her husband both for the warmth of her body and her spirit.

Sleep came like a smothering blanket and with it nightmares that zigzagged through her brain like grotesque lightning, causing her to flinch and whimper and flail at the threats and jeopardy. "No . . . no . . . where are you, Grandfather?"

All at once the coldness left and she cuddled to the warmth, her body seeking the comfort, instinctively knowing she was safe. "Tell."

"Yes, darling, I'm here. It's all right. You were having a nightmare. Open your eyes."

"No," she told him dreamily, smiling when he laughed.

"I want to make love to you."

"Please."

"I want to make sure you're awake so that you don't think I'm part of the nightmare."

224

"You couldn't be. You're my knight in shining armor."

"When was I promoted?"

"Tonight." Charity did open her eyes then. "I had bad dreams. You chased them away."

"I heard you thrashing about when I came back to our room."

"Did you come back to sleep with me?"

"Among other things."

"I don't like sleeping without you."

"It was hell for me . . . and I won't leave you again."

"Good." She took hold of his face with her hands, her fingers delighting in the electric sensations created by caressing him. "You are a very beautiful man . . . and I'm so glad you're here."

"Darling." Tell pressed his face into the satin of her skin, his mouth foraying over the smooth surface as though he had to find and mark every pore as though loving her was what he had to do.

In moments the fire that was always just below the surface with them erupted into molten passion, welding them in love, making them soar.

When Tell's mouth touched her intimately, Charity was sure she would fly apart. In passionate need to make him one with her experience, she kissed him the same way.

"Charity . . . darling . . . I need you."

In consummate splendor they loved and caressed one another, climbing the heights.

"I'll always want you, Tell."

"Then trust me, Charity, as I trust you."

Burying her face in his chest, she clung to him but didn't answer his entreaty, love and fear mixing in her like an outlandish caldron.

Whatever else there was in life for her, she knew with

225

a doomsday certainty that she couldn't lose Tell as she'd lost her grandfather and mother. Tell was the greatest love of all. Life would be a desert without him, unlivable, barren, empty. Protecting him from the specter that had taken the other Bighams was the driving force in her life now.

CHAPTER EIGHT

Tell's frustration mounted each day after the wedding. The lovemaking between Charity and him was more wonderful and they were reconciled outwardly and were very affectionate with one another. But Tell knew she was concealing something from him and it drove him wild: every time he made any overture that would lead to her confiding in him, Charity became remote again.

Driving into Manhattan without her had been another bone of contention between them that morning and her stubbornness had set his teeth on edge.

"Today is all taken up with the things I have to do here, Tell. It's ridiculous to worry about me when I'm at Bigham House. I'm with the girls, Macon, Rum and the rest of the staff." She had no intention of telling him that she was in the habit of looking over her shoulder no matter where she was.

"Need I remind you that you were the one who said that your grandfather was warning you. This house could be as dangerous for you as Manhattan and I'm damned well going to see to it that you have no more near misses."

"But you don't believe that, about this house I mean . . . and neither do I. Bigham House is my home." Charity gasped. "Tell, you're squeezing the breath out of me—"

His lips had ground into hers in a bittersweet farewell.

Their conversation went round and round in his head as his foot depressed the accelerator shooting the car up the access road to the thruway leading into Manhattan.

If he hadn't had the meeting with Jacob in the elderly lawyer's office in Manhattan Tell wouldn't have left Bigham House at all, but there had been such a note of urgency in Henry's voice when they'd talked that he couldn't let the old man down.

It had gotten to the point where being away from Charity was painful. All the fears he'd had for her seemed to swell and fester in him when she wasn't where he could touch her, talk to her.

As usual the traffic into Manhattan on a Monday morning was awful and he found himself in more than one gridlock. When he finally reached his parking area under his office building his jaw was in gridlock and he had invented a few very purple invectives that he had fired into the environment time after time.

Because he could tell that he was going to be late for his appointment he called Jacob from his own office. "Yes. I'll be there in a few minutes. You sound strange, Jacob. Are you feeling well?"

"Get here fast."

Tell stared at the phone for a puzzled second, then replaced the receiver, left his office with hurried instructions for his secretary, his briefcase with the files he'd taken from Jacob's office under his arm.

Taking a taxi was fastest though Jacob's office was a mere six blocks away. Arriving there he hurried from the cab into the building and up the silent elevator to the twentieth floor to stride along the long corridor to reach Henry's corner office. The secretary nodded when she saw him, not seeming surprised at his curt response to her greeting and that he didn't even wait to be announced.

Jacob half rose from his chair, then sank back when Tell entered the room. "Sit down, Tell."

Tell noticed Gareth at once but it was the older man that he homed in on, noting Jacob's pallor. "You found something in the files you had."

Jacob shrugged, gesturing to Tell to take the seat next to Gareth and facing him. "I don't know for sure. Cyrus could be very secretive when he chose . . ."

"The man was a sphinx, you mean." Gareth interrupted. "I never knew what he was thinking even though I admired and liked him."

Tell shot him an irritated look at his interruption. "Jacob, what are you talking about?"

Jacob pushed a folder across the desk. "Read that and tell me what conclusions you draw."

Gareth rose from his chair and leaned over Tell's shoulder reading with him. When a few minutes passed and his low surprised whistle circled the office, Jacob put his head in his hands and sighed.

Tell put the folder back on the desk waiting until Gareth sat down again before speaking. "It would seem that Cyrus believed that Jake, your son, didn't die a natural death, that he was murdered."

The older man nodded heavily. "That's how I read it."

"But Jacob, if I remember Jake, and I think I do, he was the best-liked man in the area." Gareth shrugged. "I can remember my brother Amby and me watching him play polo, or tennis or anything you could name. He was outstanding at sports and he had a flotilla of women following wherever he went."

Tell laughed harshly. "He's right about that, Jacob. I'm older than Gareth and knew Jake rather well. A happier or better adjusted man never lived . . . and with no enemies that I could see."

"Nor could I," Jacob said heavily. "I would say that it's all tomfoolery, but Cyrus makes a strong case though admitting he doesn't know who Jake's enemy could be."

Tell sat forward in his chair. "Let's assume, that however implausible it seems to us, Cyrus could be telling the truth."

"So?" Gareth looked puzzled.

"Then the next step would be to see who could identify the culprit. Since none of us can think of such a person, maybe Jake could tell us if he had an enemy. Did he leave a diary, a journal, or even an old calendar that we might peruse, Jacob?"

Jacob looked taken aback, but then he shook his head slowly. "Though Jake was a scholarly man as well as being athletic, he kept poor notes and used to tell me that was the one thing he had to struggle with in university." Jacob put his index finger to his mouth, an arrested look to his face. "Except when he went on trips, then he always kept a travel diary. He wanted to write a book one day about the West Indies and he began keeping notes any time he went on a journey, no matter how small it was. I think I might still have those travel diaries, though I can't see how they could help us."

"And they would be at your house upstate or are they at your apartment?"

"Actually, they would be here. I couldn't bear to look at his things after his accident, but I hated to part with them, so I had everything bundled up and put in an old empty law vault we have behind the law library. Someday I must go through those things and get rid of most of it."

"Meaning that in all these years you haven't gone over anything yet?"

"No, I haven't even opened the door. I'm sure every-thing would be buried in dust if it wasn't airlocked." Jacob pulled open his middle drawer and took out a small key ring with three keys on it, then rose to his feet. "Come with me, gentlemen, we'll take a look."

Tell put his hand on the older man's arm. "Jacob, Gareth and I can go in there without you."

"I'll be fine. My son has been dead almost twenty-five years and though I shall always miss him I have come to terms with his death, I assure you."

Tell and Gareth followed the erect, elderly man through the echo chamber of the law library belonging to the firm and stood behind him when he inserted the key into a metal door on the far wall, waiting until he'd switched on a light before they moved into the low-ceilinged windowless room, the stuffiness of the atmo-sphere assailing them at once.

Jacob went to an old filing cabinet that sat next to neatly stacked boxes and pulled out drawer after drawer until he came to the bottom one where he removed the contents little by little, stacking them neatly on the floor until he snatched at a grouping of leather-bound notebooks. "Ah, here they are. Good Lord, I take back what I said about my son not being a note taker. It looks like seven trip diaries to me."

"The plot thickens," Gareth mumbled at Tell's back.

Jacob turned around facing the other two with the notebooks. "We seem to be discovering facets about people close to us that we never knew; first Cyrus, now Jake." Though Jacob smiled there was a tremolo to his voice that was unmistakable.

"Why don't you read them first if you like?" Gareth suggested, aware that Tell had stiffened at his words.

"No." Tell's hands curled into fists. "We're not even sure these can help us but we can't afford to waste time

231

with amenities." Tell's voice cracked. "My wife could be in peril."

"Tell's right to feel an urgency about this and I must admit that I do myself. We'll split them up as we did before with Tell taking three and you and I two apiece, Gareth."

Gareth looked at Tell and saw that beneath his polite veneer he was churning. "I'll get on these tonight, Tell, and call you tomorrow."

"If you find out anything before tomorrow call Bigham House. I'll be out there; you too, Jacob."

"Don't worry, I will."

Tell returned to his office, leaving Gareth and Jacob as soon as he could.

Instructing his secretary to hold all calls, he entered his office, locked it, stripped off his tie and jacket and sat down to read the travel diaries of Jacob Henry II.

Charity had found herself very busy right after Lionel and Jennifer's wedding. She was immersed in helping Rita with her course selection for Russell Sage College, the other girls needed lessons, checkups from their doctors and there were a couple of days that she had to drive into Manhattan to confer with the staff at Promise House.

So it wasn't until almost a week after the wedding that she had a moment to think about finding the secret stairway leading from the closet in the master suite down inside the house.

Charity had a powerful wish that she and Tell hadn't argued that morning and that he was here with her instead of in Manhattan.

That afternoon when Rita was with her father choosing furnishings for the new house they would have, the girls were napping and Kathleen had gone to a bridge luncheon with some friends, Charity was at loose ends.

Finding a flashlight in the kitchen, she rustled around until she found a small claw hammer, feeling comforted that she had a weapon if she were to encounter bats or some creepy crawly thing.

Lyle Clausen watched her approach him as she came out of the kitchen and walked down the main center hall leading to the front door. "Going into the attic, Charity? You used to love it there when you were a girl."

Charity smiled at the memory. "How did you remember that? I suppose it was because one day you covered for me when Grandfather was going to give me a thrashing for going up there."

"That was because some dampness had gotten into the boards and they had weakened."

"I hope I thanked you for sparing me the spanking."

"You were always a very polite young girl."

Charity laughed, noting his boots and crop. "See you at dinner. I guess you're going riding."

"I usually exercise Diablo at this time."

"Be careful of him, Lyle. I understand he's well named . . . the devil. The stable boys treat him with great respect."

"I will."

Charity parted from him, relieved that he hadn't pressed her for an explanation. If he thought that she had gone into the attic so much the better. Lyle had always been nice to her but she didn't want to confide in him where she was going, not that she knew where the staircase led.

In minutes she was in the master suite with the door locked behind her as a precaution.

Charity's palms felt sweaty as she donned old, faded jeans, a long-sleeved cotton shirt, and a kerchief tied over her hair. Her throat was dry and she had to exert all the willpower she had not to listen to the voice inside her that told her not to proceed. She donned serviceable ankle-length climbing boots and faced the closet, flashlight in hand, inhaling deep breaths.

Pushing open the back of the closet with one hand, Charity stared down into the depths of the winding stone stairway. It was amazingly cobweb-free from what she could see and looked relatively clean. Somehow the thought that someone seemed to be housekeeping the silo-shaped area was not a comfort to her.

Taking the first step was the hardest, but when she'd taken it she as quickly stepped back, looking suspiciously at the hinged door that had begun to swing shut on her the moment she'd taken her hand from it. Caution dictated that she guard her back. Looking around her, she spied Tell's favorite putter that he often used to hit golf balls across the carpeting of their bedroom. It was a way he had of relieving tension and the mindless concentration had proved to be a problem solver for him on more than one occasion.

Jamming the club into the opening under the hinge effectively provided the failsafe to her returning to where she'd started safely. Swallowing, she began again.

Though her boots were rubber soled, they made a hollow, echoing sound in the narrow silo-like area in which the stairs had been encased. Charity moved slowly, her flashlight touching every step and shining all around her, at times glinting on the stone and refracting the light back to her. It was a very clean atmosphere and there was no trouble with breathing, signaling to her that there was adequate ventilation in the stairwell.

Her heart thudded in slow, painful cadence as she questioned herself silently about the wisdom of continuing with each step she took downward, but she didn't stop. It was though she had to go on, that the answers she sought could be ahead. Down, down she went.

Once when she inhaled she caught the distinct odor

of fresh bread and assumed that she had to be in the vicinity of the kitchen to get such a strong whiff of Rum's baking. Step by slow step she continued down . . . until she began to get the feeling that she could be below the first floor, maybe even at the basement level. Charity experienced a shiver of disorientation and paused for a second before continuing.

When her flashlight picked up a doorway in the stonework, her heart flipped over, the flashlight sending a distorted beam of light over the wall as her hand shook in reaction. Steadying herself was an effort, but she remained still until she was. Then placing the flashlight in her left hand she used the right to turn the metal handle. Nothing. Putting the flashlight between her knees, she grasped the knob with both hands and strained to turn it. Locked! She saw a keyhole and then scanned the walls for a key that might have hung there, but there was none. Wherever the door led it couldn't be opened on her side. She would have to try and trace the location outside, perhaps then there would be a way to open it.

Going down a few more steps she was about to make another turn in the stairs when her flashlight focused on the bottom. There was a cement floor and another doorway. As she was about to proceed to the door to try it, Charity heard a low hissing, scraping sound and froze in place. *No!* It was not her imagination that the ground-floor door was opening.

"My God," Charity whispered, stepping back and upward, her hand flicking off the switch of the flashlight, a primeval fear seizing her. A cold force outside herself seemed to be telling her to run, to escape. Feeling her way she moved as rapidly as possible, putting down her feet with great care in order to avoid making any sound. The darkness was like a smothering cloak around her and she had to fight not to gasp every breath.

Below her there was the unmistakable sound of someone moving into the silo and closing the door, then there were footsteps moving upward . . . toward her.

Charity could see the shadow of a light moving toward her as she continued to move rapidly backward, not daring to turn around and run as she wanted to do for fear of disclosure.

When there was a scraping sound and then a muffled curse and the bumping of something falling, then the light going out, she whirled around and lit her own torch hurrying now, stumbling up the stairs, aware she could be heard, the breath rasping painfully from her body as she struggled to reach her own room, slam the door and somehow put up a barrier that would keep the intruder from finding her.

Catapulting through the opening into the closet, her momentum carried her out into the bedroom so that she stumbled and fell to the floor, her fingers curling into the Aubusson carpet as though the familiarity of the precious goods was somehow a sane protection against the unknown.

"Charity! Are you hurt? What the bloody hell are you doing? Where did you come from?"

Looking up from her sprawled position on the floor, her throat dry and her breathing uneven she stared at her husband. "Tell, close the door. Barricade it. Keep it out."

"Keep what out? Where did you come from?" Tell's eyes followed in the direction she was pointing. First he had moved toward her, but now at her words he checked it, changing direction and going to the closet. He saw the opening at once and when he put his head in there he heard footsteps and saw the shadowy light. "What the hell is going on? Who's there? Damn you, speak up."

236

The light coming up the stairs stopped, then it turned and rapid footsteps telegraphed retreat.

"Come back here." Tell stepped through the opening.

"No! Don't go down there, Tell. Someone is there. Please, don't leave me."

Her entreaty was a brake to his forward motion. He took one last quick look down the stairway, then went back to his wife, sinking to his knees and lifting her into his arms, his hands going over her quickly, his fierce gaze fixing on her as he carried her to their bed, then went down beside her. "Are you hurt?" At her negative he kissed her. "Wait here. No, no, it's all right. I'll be right back." Tell left her on the run, sprinting through the opening and down the winding staircase pell-mell.

He heard the clang of a metal door slamming shut and he was in total darkness but he followed to the bottom, trying the door, then throwing himself against it to no avail.

Reversing himself he hurried up again as fast as he could in total blackness, back into the room and across to Charity, who was still on the bed with her gaze fixed on the opening in the closet.

Going down beside her he took her in his arms. "Charity, I want the truth. All of it. Start talking." Tell kissed her face, letting his lips slide over her skin, down her neck, probing her ears, feeling the sensations of shock rippling through her body.

"Close the door to the stairway first." She shivered.

Tell rolled off the bed, approached the hidden doorway and pushed on the mechanism, closing it. "Amazing," he muttered before hurrying back to Charity and beginning to caress her fiercely. "Talk."

"I thought you didn't want me to talk when we were going to make love."

"Damned little devil, I want no more evasions." Though she smiled at him, he heard the tremor in her voice, his heart sinking at the danger she could have been in the past hour or so. He gave her a hard kiss then leaned back from her, his arms keeping her supine on the bed. "Talk."

Charity could tell by the steely look in his eyes that he would tolerate nothing less than the whole truth. "I found something."

Tell nodded. "I guessed that. Why didn't you want to share it with me?"

Charity touched his cheek, the velvet roughness of his jaw a familiar joy. "I was afraid for you . . . and I wasn't quite sure if you would think it credible . . ."

"But you do, don't you?" Tell kissed her cheek, relief like a flood in him because he had her in his arms.

"Yes. I believe every word."

"And?"

"I was afraid you might be in as . . . ah, in danger."

"You were going to say 'as much danger as I am in.' Correct? Answer me, Charity."

"Yes." Her hands seemed to have a life of their own when they lifted and threaded through his crisp, thick hair. "I don't want anything to hurt you."

"Do you love me?"

"Yes, I bloody well do."

Chuckling, Tell pressed his face into her neck, his mouth worrying the soft skin there. "Go on."

Settling herself more comfortably into his arms, feeling soothed by the warm body of her husband, Charity told him about the time in the library when she'd discovered the note in the pages of the book.

"Written in Cyrus's handwriting?"

Charity nodded. "Oh yes, it was unmistakably his. Grandfather wrote to me almost every day when I was in college. I know his handwriting very well."

"Will you show it to me?"

"Yes, but you must promise me that you'll be careful.

238

I think that the person who is after me is the same one who was coming up the stairs. Oh, Tell, don't look like that." He'd gone grayish in color, his golden eyes hardening to metallic.

"Gareth and I didn't see anyone when we came up the drive. He went down to the stables and I went directly to the library. I'll get in touch with him and see if there was anyone in the paddock area."

"Not to worry. Lyle was going in that general direction. If anyone was around he wouldn't be slow to chase them. Despite the fact that he's very easygoing he never liked trespassers and often disagreed with Grandfather when he would allow the town people to cross his property."

Tell looked thoughtful. "You're right. I can remember them exchanging words about it. Lyle thought that Cyrus was being careless with your welfare."

"Grandfather was adamant that I would never come to harm at Bigham House . . . from anyone."

"Yet in the final analysis, he felt he had to warn you against the dangers here, so much so that he felt that his own death would be murder."

Shivering, Charity cuddled closer to Tell, her hands slipping around his waist. "It's madness, Tell. If I hadn't trusted my grandfather so implicitly I would say it was pure raving."

"Damn, how I wish he'd had some inkling of who this madman is." Tell kissed her gently. "I will not let you out of my sight, Charity. And I mean it this time."

"You don't have to convince me. I don't want to be apart from you."

"Good, because you won't be. If there's business in town we'll handle it together, otherwise we stay here."

"Fine."

"And you don't think now that I could be part of this conspiracy against you." He smiled down at her. "Oh yes, my darling, I could tell that you had questions about me."

"I was frightened and confused, Tell, and getting paranoid about everyone, but I don't think I ever really doubted you because when I was with you was the only time I felt safe."

"Thank you for that." Tell pushed his face into her hair.

"Are we going to talk or make love?"

"Both."

"You have changed."

"I've discovered I like the little kitten sounds you make when we're making love."

"Me? You're the one who growls like a tame tiger."

"Kiss me, darling, and we'll worry about the sound track later." Tell was so grateful he had her in his arms, his fierce possession of her was total as though by making love to her he could drive the world away and keep her safe.

Charity was eager to embrace him, to clutch to her the wonderful opium of Tell's lovemaking that allowed her to put aside all fear, closet any trepidation. "Oh Tell . . . please . . ."

"That's the idea . . . pleasing you, my love."

Charity's languorous body took on an attitude of attention at his words. Then she took hold of his face with her hands. "Pleasing? That's the name of the game, you say?"

"Pleasing you is everything to me, Charity." Despite the hold she had on him he was able to push his face into her breasts, nuzzling there, muttering love words that had the ferocity of curses.

"Good." In a nimble twist she was free of him, almost laughing at the stunned, glazed look to his features when she rolled atop him. "Then it's my turn to do the pleasing."

240

"Is it? It seems you do that most of the time now, love." Tell was bemused by the hot amusement in her eyes, his own growing mirth quickly dispelled when she began to make love to him, her hands and mouth magic on his body. "Charity . . . darling . . . don't."

In a surge of sexual power that almost undid her she felt his body do a mini-jackknife as she worked her way in slow, deliberate exploration down his body. When he called out her name it was as though all at once the electric shock emotion he was experiencing went through his skin in a sensual osmosis into hers. He was setting her on fire as he always did!

"No more." Tell lifted her off him and flipped her onto her back, none too gently, the hurricane surrender she engendered in him causing shockwaves to his system. Never before had he been out of control with a woman! Not until Charity had become his wife. In the most casual ways of smiling, chatting, laughing she had been able to put him off stride. Now even their love-making was making him slip off the planet and the lack of being the driver of his own destiny was a leveler to him. Loving Charity was a threat to him and the emotion was growing stronger each day!

In a kaleidoscope of sensuous color and feeling they climaxed together in joyous and explosive harmony, both of them crying out their delight in the love they shared.

Long minutes afterward they were still curled together in a loveknot lethargy that soothed and softened all the rough edges, making the most impossible barrier seem like a mere step along the way.

"Charity, how far does the stairway go?"

Jarred out of her rosy aura, Charity realized that her husband, a man of bulldog tenacity, had been only diverted by their lovemaking, not deterred. "To the ground, I think. There are two doors leading from the turret but I'm not sure where they go."

"Turret?" Tell stiffened.

Charity craned her neck so she could look up at him. "What is it? I just called it that because it's so round, like a silo, if you know what I mean."

"I know exactly what you mean, Charity. Don't you know, too?" Tell turned her to face him, so they were face to face, their nude bodies touching. "Of course you do. What looks like a turret at Bigham House, darling?"

Charity stared at him for a moment. "The gate-house." At Tell's nod she continued. "The stable and the . . . corner of the house where this suite and the library are situated." Her voice faded away, her head moving in a negative way on the pillow. "All these years I've looked at Bigham House and I've never seen the obvious, I mean I knew the architecture but it never registered when I was going down that stairway."

"I never made the connection until this minute, darling."

"But someone besides Grandfather knew about the staircase."

"Yes . . . and I intend to see that the stairway is sealed off until the time we discover who has been intimidating you."

Charity saw the tight, glassy look to his face. "Are you thinking that a pimp or a junkie in the vicinity of Promise House would not know about the turret?"

Tell's arms convulsed on her. "Darling! Please don't dwell on that."

Charity was going to say more but the agony in his voice gave her pause. "We have to find out who it is, Tell. What if this person did kill my mother and grandfather?"

"We'll find out everything, I promise you, my sweet one." Tell's body pearled with a cold sweat at the thought of her being subjected to the same cold-blooded "accident" that had happened to her mother. The memory of the boating incident was as fresh in his mind as though it had just occurred.

"Tell? Tell, let's not talk about this anymore. We'll close up the stairway and that will be an end to it." Charity was well aware that neither she nor Tell thought that was true.

The next day when Tell was busy working in the library, Charity decided to go horseback riding. Despite Tell's adjurations that he was to be with her at all times, she dressed in her riding clothes feeling a desperate need to cleanse her thoughts, breathe fresh air. Penning a short note to Tell, she told him what she was doing.

She hadn't been able to do much riding because she was usually involved in something, but right at the moment she had free time and decided to take advantage of it. After pulling on her boots and getting her crop from the closet she retraced her steps down to the front hall to be met by Macon, who handed her the mail on a silver tray.

Glancing through the sheaf of envelopes she was caught by the name of a law firm on a letter head. March and Day. Wracking her brain she came up with the answer to her mental questioning. Kathleen had been the one to mention the firm on the day of the funeral. They represented her.

Opening the letter, Charity read it twice before she comprehended the meaning.

"Miss Charity, are you all right? You're so pale, miss."

"Where is Mrs. Bigham, Macon?" Charity knew her voice was tight and angry but she couldn't explain to the old retainer she wasn't irked with him. She had a feeling she would crack apart if she said too much.

"In the small sitting room, Miss Charity. She's writing letters, I believe."

Before he was quite through Charity was striding down the wide corridor that took her to the airy, often sun-filled room beyond the dining room and close to the solarium.

Storming into the room she strode right to the Queen Anne desk near the window where her stepgrandmother was busily writing and tossed the envelope on the desk top. "Why did you do it?"

Kathleen looked up slowly, studied the missive, then gazed at Charity. "I do not feel that you have handled the property bequeathed to you by my husband in a responsible manner. Under the laws of this state I am perfectly within my rights to question this no matter what the terms of Cyrus's will state to the contrary." The cold, practical, perfectly enunciated words seemed an intrusion in that room of soft light. "It is not a personal vendetta, Charity, but a well-thought-out judgment on my part."

"Since a move like this was anticipated by Jacob Henry, we have taken steps to circumvent it, Kathleen," Charity said tightly. And she thought she'd been on better footing with her stepgrandmother. "One way was to sign all my possessions over to my husband. That will be done this afternoon, Kathleen."

"That is irresponsible and you know it. Cyrus would not have wanted such a thing."

"Nor would he have wanted you to destroy the terms of his will as you have been trying to do, Kathleen. Please believe I will fight you on this."

"Wait, Charity." Kathleen stared at her stepgranddaughter's back. "Please don't think this was a type of revenge. I truly don't believe you know how to handle property. I do feel that you have done a good job with the girls. I have every intention of continuing to work

244

with Promise House because I feel that the work is worthwhile if this case is adjudicated in my favor."

Charity spun around to face the other woman. "Is there no end to this? Must you have everything before you are satisfied?"

Twin flags of color touched Kathleen's cheeks. "It is the principle of the thing, Charity."

"No." She shook her head. "It's the jealousy that you can't bury. You still resent the fact that my grandfather loved me."

"Obsessively." The word hissed from Kathleen's mouth like a curse. "It didn't bother him one bit that you were illegitimate. His love for you was indecent."

Charity shook her head wearily. "Kathleen, it was not my fault that my grandfather loved his first wife so much, then his daughter and me. Can't you see that?"

Kathleen's fists clenched, her face whitening. "I was his wife. I loved him and he lived in the past."

"I'm sorry, but I am going to fight you on this and I will win."

"Then let the games begin," Kathleen pronounced coldly.

"So be it." Charity left the room at a run, going up the back stairs off the kitchen to the sitting room of the master suite.

Dialing and reaching Jacob Henry took minutes but to Charity it felt like a small lifetime. "Jacob? It's Charity Layton. I want you to move on that plan we had to change all my properties and monies over to Tell. Kathleen has had me served with a show cause order."

"I'll do it right away." The older man paused. "Charity, let me ask you something while I have you on the phone. Tell, Gareth, and I have been going through your grandfather's papers hoping we would come up with something that would give a clue to the identity of the person who . . ."

245

At Jacob's hesitation, Charity spoke. "The person who might be causing all the 'accidents.' I know. Did you find something?"

"No, but I did find a note to me, informing me that I would discover something about Jake if I looked into the turret safe. Do you know what he means by that, Charity? With the letter is a large key taped to the sheet."

Charity felt hot and cold all at once. "Jacob, could I come into town and get the key?"

"No need, child, I'm at my house outside Bigham Park . . ."

"Good. I'm going riding. I'll cut across the fields and get there faster than I would in a car."

"Do you understand Cyrus's cryptic note, Charity?"

"I think I do, Jacob, but I don't want to discuss it on the phone. I'll be there in a few minutes. Look for me."

Charity lifted the note she'd left for Tell and crumpled it in her hand. She could be back before he looked for her. She ran from the room and went back down the kitchen stairs again. "I'm going to see Mr. Jacob, Rum, if my husband is looking for me."

"You be careful on your horse, young lady, and don't take the high fences."

"I'll be back in time for dinner."

Charity ran all the way to the stable but she didn't feel winded, only exhilarated, when she reached it and ordered her horse.

"She'll be wanting to gallop, Miss Charity, but you hold her in. Some parts of the meadow have chuck holes that I haven't filled as yet."

"I'll do that, Mr. Davis. Thank you."

Mr. Davis watched her hop into the saddle. "Mr. Tell was wanting my son to go with you anywhere, Miss Charity. If you would wait for just . . ."

"It's all right, Mr. Davis, I'm just going over to Mr.

Henry's. I won't be long." She smiled at his doubtful look and whistled at Darcy.

It felt good to be riding again. There were so many times that she had longed to get back to it, but the pressures of work and the added responsibilities of running Bigham House had curtailed much of her recreational activity. When she'd been young her mother and grandfather had entered her in dressage classes and she had gloried in it.

Giving Darcy her head, Charity kept in mind what Mr. Davis had said but she was also perfectly aware of Darcy's sure footing and her love of galloping. There wasn't a horse in the stable outside of Diablo that had the heart of the high-stepping mare. She would have slower going on the way back because it would be almost dark but since the horse was very familiar with the area there wouldn't be too much of a problem. But for now she felt great glee in letting the mare go, tearing over the rolling land that was as familiar to her as the palm of her hand.

With the wind in her face and pulling mightily at the kerchief she'd worn to confine her hair, Charity could have laughed out loud with the freedom of it. Like a child she exulted in being carried back to the carefree days of childhood. For a few moments she could put the many unknowns in her life behind her, the multitude of fears packed away, in the short time it would take her to cross the meadows and get to Jacob Henry's house.

"Beautiful Darcy," she crooned to the mare, her words lost in the rush of air around them.

As if watching a movie, she could hear her mother laughing beside her as the two of them galloped over the meadows, picturing the streaming dark blond hair of her mother and how happy Charity had been with her. Her mother had been a bruising rider and taught Charity very early to take her fences with ease and style, to

247

become one with the animal, give trust and receive it back in the very special relationship that could be had between horse and rider.

Charity recalled sharply that it was her mother's favorite ride in just this direction, over the rolling meadows to Jacob's property.

"Why do you like it so much, Mother?" Charity had asked her one day when they had rested their mounts under a shady tree on a knoll that gave a view both of Bigham House and Jacob's property.

Julia had smiled at her young daughter. "For a very romantic and wonderful reason that I will tell you all about one day."

"Is it about my father?" Charity had always asked a great many questions about him and though her mother was very free with information she had never disclosed his identity to Charity.

"Yes, dear, it is and you will like the story very much."

"Then I would like to hear it right now."

"Soon, soon." Julia had laughed and kissed her daughter.

It had always been such a frustration to Charity that she had lost her dear mother before the story could be told, and the romantic fantasies she had woven about what it could have been were legion.

Down through the years she had often dwelt on the probable identity of the man who had fathered her, what kind of person had he been to elicit such deep, lasting devotion from her mother who had never seemed to care for anyone else, though, even as a child, Charity had been aware that her mother was a very attractive person.

When Charity had approached her grandfather after her mother's death and asked him about her father, he had shaken his head sadly.

"Your mother was very much like me and I was proud of that, but her secretive ways in some areas of her life were a source of irritation, too. Many times I asked your mother who it was, but she never said." He had patted her head and taken her hand and squeezed it. "Though your mother never told me straight out who your father was, child, I did know that she never loved anyone else, and that she had loved him dearly. In that way she was like my Faith, your grandmother, steadfast and loyal."

"Why didn't she tell us, Grandfather?"

Charity recalled her grandfather had frowned. "Something was bothering Julia; something that nagged at her and I didn't know what it was, but I think there were times when she wanted to tell us."

What had brought all that back to her now? One hand left the reins and touched the sapphire heart at her throat. She needed Tell's strength.

All at once Charity felt her mother's presence very strongly, so much so that she glanced around her as she rode, not slowing down Darcy's eager speed, but feeling as though she were being watched. Charity had an uncanny sense of her mother urging her to go faster and with that as a goad, Charity dug her heels into the mare's flanks, the answering surge of speed coming from the animal at once.

At Jacob's gate, Charity didn't pause but urged the fleet-footed mare right at it.

Knowing what was expected of her, Darcy gathered her lithe body and thrust herself upward, clearing the gate by many inches easily and never breaking stride.

"Good girl," Charity called to the mare, laughing in the joyous freedom of being one with such a wonderful creature.

Slowing the headlong rush of the mare with gentle words Charity cantered toward the stables behind the big white house, pleasure rippling through her at the familiar sights.

Despite the chilly breeze Jacob was standing on his back terrace, his hands shading his eyes from the western sun as Charity, seeing him, veered her course from the stables and cantered down the drive toward him. "Charity, my child, you took that fence just as Jake used to do. I had such tremendous déjà vu at that moment because you ride the same way as he did, with great verve and dash."

Charity dismounted handing her reins to Milo, Jacob's stableman, whom she'd known since childhood and who had hurried across the stableyard when he had spotted her. "Rub her down well, Milo, she's had a good run."

"I'll cool her down first, Miss Charity," Milo said. "I'm sure Mr. Davis told you about the chuckholes, yet there you were flying over the meadow like some wild banshee."

Jacob took her arm, chuckling. "You will never be anything more than a child to my staff, I fear, Charity."

"She does ride like Mr. Jake, though, has his very seat, she does, even though he wouldn't be quite so foolhardy." Milo glared at his employer and Charity as though daring them to argue with him.

Jacob was still laughing when they walked through the french doors leading off the terrace and along the center hall of the house leading to his study.

Charity stopped just inside the door of the book-lined room with its leaded glass window doors overlooking the garden, gazing around her with a satisfied sigh. "You and Grandfather have always had the best studies, filled with wonderful books. It's like being walled off from the world, safe and warm."

Jacob smiled at her. "I used to catch you climbing to

the top shelf to get the books that were a little too . . . er, ah, advanced for you."

Charity smiled. "I kept trying to get your copy of *Tom Jones,* but you always caught me." She saw the glint of the large key on the desk. "Is this it?"

"Yes. Do you think you know where it fits?"

"I do. Would you like to join us for dinner then we'll try the key after that?"

Jacob rubbed his hands together, grinning at her. "I was sure you wouldn't ask so I was preparing to ask you."

"Good. Let me call Rum and tell her you're coming, then you can drive over and I'll ride Darcy back." Charity dialed the kitchen number of Bigham House. "Rum. Set a place for Jacob at the dinner table. He'll be joining us. No, I'm riding back. Yes, I'll be careful."

"You could ride with me, Charity, and we could send one of the stable boys back for your horse. It does get dark so early in late autumn."

"I'll be fine. I'm not staying that long, Jacob. There will be plenty of daylight left." Charity smiled at the older man, seeing that he wasn't convinced. "I'll be careful."

"All right." Jacob snapped his fingers. "Before you go, I want to show you something that I've found in Jake's papers that I had at the vault in my office. It has convinced me that I must go through his things very carefully now. I have a feeling that I've done my son a disservice by hiding things away and not looking at them."

Charity went to look over Jacob's shoulder as he seated himself behind his desk and shuffled through some papers before bringing out one and holding it so that she could see it clearly. "It looks like a will."

"It is and I never knew he had one. It's very short and precise. You see all of the estate, properties, and monies that belonged to him have been monitored by the firm since I knew that they were executors anyway, but since I have never needed his money or property such profits that accrued were plowed back into his holdings. That much I knew. This I didn't know." Jacob pointed at a line midway down the first page. "I am custodian of all he owned to be kept in trust for his beloved wife."

"I didn't know Jake was married."

"He wasn't but obviously he intended marriage and in the very near future just before his death." Jacob sighed.

"And you don't know who it was."

"No, but I'm going to keep searching now that I've found this. I want to follow my son's instructions to the letter and I have a great hankering to know the woman who would have been my daughter-in-law."

Charity nodded, patting Jacob on the back. Then she glanced at her watch. "I'd better go. Bring old clothes with you this evening, Jacob."

Jacob's eyes snapped with interest. "Very intriguing. Will we be digging in a basement?"

"I'll show you when you get there."

"Charity! That's unkind to keep me in suspense." Jacob pressed a button on his console and ordered Darcy to be brought around to the front door. "I assume you will be going the old road rather than the meadows."

Charity nodded, getting her riding gloves out of her pocket. "I'll have plenty of light going that way."

"But be careful, it's a winding old cart track in some spots and not in the best repair."

"Until I reach Bigham Park. It's good smooth macadam from there."

Jacob leaned up and kissed her cheek. "Cyrus would be so proud of you, Charity. You're like him in many ways."

252

"And I ride like Jake. Heavens, I am a split personality."

Jacob laughed, admiring the easy way she mounted, waving at her as she cantered down the drive. "She's beautiful, is she not, Milo?" Jacob spoke to his retainer and friend who was also watching Charity.

"Not bad, as I say she has a very good seat . . . every bit as good as Jake, I'm thinking."

The ride back was in fading daylight but still clear enough to see. The cold had increased with the disappearance of the sun and the mare, sensing she had a fine dinner of oats awaiting her, was trying to break into a gallop.

"Easy girl. You'll get there." Charity laughed at Darcy's antics.

As she trotted along Charity strained her eyes to watch for any potholes that could entrap the animal.

It was a relief to turn onto safer Bigham House property with its well-kept roads.

Halfway up the access road that would take her to the main drive, she heard the distinct crack of rifle, then the thud of a bullet burying itself in an oak just behind her head.

"Dammit! Hunters trespassing on our land! Go, Darcy. Hurry, girl. They'll hit us if we don't get out of here. Damn them!" Charity leaned over Darcy's neck praying that the horse wouldn't stumble over something in the rapidly growing darkness, urging her to full gallop.

CHAPTER NINE

Tell had searched the stairway on his own that afternoon, armed with an industrial flashlight with a strong beam and a small packet of useful tools. He had inspected every inch of the walls from top to bottom, coming back again and again to the smaller of the two doors. Examining it minutely, then measuring from the ground to the door and studying it again convinced him that it opened somewhere on the main floor. Tell had every intention of tearing the thing apart brick by brick to see exactly what it contained and where it led. He knew a couple of men who could do the job for him and get him some answers.

When he returned to the bedroom, he put away the tools he'd carted with him, then showered and readied himself for dinner.

It was when he began looking for his wife that he was stymied until he went to the kitchen and talked to Mrs. Rumrill.

"Yes, Mr. Tell, I know she shouldn't have gone over the meadows at this time of day but she does know every bit of ground and she will come back by the road, I'm sure, since she was just going to Mr. Henry's."

"Thank you, Mrs. Rumrill." Tell hurried to the front of the house, flinging it open, catching the slicing cold November wind right in the face. Unmindful of it he stepped out on the fan-shaped steps, noting the gray of approaching night. If she wasn't there, in front of him, in five minutes . . .

He saw her galloping up the drive, leaning over her horse's neck, throwing quick glances behind her. "What the hell . . . Charity! Wait. Pull up."

Charity saw her husband move almost in front of her and sawed on the reins, pulling Darcy back so that the horse reared. "I'm sorry, Tell. Someone was hunting in the west wood and I got out of there fast. I'll have to tell Davis to check it out."

"Someone was firing? Near you?"

At the same time jagged lightning pierced the sky followed by a roll of thunder, then rain pelting down over them, increasing to a cascade in seconds.

"Lightning? In November? Has the world gone mad?" Charity stared up at the sky, then down at her husband feeling as out of sync and control as the weather. "No, don't pull me off, Tell. I have to get Darcy under cover and rubbed down. She'll get a chill."

"I'll call the stable and they'll send someone right away and I'll inform them of the poachers too. Come on." Who had been shooting so close to the house? At his wife? Lifting her from the saddle he was struck anew at how light she was.

"Actually all you have to do is slap her rump and she'll trot to the stables by herself, but I do want her rubbed down and curried . . ."

Tell kissed her quickly. "We'll call now." He slapped Darcy and the horse whinnied, shaking her head, and trotting off to the stables. "Let's get inside. We're both soaked."

Dripping on the marble foyer, Tell and Charity held each other, laughing while he called the stables and gave terse instructions to the person who'd answered. "And I want someone out there now, Mr. Davis. There is no hunting on this property. Thank you."

"Good heavens, Charity. You and Tell have left a puddle." Kathleen was poised halfway down the stairs, her well-made-up face creased in a frown.

Macon appeared from the kitchen area, his eyes flickering over the three people in the foyer and sizing up the situation before he went to the intercom and spoke into it quietly. Then he approached Tell and Charity. "Perhaps, Mr. and Mrs. Layton, you should go up and take a hot bath. I shall take care of this."

Tell smothered a laugh at the pompous tones of the butler. He couldn't be sure if Macon was lecturing Charity and him or Kathleen. "Fine. We'll do that."

"Dinner is less than an hour. I hope you'll remember that," Kathleen said tartly.

"It's all right, Mrs. Layton," Macon said woodenly. "If you like I'm sure Mrs. Rumrill can put things back for you."

"Thank you, Macon, but we'll be on time."

"Damn, Charity, you might have taken advantage of that," Tell muttered in her ear, when they were in their own bedroom. "I'm planning on taking you into the hot tub and it would have been wonderful to linger there." Tell's mind rattled with what she'd told him earlier, but he masked his angst and tried to distract her too.

Charity chuckled when he lifted her in his arms and strode through to the large bathroom where he placed her back on her feet before turning to the switch for the hot tub. She was glad to strip the clothes from her body and join her husband in the hot swirling water that took the chill from her bones.

Dressing was fun. Tell and Charity stayed close to one another, touching, embracing, kissing.

"Damn dinner and that whole family. Let's skip it and go to bed."

"That sounds wonderful, but Jacob Henry is coming and I don't think we should be impolite to him."

Tell groaned, his mouth caressing the soft skin under her ear. "I'll be a mess during dinner. Promise me that we'll retire early."

"Promise." Charity noted the thoughtful look behind his grin.

Tell hadn't forgotten what Charity had said about the shooting in the west wood and as soon as he could after dinner he was going to talk to Davis and his son about it.

They left their room and went down the stairs arm in arm, seeing no trace of the puddles they had made on the parquet floor.

Dinner was almost comical to Tell. When Kathleen asked Jacob for the second time what he was doing there for dinner, he intervened. "Charity invited him, Kathleen. We have papers to go over this evening."

"I see. I think it would help if I knew in advance who was going to be at my table." Kathleen dabbed at her mouth with a damask napkin and signaled that her plate be removed.

"Mother." Gareth looked irritated. "Lionel and Jennifer will be back from their trip next week. I'm in my apartment in New York now and I think you, Lyle, and Amby should consider your move to Palm Beach." Gareth shot a look at the girls who were listening to everything though they didn't pause in their eating. "Charity has been most patient with all of us and . . ."

"Mother doesn't need you to instruct her in anything, Gareth." Amby threw his napkin down on the table, ignoring the luscious marble mousse dessert in front of him.

Tell rose to his feet, glancing at the girls, then at Ambrose. "We'll take coffee in the living room. Jacob, if you like you can take yours with Charity and me in the library."

"Capital."

Tell looked at a quizzical Gareth. "Coming?"

Gareth jumped to his feet, grinning. "You bet."

"Should we all come to the library?" Lyle went to his sister's chair and helped her from it. "Sounds intriguing."

"No need. Why don't you, Kathleen, and Ambrose have your coffee in the living room with the girls."

Without another word, and seemingly impervious to Kathleen's sputtered protests, Tell took his wife's arm and led her from the room.

Charity expelled a great breath of relief when the library door closed behind them. "Tell, I don't know if you really have any papers to show Jacob but he gave me a key today and I think it might fit one of the doors in the silo."

Tell stared at her for a few moments, then nodded. "Let's go up the kitchen stairs and we'll have a look." Tell whispered to Gareth and Jacob all the way to the second-floor master suite, informing them in terse sentences about the turret room.

Though Charity had assumed that Tell had informed both men what was in the closet, she heard the gasps behind her when she pushed the panel to expose the spiral staircase.

"Where's the key, darling? Gareth and I will go down there and try it on the doors. You and Jacob stay here."

Charity was disappointed that she wouldn't be going with the men but she also knew that there wasn't room in the round enclosure for more than two people.

Jacob took her arm and led her to a grouping of chairs by the window where they could relax but still could see the closet and could hear the men's voices.

258

"My child, this is very interesting to me. I knew that Cyrus could be eccentric when it came to secrecy, but I never dreamed of anything like this."

The knock at the door startled them.

"It must be Macon with the coffee. I told Rum when we passed through the kitchen where we would be."

Jacob nodded but said nothing as Charity rushed to the closet to shut it before answering the door and taking the coffee tray from Macon.

Charity seated herself again, pouring the hot, fragrant liquid and listen to Jacob's many anecdotes about her grandfather, cocking her head to one side when he paused, an arrested look on his face. "What is it?"

"I just recalled that Cyrus once told me that he had a hidden safe in his library." Jacob nodded, smiling with a faraway look to his eyes. "I wonder if it could have anything to do with the key I gave you."

Charity jumped to her feet, knocking against the table holding the coffee cups and almost spilling them. "The silo door could lead into the library since it's right beneath us." Charity clapped her hands. "I'll bet it does. Jacob, you wait here for Tell and Gareth, I'll be right back."

"Charity, wait . . ."

Gareth used his arc lamp flash to light both their ways, the beam penetrating every nook and cranny as they descended the stairway. "This is something. What Amby and I couldn't have done with this when we were kids."

Tell was so intent on getting to the small door he barely grunted a reply. "Ah, here we are. Hold that lamp high, Gareth." Inserting the key, Tell turned it carefully, fearing to break it, but the lock was well oiled and turned easily. As Tell opened the door, something fell at his feet, making a soft thud on the steps.

Gareth picked it up and held it in front of the lamp. "I recognize this."

"So do I."

The two men stared at each other for a few heartbeats, realization coming at them like a thrown punch.

Turning, they began to run back up the stairs. The voices arrested the movement.

"That's Charity with him," Tell muttered between his teeth, his voice barely audible. "Hurry, Gareth, hurry."

An instinct for survival made suspicions grow when the others hadn't returned to the living room to join them for coffee. There was enough going on in the sitting room that no one would notice one less person.

The library! That was the logical place to begin. It wasn't wise to try the stairway again. Damn them for discovering it.

The library door was ajar. Pushing it open a bit more allowed for a view of Charity and her provocative pushing and tugging at the turret wall.

When the opening appeared, the hidden safe revealed at last, it was time to move, to kill, to rid the world of Charity Bigham Layton.

Charity had gone down the kitchen stairs again, not wanting to take the chance that anyone in the living room would come out and question her.

Once in the library she went to the corner that had a stonework, concave wall adjacent to the window. Why hadn't she ever suspected the turret and its secrets before this moment? Charity stared at the surface and the artifacts that were on it. No door. After putting her ear to the stone and listening and hearing nothing, she deduced that she had come to an erroneous conclusion about an opening to the silo in the library.

260

Just to satisfy herself, Charity pushed on some of the bricks, with no effect. Then, one by one, she began to remove the many wrought-iron trivets that hung there. She always thought them a jarring touch in the library, but her grandfather had been very fond of collecting them.

When one of the trivets wouldn't move, she tugged at it and it turned in her hand, part of the stonework moving and opening at the same time. Then for a moment she heard Tell conversing with Gareth, then there was silence. She was about to call out to them when something distracted her.

Her gaze was caught by a suede packet lying in the small niche behind the bricks. Reaching for it she was about to call to Tell so that he would know she had discovered something when someone grabbed her from behind gripping her jaw in a fierce hold and cutting off any sound she would make.

"That's right, Charity. Stay still. Don't move."

Charity managed to slant her eyes toward her assailant when he reached around her for the packet.

Because he had to reach, his hold on her loosened, and she broke free of the hand across her mouth. "Lyle, what do you think you're doing? That's mine."

"Don't struggle, Charity . . . not unless you really like pain." Lyle tightened his hold, noting her wince when he did.

Charity stared into the face of a man she'd known since childhood and saw a death mask where there had always been congeniality. He was a stranger, a very dangerous and angry alien. "What are you doing, Lyle? Stop this."

"Damn you, stay still. It's time I was rid of you, you annoying bitch."

Stunned, Charity stared at him. "Are you the one who has caused the accidents, the other weird happenings?" When that lazy, malicious grin widened she shivered.

"That's such a very simple statement for a very convoluted involvement, my dear Charity. Now back away from there. I want to close that little trap door you have discovered. Damn Cyrus! I have searched for his hidden papers for years." His low laugh had no humor in it. "He was on to me, but he didn't know how I was getting to his room to flavor his food and remove the dishes afterward." Lyle laughed out loud at her horror-stricken face. "He was a bastard. Only his precious Julia and you ever meant anything to him. Not even my sister could hold his affections for long."

"Whatever your game is now, Lyle, you won't get away with it. The house is filled with people who would come if I screamed once. Give it up." Charity's fear was fast turning to acidic anger. This man had killed her beloved grandfather.

"In this room? Don't try to smoke me, my dear. This library is as soundproof as a vault. Have you forgotten that I have lived in this house for many years . . . and if it hadn't been for you it would be mine now."

"Jacob knows where I am. He'll tell my husband."

"Ah, yes, the illustrious Griffith Tell Layton who has been fawning over you since your childhood. He has stood between us too many times, Charity. I owe him for that."

Fear for Tell galvanized her to action and she tried to free herself again. "Ow, you're hurting my neck."

"Then stop wriggling. I can easily break it for you, Charity, but I'd rather not do it yet." He threw the packet down on the desk, his attention fixed on it.

Charity feeling his hold loosen once more, thrust free of him, running for the door, but as she turned the handle and had it partially open, she felt Lyle's strong arm around her throat, throttling her. Air rasped from her lungs as she was dragged backward.

As Lyle turned his body to kick the door closed again, it was thrust open and Tell stood there, panting, crouched, his fingers flexing into fists, his facial bones working spasmodically under the pallor of his skin.

"Let her go, Clausen." Tell's voice rasped from his throat as though he were in pain.

Gareth was out of breath and running when he almost stumbled into Tell in his hurry to get into the room. "Lyle, listen to me." Gareth took a deep breath. "Whatever you've been involved in, it's over. Do you hear me? Over. Release Charity, for God's sake."

"How did you know to come to the library?" Lyle quizzed petulantly, his hold tightening on Charity, not seeming to notice her hands clawing at his choking arm, the guttural sounds of stress she made. He lifted Cyrus Bigham's gold letter opener shaped like a sword from the desk, holding it high in his one hand.

"What's going on in here? What did you hear when you were in the turret?" Jacob burst in the door, pulling Lyle's gaze his way.

At the same moment Tell leaped, his one hand claw-like in reaching for the garroting forearm that was impinging on his wife's windpipe, the other like a homing device on the hand that held the letter opener. Sheer force broke the hold, even as the weapon that Lyle had in his other hand was thrusting downward against Tell's hold.

Through the red haze in front of her eyes and in spite of having to fight for every breath, Charity saw the lethal descent of the letter opener and not the strong hand that was fighting its aim. "No!" Her hoarse croak was accompanied by her upthrust arm that caught the blade and sent a deep scratch down her arm before her husband could deflect it.

At the same moment Gareth flung himself across the room, his full weight bearing back his uncle, wrenching the arm upward, cursing him.

"Why all the noise? What happened?" Priscilla put her head in the doorway, all agog, the other girls right behind her, and Kathleen and Ambrose behind them.

"Gareth, what are you doing to your uncle?" Kathleen pressed her way past the girls, her voice surprised and agitated. "Tell, stop that at once. You'll kill my brother."

Charity, who had been tossed back on the floor cradling her arm, saw that it was true. Tell had pushed Gareth aside and had his hands around Lyle's neck and he was shaking him like a terrier with a rat. She crawled to her husband, pulling on his arm. "Tell, please don't. Help me."

Tell's head swung her way, the death grip he had on Lyle's throat loosening. "Darling, are you hurt?"

"My arm." Charity watched Tell lean back, scowling at the long scratch, but not moving from his position astride Clausen.

Lyle heaved upward trying to get Tell off his chest but it didn't work and with Gareth pinioning him he finally conceded and stayed still. "Kathleen, tell your son to release me at once."

"Gareth, do as you're told."

"No, Mother. If you move, Uncle, your shoulder will separate from your body."

Tell checked to see that Gareth had the other man securely before moving free of him and standing. Then he scooped Charity up into his arms, kissing her forehead and lifting her arm to his lips. "We'll get something for your arm."

"I'll get something." Priscilla left the room with Marybeth.

264

Tell looked at Kathleen. "If Gareth releases your brother, I'll kill him with my bare hands."

"If you don't, I will." Gareth hauled his uncle to his feet. "Jacob, call the police."

"I did it upstairs when the two of you came out of that turret like an explosion. I figured something was up."

"Turret? What turret are you talking about?" Ambrose looked belligerent.

"You'll know in time, brother." Gareth gave a mirthless laugh.

Macon came to the doorway blinking at everyone. "Miss Priscilla said that you needed this, Mrs. Layton." With Priscilla, Marybeth and the other girls behind him he moved toward Charity with the antibiotic cream which she applied to the scratch.

"I will explain it to you tomorrow, Macon, but now I would like you and Mrs. Rumrill to take the girls upstairs and stay with them while the police are here."

When the girls protested, Tell spoke to them kindly but firmly and they went with the butler.

"I want an explanation." Kathleen shot quick glances from her brother to Charity, then to Tell.

"Ambrose, go to the kitchen. There's rope in the butler's pantry. No one's doing or saying anything more until my uncle is securely tied." Gareth's bitter voice effectively silenced his mother when she would have spoken again.

Ambrose looked at his brother as though he were staring at a stranger, then he left the library.

No one spoke while he was gone. Tell busied himself with his wife's arm, nodding when his wife murmured soothingly to him. Lyle's labored breathing seemed cacophonous in that silent room.

When he finished with her arm Tell poured cognac from the decanter on the library table and insisted his

265

wife sip it. "It will help your throat, Charity." His fingers touched the red marks under her chin.

Charity could see the tautness behind his smile. "I'm all right, really I am."

"That bastard has been threatening you, all this time, trying to hurt you." Tell shook his head, pulling her close to him again. His eyes went to Lyle Clausen who stared back at him unblinkingly.

"Here's the rope, but I think this is foolish . . ."

"Shut up, Amby, and bring me that rope." Gareth's growled words elicited a gasped reproof from his mother.

Tell released Charity, kissing her cheek lingeringly before going over to help Gareth bind Lyle Clausen.

"Is that necessary, Tell? I don't understand any of this but it doesn't seem to me that you have the right to accuse my brother of anything. What has he done to deserve this?"

"I should kill him." Tell's words dropped into the room like stones.

"Explain that, damn you." Ambrose glared at Tell and Gareth.

"These will." Charity's voice still had a painful huskiness as she walked to the desk and lifted the leatherbound packet. "I'm sure of it." She opened the packet and took out some letters, legal documents, and loose papers. Her hand fell on a letter with her name on it and she picked it up.

"No! No!" Lyle Clausen screamed as though in pain. "That belongs to me, you damned little witch."

Gareth turned to his uncle quickly, going over the knots that bound him to the chair. "Shut up. Nothing in this house belongs to you, Lyle."

Lyle's laughter burst around the room like a hail of bullets, making Kathleen jump and stare at her brother.

"Is that right? Well, what if I tell you that I'm Charity Bigham's father, then what would you say?"

"Lyle! What are you saying?" Kathleen was helped to a small couch by her son Ambrose.

"No." The whispered negative was like a curse. Charity sank into the chair behind the desk. "That can't be."

"Why not, Charity? Why wouldn't I be the one who was fooling around with your whore of a mother and getting her pregnant?"

Tell pulled a handkerchief from his breast pocket and stuffed it in the other man's mouth when he would have said more, ignoring Kathleen and Ambrose's protests. Then he turned to his ashen-faced wife and went down on his knees in front of her chair. "He's lying. If he's truly the person we think he is who has hurt you and tried to kill you on more than one occasion, then lying would be nothing to him. No father would do what he has done to you, Charity. You can believe that."

Charity nodded numbly.

Gareth had been perusing the papers that lay strewn on the desk. He picked up a document that had a notary stamp on it. "Wait a minute, Charity, this is a deposition signed by your mother stating that your father was . . ." Gareth looked up, his mouth agape, his gaze sliding to Jacob. "Jacob Henry II was your dad, Charity, according to this deposition . . . and if the date is correct on the letterhead, Cyrus received this shortly before his death." Gareth waved the envelope. "From Street Detective Agency and marked *very confidential.*" Gareth gazed at a stunned Charity compassionately. "Cyrus must not have had time to inform you before he died, Charity."

Silence fell over the room like a strange light, touching its occupants and bronzing their stillness.

Tell took hold of her arm, but Charity didn't notice.

She was looking at Jacob who was watching her, and nodding, a sheen of tears in his eyes.

"It could be . . . must be true, child. You're so like Jake in so many ways."

Gareth coughed and continued. "This also states, according to letters of your mother's, that your mother and father had intended to elope because of her pregnancy and that he was killed the day before they were to marry."

Jacob crossed the room to Charity, his arms outstretched. "My darling child, I'm so happy. There was so much in you that was like my Jake but I never guessed."

Charity rose and hugged the older man, feeling the tremor in his frame.

When Lyle began moving and struggling in his bonds Ambrose crossed the room and pulled the handkerchief from his mouth, then stared defiantly at Gareth and Tell.

Lyle coughed. "You're a bastard, Charity, don't forget that." He laughed harshly. "When I asked your mother to marry me she said no. I even knew she was intimate with Jake but I still asked her, then she said she was marrying him in a few days, but I took care of that. I would have killed her when she refused me after his 'accident' but I didn't want an investigation into Jake's death . . . so I waited."

Charity felt Jacob stiffen and she put her arm around his shoulders. "Are you saying that you killed Jake . . . my father?" The look of benign satisfaction that rippled over his features had her shuddering. "You did do it."

"My God! My son! I thought the car had been defective," Jacob exclaimed.

"It was. I tampered with the steering mechanism. That's why he went over the bluff," Lyle explained gently.

"You bloody bastard!" Tell moved toward him. "And Julia? Did you kill her too?"

"I asked her to marry me some years later and she said she'd never marry, that she could only love one man. You should have seen her face when I swam out to her that day. At first she was a little irked because she wanted to be alone. When I jabbed her behind the ear with the syringe, she looked stunned." Lyle smiled. "A friend of mine is a medical examiner upstate. I invited him to New York for dinner and a show. Over drinks I prodded him about certain chemicals, untraceable poisons to be exact. He was so flattered that I was interested in his work . . ."

"Damn you . . ." Gareth went for his uncle, grasping him around the neck, almost lifting him from the chair.

Tell pulled him off Lyle. "I would help you throttle him if I didn't think it would be a greater punishment to him to go through a trial and become a pawn of the penal system, and I damned well will do everything in my power to see that he's there until he dies." Tell stared down at the bound man, who was red-faced and coughing. "You're a vermin, Clausen. Julia was the sweetest woman who ever walked outside of my wife and you took her life. But I don't think you killed her just because she turned you down. Hadn't she begun suspecting that you had had something to do with Jake's death?"

"No! No, she never knew. She was stupid to cling to a dead man, and I told her so. Her eyes gave her away then, I could see that she was thinking of Jake and his death. That's when she swam away from me, trying to be alone with her thoughts. But again she underestimated me, because I caught her . . . and made her pay." Lyle looked thoughtful. "When I grabbed her and she realized that I was going to kill her she didn't plead for herself but for her little girl. The fool."

"Good God." Ambrose went to his mother who was making soft sad sounds in her throat. "He's sick, Mother."

"Sick?" Lyle struggled mightily against his bonds. "Don't you say that about me, you whining wimp. Sick? Never. I outsmarted them all. When Cyrus began looking at me strangely, I knew he had gotten something else from that detective agency he was always using. It was time to finish him as well, and I was smart about that too. His doctor never suspected a thing and neither did you, Kathleen." Lyle beamed triumphantly at his sister.

Kathleen reeled in the chair, her eyes starting from her head. "You killed my beloved Cyrus?"

"Beloved? Don't make me laugh, sister. He never saw you when Charity was around . . . and he would never have married you at all had Julia lived. Those two were the stars in his heaven."

"I loved him." Kathleen's shaky cry reverberated around the room.

"You loved his money as I did. I was able to put away a sizable nest egg for myself by manipulating Cyrus . . . and so did you and your progeny, Kathleen."

"Don't lump us with you, you cur dog." Gareth made a move toward him again, deterred by Tell's hand.

"He's baiting you, Gareth. Think how frustrated he'll be when all the money he's made off Cyrus's generosity goes down the drain to pay the battery of lawyers he'll need in the days ahead."

The strangled sounds that came from Lyle Clausen's throat sounded as though the Bulls of Bashan were in the room. Curses rolled from his twisted lips. "I should have killed you, Layton, when I had the chance."

"How? Not face to face, that's for sure, you pariah."

Tell's tight features telegraphed how he held himself in check. "You would have had to try and run me down with a car, or stab me on the street as you tried to do with my wife." Tell hugged Charity close to him, anger building in him as he listed Lyle's lethal actions.

"Don't forget the incident with the rifle the other day, Layton," Clausen said silkily, his lips drooping in pleasure when Tell stiffened. "Oh yes, I almost got her then, but her damned horse sidled, then she was able to get away."

"I thought it was poachers," Charity said softly, her hands clutching Tell. "Now I fully understand why Grandfather used the story *The Man with the Twisted Lip* to give me a message."

"What are you talking about, Charity?" Gareth approached her.

"I'll tell you and Jacob everything later. Go on, darling." Tell kept her close to him.

"*The Man with the Twisted Lip* is about a man in disguise. Grandfather was telling me that the enemy was a two-faced person who was after me." Charity pressed a hand to her lips to stop their trembling.

"And there were other times when I almost succeeded, Charity." Lyle looked around him as though to be sure he had everyone's attention. "Let's not forget the first day you went down the hidden stairway . . ."

"What stairway?" Ambrose blurted then subsided when his uncle glared at him.

"I knew what you were going to do when I saw you in the main hall that day, Charity, carrying the flashlight and trying to be so mysterious. I deduced that you had discovered the secret way I had gotten into Cyrus's room." Lyle frowned. "But I don't know how you opened that smaller door. I was never able to do it."

"That was why there were so many marks around the

271

keyhole, Tell, and why we had a hard time turning the key." Gareth hit the palm of his hand with his fist.

"But when we did get it open we saw the packet disappear and heard you threaten my wife, Clausen. You see the hiding place could be opened from the turret or the library." Tell finished the tale, the black satisfaction he felt at seeing the nemesis disconcerted, very fleeting.

"I should have gotten her with the fallen tree. That was foolproof." Lyle's voice had a reedy shrillness when he laughed. "You remember that, don't you, Charity?"

"Yes."

As Lyle opened his mouth to say more, there was a slight ruckus at the door and Macon entered stiffly. "The police are here, Mrs. Layton."

"About time," Gareth muttered.

"Gareth, don't say that. Lyle is your uncle. You must defend him." Kathleen sobbed into her handkerchief.

"Mother, don't ask that of me. I won't do it. I will give him the names of some good criminal lawyers, none of whom will be connected with our firm." Gareth looked at the man who'd been his mentor since he'd begun practicing. "I couldn't do anything more."

"Nor would I stand for it, but thank you for saying that, Gareth." Jacob spoke firmly, flashing Charity a wan smile when she took his hand. "My granddaughter and I wish to see justice served."

Tell kissed Charity's cheek, then moved to speak to the policemen who'd been ushered into the room by Macon.

Questions followed. Everyone—including the girls who were asked to come downstairs—was queried about what they knew.

Tell did as much as he could to shield the girls from the sordid details because he saw how shocked they were to see Lyle put into handcuffs.

272

When two policemen escorted him to the door, Lyle paused and turned around to gaze across the room.

"Don't get too comfortable, Charity. I might show up again like the proverbial bad penny."

Charity stepped in front of her husband when he would have moved toward Lyle. Looking over her shoulder at Clausen, she shook her head. "Your days of intimidation are over, Lyle. I'm not afraid of you . . . and neither should anyone else be. Once a weasel has been drawn from his hole, he can be dealt with quickly. You've just been exposed and your teeth pulled, Lyle."

"You damnable bitch. I should have gotten you with the boat. It would have been poetic justice if you had died like your mother." The two policemen tightened their hold when he screamed at Charity.

Kathleen sobbed, cuddling closer to her elder son.

One of the policemen was jotting in his notebook, all the while shooting impassive glances from Lyle to Charity. "Get him out of here," he instructed another detective. Then he faced the others. "Some of you will have to come to the station. From the sound of it, this case is very involved."

"I will speak for the family, Detective Shaeny, at least for preliminary questioning. Would that be permissible? Since you've been able to get statements from everyone who was here today, I think it might make it easier on the family that way." Gareth spoke hurriedly at a nod from Tell.

"It might not be enough, Mr. Beech. There will be an exhumation by the sound of it, plus other legal steps we have to take." The detective stuck to his guns, his gaze swinging toward Kathleen when she gasped a negative. "I'm sorry, ma'am, truly I am, but if there's some question how your husband died . . ." He shrugged.

"There won't be a need for exhumation, detective. Get in touch with an address I will give you. Cyrus had his body secretly sent to a laboratory in France for examination because he feared that he would be poisoned." Tell looked at Kathleen, who had sagged against her son. "I'm sorry, Kathleen. Neither Charity nor I knew this until a short time ago."

"It will be all right, Mother. I shall get our own lawyers to check this." Ambrose looked at the others stiffly.

"Give it up, Ambrose. Can't you see that our family has been the cause of grave anguish to others? That we deprived Charity and Jacob of their loved ones, not to mention what was done to Cyrus?" Gareth's voice rose angrily. "Our uncle is a monster, Amby, a damned Frankenstein."

"You're fretting Mother." Ambrose's face reddened. "You've never been loyal, Gareth."

"Not to him, never to an ogre. He deserves the judgment of his peers and that's what he shall get, but in some areas of the world he would have been taken out and executed without a trial for just half of things he's done."

Kathleen rose to her feet, pale but chin held high. "It is unforgivable if he has killed my Cyrus, but he is my brother and he must have proper representation." She looked at Charity. "I am deeply sorry . . . for all that has happened and, of course, I will move out of this house as soon as possible, and make no more legal moves against you concerning the estate."

Charity nodded, not able to answer the other woman. She was sorry for Kathleen, but she wanted and needed the company of her grandfather and her husband now. It was their comfort and solace that she sought.

Ambrose looked at Charity. "I will go too, Charity, and I, too, am sorry for what has happened."

Charity coughed to clear the huskiness from her throat. "Please believe that I blame no one for what Lyle has done, except Lyle."

274

"I have the same feelings as my granddaughter, Kathleen. I blame no one but Lyle and do not bear you or any member of your family ill will." Jacob's sad voice had a tiredness to it that drew Charity closer to him. "I will always grieve for my son, but now I have a consolation that I had never looked for . . . my granddaughter."

"Thank you, Charity, Jacob." Kathleen smiled, her pallor pronounced, then glanced at her older son. "Ambrose, I think I'll go to my room and lie down for a short time. Perhaps you will see to your uncle."

"Mother." Gareth touched his mother's arm. "I'm very sorry that you had to be put through all this, but he had to be stopped."

"Yes, I know." Kathleen put her hand over his. "It's just such a shock. Lyle had his moods, but I never suspected this."

"None of us did, Mother. I will see to it that he has a lawyer who will meet him at the station. Don't worry."

Kathleen nodded, putting her one hand up to his cheek. "You have facets to you that I have never known, Gareth. It saddens me that I never realized the depths of courage and caring you have."

"Mother." Gareth's voice broke as he took her hand and kissed it gently.

"Ah, I will take Mother to her room, and then I will accompany you to the station, Gareth, unless you would rather I went alone and talked to the lawyer you'll have there." Ambrose shrugged, looking ill at ease, as though he had reached a new and uncomfortable plateau with his brother.

"We'll both go there and see about Lyle, brother."

Ambrose nodded once and took his mother's arm, leading her from the room.

The silence, after the others had left, was broken when Tell slapped his hand against the leather back of

Cyrus's chair, the sound like a pistol shot in the stillness. "Dammit, Gareth, don't expect me to echo soft sentiments about your uncle. I can't. He damn near killed my wife, more than once."

Gareth nodded. "I know, and I don't see any cause for leniency, nor would I seek it. Other than getting him representation and a hearing, I intend to do nothing. Lyle is a monster and I hope he is out of my family forever." Gareth moved toward Jacob Henry. "I never guessed he could do such a thing to Charity or to you, Jacob, and I will understand if you would like me to seek out another firm."

"Never." Jacob grasped his upper arms, shaking him slightly. "You have become like Jake to me, Gareth, and I will never forget all the hours you put in to discover who was intimidating my grandchild. You would hurt me terribly if you left us."

"Thank you, sir," Gareth said huskily.

When Gareth turned to Charity and took her in his arms, she hugged him back. "I agree with Grandfather, Gareth. You are too important to be out of our lives. Don't let it happen."

"I won't, little sister, you mean a great deal to me also, and you are one very brave lady." Gareth stepped back from her. "I think I'll call Brad Collins to represent Lyle, Jacob. What do you think?"

Jacob nodded. "He's good."

"I'll call Brad from my brother's room. Excuse me."

"This has hurt Gareth, too." Charity sighed as she watched him leave the room, then she looked up at her husband. "Lyle was the man in the black jogging suit I saw in New York and at the boat house. It seems unreal."

"It's over now, darling."

Charity nodded and turned with a shy smile to Jacob.

"I hope you will want to play a big part in my life too . . . Grandfather."

Jacob went to her, enfolding her in his arms. "I never hoped for such a boon in my life, Charity. I have loved you since you were a child and often wished that you were mine and now you are. I shall want us to have constant contact. You are my blood, my only heir. And your children will be of my blood . . . if you and Tell choose to have a family."

"I think the decision may have been taken out of our hands." Charity laughed, then she spun around to look at her husband who was staring at her, his eyes wide, his face ashen. "I'm not really sure," she told him hurriedly. "Tell? Say something."

"We've only been married a few months."

Jacob smothered his laugh with a sudden cough behind his hand, muttering something about talking to Macon about some tea, then he left them alone.

"Tell, look at me. You're not angry that I blurted it out like that, are you?"

"Angry? I think stunned is a better word. Dammit, Charity, we were going to wait. We have so many things to settle between ourselves before we consider a family."

Charity lifted her chin. "I'm not interrupting this pregnancy for anything or anyone."

"I never suggested such a thing," Tell shot back, his face mottling angrily. "What makes you think that you would be more protective of our child than I would?"

"You don't want our child." Charity gulped back a sob, the events of the day piling one on top of the other and spilling over into tears.

"Charity, for God's sake, be reasonable. That isn't true and you know it."

"Leave me alone." She whirled from the room, running along the hall to the foyer and up the stairs to their suite of rooms, hating Tell with an emotional passion at that moment.

A month later Charity had begun to fill out, her waist thickening, her mornings sometimes wretched with nausea.

Not all Tell's persuasions and coaxing had quite convinced her that he wanted the child, but he had succeeded in talking her into taking a vacation in Barbados with him after the initial legal business with Lyle Clausen was settled. Though they would have to return from the beautiful West Indian island and face the trial, somehow all that seemed far away to Charity as she reclined on the sand in front of the condominium that Tell had borrowed from a friend, a leafy plum tree planted in front of the condo shading her from the strong sun and allowing the soft western breeze to cool her.

Tell walked toward her, his skin already tinted a light mahogany, his body dripping with sea water from his swim.

"Be careful. Even through the leafy trees you can get burned, Charity. We're not that far from the equator here." He stared down at her, his heart thudding against his ribs. Tell wanted her every time he looked at her and her more rounded body was more sensuous to him than anything he'd ever seen. It drove him crazy that he had been unable to bridge the gap between them, that every overture had been snubbed by Charity. Damn, how could she not know he loved her!

Charity kept her eyes closed, knowing that when she opened them she would see the tight, stiff features that had become familiar to her. She and Tell spoke and they even made love but the relaxing oneness that they'd shared since their marriage had dissipated.

Charity blamed herself for flying off the handle with him the way she'd done on the day Lyle had been arrested, and she wished with all her heart she could mend the rift between them, but she was so uncomfortable with him she was sure he would rebuff any overture she might make.

"I thought I'd go snorkeling out by the wreck. Would you like to go, Charity?"

"Yes." She was so glad to be included. Yesterday Tell had gone parasailing by himself; not only hadn't he asked her, he hadn't mentioned that he was going.

Charity had been sitting on the covered terrace of the condo idly looking at a passing boat using Tell's maxi-strength binoculars. When she'd seen the powerful pull boat speed by towing the para sailer who was a couple of hundred feet in the air in the body trap with the multicolored parachute billowing over him, she had focused on the flyer and almost fell out of her chair when she recognized Tell.

When he'd returned she'd faced him at once. "How many other things will you be doing without me? I'd like to know then I could schedule my day."

"Charity, I didn't think you should go parasailing in your condition . . ."

"Hah!" Charity's temper had erupted at once.

"Nor do I intend to let you go scuba diving or water skiing either. You can always do those things when we come again."

"If we come again."

"I'm considering purchasing this place."

"Then you come by yourself."

"As you say." Tell had stormed from the condo and she hadn't seen him until dinnertime.

Charity had smelled the rum on his breath when they'd been dressing for the evening meal.

They had dined at the Bagatelle Great House up in

279

the highlands of Barbados, away from the coast. The food was luscious, the atmosphere romantic, but they spoke little and neither one had finished the succulent meal.

Tell watched her rise gracefully from the lounge chair, noting the slight heaviness of her waist, his heart thudding heavily with want as he watched her move toward her gear. "Let me get it for you." He was delighted that she was coming with him.

"No need. It isn't heavy."

They walked to the water's edge before donning mask and flippers, then they walked backward into the sea, a method used by snorkelers that simplified the cumbersome task of walking in flippers.

At once Tell turned toward Charity and watched her as she began the slow, languorous kicking that moved her so swiftly through the water.

It had never ceased to amaze him at how agile and athletic she was, how at home she was in the sea. Reaching out he grasped her hand and tugged her gently close to him, seeing her look of surprise. But she quickly accepted that he wanted her to swim near him in the water, adopting the "buddy" system that was a safety precaution.

The wreck was beautiful with the crystal-clear aquahued water creating a fascinating aura. As usual schools of fish moved around unconcernedly, their blue and gold tints glinting jewellike in the depths.

When they reached the raft that had been anchored out over the wreck, Tell gestured to her to get up on the raft, but Charity shook her head, pointing downward that she wanted to have a closer look at the wreck.

Without waiting for him Charity took a deep breath and dove downward.

Tell was immobilized by surprise for a second, then he

too doubled his body and thrust downward. When he saw that she was moving slowly over the sunken barge, he wasn't too worried, but when her hand went out as though to touch something in front of her, he kicked furiously toward her.

With a strong push his hand went under hers. He had spied the sea urchin undulating with the movements of the water. He was almost able to pull up her hand. Then he felt a stinging as though a lit cigarette had been touched several places on his hand before it went numb.

Still managing to get to the surface, they both blew their tubes, then Charity wrenched off her mask.

"Tell! The urchin got you, didn't it?"

Tell nodded, gesturing to her to replace her mask. He removed his breathing tube. "Let's get back to shore and I'll put some fresh lime and candle wax on it. That'll take care of it." Tell had lost feeling in his fingers and he kept that hand away from her because he didn't want her overly concerned.

Near the shore, Charity yanked off her equipment and though she was rolled off her feet by the swells more than once, she was able to get to Tell's side quickly. "Hurry. Oh my God, Tell, your hand's blue and so stiff." Fear had her gasping.

"It's all right, I've been hit before, Charity. Darling, please don't get upset." Bending down, he scooped up her equipment as well as his own with one hand and accompanied her up the beach to the condo.

"Hurry, Tell, we must get a doctor."

Inside the two-story dwelling that had shutters open to the out of doors except where the sun hit and the blinds were drawn, Tell had to show her what the lime and wax would do even though she wouldn't stop pleading that they see a doctor.

"There. Now do you believe me? You can see that the

marks are dissolving and the feeling has come back into my hand."

Charity held his hand in both of hers, tears spilling from her eyes. "I was so afraid of losing you. That would kill me."

Ignoring his throbbing hand, Tell scooped her into his arms and sank down on the bed. "How do you think I would feel if you were gone from me, Charity? You're my life. Nothing else is important to me without you." He bent his head and kissed her quickly. "I've loved you since you've been a little girl and since our marriage I've loved you more. Living without you would be impossible." He kissed her more lingeringly. "How could you think that I wouldn't love having our baby? I was afraid, at first, because you're so slender but several doctors have told me that my fears are groundless in light of your past physicals."

"Several doctors? Past physicals?"

Tell reddened to the roots of his hair. "I know you have your own physician, but I consulted with some specialists and . . . Why are you laughing?"

Charity fingered the sapphire heart that she had never removed since the day Tell had given it to her. "You do take very good care of me, just as everyone has said."

"Damn them, they told you I was obsessed with you."

"Are you?"

"Yes."

"Good, because I'm obsessed with you." Charity lifted the hand stabbed by the urchin quills and kissed it. Then she placed her hands on both sides of his face. "I didn't mean to lash out at you the way I've been doing. I do love you so much, Tell. Sometimes I can't believe my luck at landing you."

"Landing me? Is that what you did? I thought I hijacked you into marriage." He leaned back on the bed, taking her with him. "I want to make love to you. Is it safe?"

Charity laughed. "Of course. I hate to be the one to explode all your myths about delicate conditions, but I'm healthy as a horse. I could even have twins."

"God! Charity, take it easy. Let's have one at a time . . . but let's think about that later. Love me now. I need you."

With a sigh of joy, Charity began a loving exploration of her husband. How she had missed touching him! And how she needed him!

Seven and one half months later Charity gave birth to a boy in Mount Olivet Hospital in Bigham Park with her husband in attendance and her grandfather and Gareth pacing the corridor.

"Would you mind if I call him Griffith Henry Bigham Layton?"

"What an imposing name, Mama." Tell buried his face in her neck.

When Charity felt his tears on her skin, she cuddled her baby with one hand and turned her face to find her husband's mouth. "I love you, darling husband," she murmered.

"I love you too, Charity mine." Tell kissed his son then he lifted his head and smiled at his wife. The sapphire heart sparkled brilliantly against her neck.